Sharon O. Lightholder

The Paris Draft

A Novel

The Road Back From Dementia

Also by the author:

Fiction

The English Rendition
The Baldwin Portolano

Non-Fiction

Vietnam: The War Zone Dictionary In their Own Words
The comprehensive dictionary of the words and phrases used during the Vietnam War by American and Allied troops, contractors, and non-combatants including journalists and Red Cross volunteers, in both official documents and slang

Dedicated

To Ann's Memory

Chapter № 1

Mid-September 2017

Jack flinched when his iPhone 4 hooted like a submarine's diving alarm. Most of the Cutty Sark he was pouring hit the short tumbler, but some pooled on the scarred kitchen table in his lakeside cabin. He didn't need to look at the caller ID, which flashed *Spawn of Satin*, to know it was Max. Any other call rang like a real telephone. He had intended the caller ID to read *Spawn of Satan* but never bothered to fix it. That's what editors did. Made his stuff look good. Satin. Satan. He shrugged. Slippery fabric or the devil, a simple typo. His intent was clear, even if his spelling was wrong. Maybe he'd just rename Max's contact as 666, if he could just remember how.

He grabbed the phone as it vibrated toward the amber puddle and hit the green button. "Hi Max, happy Friday. How..."

"It's Thursday. And it's almost October."

Jack tapped the speaker icon and pushed the phone to a dry area of the table past the newly oiled Winchester Model 70. He stared at the ceiling and shoved his hands into the pockets of his wrinkled khaki cargo pants. "Really? Is that why all the summer people left the lake?"

Max leaned both elbows on his glass desk, looked over the New York City skyline, and shouted at his office phone, "Come on, Jack! You can't just hang out at the lake, commune with nature, and wait for deer season to open so you can play Hemingway. Where is it? I gotta get your draft to Isabel. She's waiting for it! And you know I need a few days to run it through a data entry technician to get it digital for her."

"Just a few more finishing touches," Jack called over his shoulder as he reached into the freezer.

Max ran his hand over his short wiry hair. "You know, I'm going to lose Isabel to other projects if you don't give me your manuscript soon. She's just finishing off a Pulitzer winner's latest history and a sex on the beach kinda book, so she is ready for you. And I'm already getting other offers..."

"But she makes my work so..." He spoke as loud as he thought he could without screaming and silently slid an ice cube down the edge of the glass.

"I know! She gets you. She's a real genius, but if you don't give her pages she can't edit bupkis."

"Yeah, I know." He wiped the dribble of scotch off the table with the hem of his black Rolling Stones concert T-shirt.

"Look, she's as independent as you are, but if I can't get something to the imprint by the end of October, you're going to default on your contract. In case you forgot the deal I got for you, I'm gonna read it to you. Blah blah blah, yeah, here it is '...*before* November first, a serviceable draft of a literary work...'"

"I know! And If I don't send it in on time, the next two book advances go down the crapper."

"And you have to return your advance. That's the deal. You've got potentially a million bucks riding on this, pal."

"Do they know about her?"

"Isabel Ross? Nobody does. She just edits your stuff invisibly from her house on Long Island, like always. Doesn't even want to be mentioned in your acknowledgments, just wants first crack at your next book." He laughed. "As if we could get anyone better! Remember when you started? We had to use real messengers to drive your stuff out there. Her neighbors probably thought we were schlepping drugs or laundering money. But now, the magic of the Internet allows her to..."

"So, you've never met her either? I thought you had. Didn't you vouch for her when we started?"

Max stretched and pulled his vest down over his expanding gut, thinking he might actually take a spinning class, not just use the steam room at his gym. "What's it matter now? It's been a great twenty-year run. A thriller a year for Christmas sales. You know, I've got other cli-ents, but it's really thanks to you two that I'm getting the last of my kids through college next year."

"Ya shouldn't have had 'em so late. I had mine early so she could hate me longer." Jack paused, looking at his drink. "Seriously? You've never met Isabel? After all this time?"

"Naw. Why bother? All I need to know is that she knows your style almost better than you do. You can set your watch by her on any project I've ever given her. She's never let us down, so why bother her? She's kind of a hermit or a what-da-you-call-it?"

Jack frowned and dug for the word. "Anti...anomo...agoraphobic?"

"Yeah. That's it. All I need to know is that she can make your work sparkle so I can pitch it with ease."

He looked at the chipped porcelain ashtray next to the rippling amber liquid in his glass, reading, "The Ritz. Paris." He smiled as he re-membered how he had pocketed it when his first book hit the *New York Times* bestseller list. That night, he and the other boys with more beard and ego than sense, went off to celebrate. Jack shook his head when he recalled how they stuck him with the bar bill. It was only one drink each, but somehow it had totaled his rent money for the month. That's when he took the ashtray. It was when his wife loved him and Paris was afford-able. It was when he was brave and his hair was chestnut, his muscles toned, and he wrote balls to the wall every day.

He stared at the ashtray, now holding three pennies, a bright brass .257 Roberts cartridge, and a bent paper clip. Then it hit him: location. "Paris, Max. I need to go to Paris for a last bit of research and polish. You know how atmospheric I can get and how the ladies love that. I hear that all the time on tour." He pushed his voice to a mincing soprano, "I just love your locations, Mister Forrester! I almost feel like I'm there..."

"Paris?"

"Yup. Don't you listen to yourself? The demographic is shifting. My thrillers can't be all spy-craft, sweaty balls, karate, and car chases. I gotta get more *location*...travelogue, atmosphere, and screwing...uh, romance, not just *that* kinda screwing. I want to get that Paris feel in the..."

Max huffed. "It's all gone *bobo* now. When I visited my cookbook authors there this summer..."

"What's bonbo?"

"No! *Bobo. Bourgeois bohème,*" he said with an accent inexcusably forced into the mush-mouthed variety of faux-French that Jack hated. Actually, today Jack hated much about his literary agent, his latest contract, and his life. But this was no time to air grievances. He took a sip and regretted it immediately when the cube clinked.

"Ah, Jesus, Jack! You're not drinking, are you? It's not even noon."

He looked at the pale amber in the glass. "Iced tea," he said pronouncing the "d" with care. "Just finished a run around the lake. Need to hydrate."

"Really?"

"Really," he lied again. "You know, I was just thinking that I did my best work in Paris years ago. But I'm still using that old version of the city in my books. I need to freshen up the references. It's just the spark I need to finish it. Make it shine. Can you book me one of those A-B things and get a ticket from JFK? Delta or Air France, preferably."

"Do you mean Air-B-and-B? You want me to rent a room or an apartment? Why not just stay in a hotel?"

"Nope. I need my privacy. I need workspace, a coffee machine, and lots of typing paper. The readers! My fans, you know. They recognize me from the back cover PR shot." He grinned at his surge of creativity and hiked up his sagging khaki cargo pants, reminding himself to find his belt.

"You think I'm your personal assistant?"

"No, but you have one and I don't. Think, Max. The sooner I get there, well...the sooner you'll have your—"

"A week?"

"I'll need all of October."

Max looked at the calendar on his computer. He smiled. "Hey! I got clients with an apartment in Paris. They'll be on a book tour all month. Maybe they'll let me—"

"What? Speak up. You're mumbling."

"My cookbook authors. Got a great apartment there. He's the sausage guy. She does breads. This is their first co-authored book."

"You make it sound like they've invented the hot dog and bun." Jack laughed at his own remark. "People buy those books?"

"By the carload. Christmas sales are big, so I have them doing a coast-to-coast tour with signings in high-end cooking stores and morning show TV demos. The whole ball of wax. Huge books, brilliant photos..."

"Do people actually cook stuff from that kinda book?"

"I don't care if they shred them for mulch around their azaleas as long as they buy them."

"You are a heathen."

"But I'm *your* heathen. Didn't I get the delivery date pushed back like you asked? They're still moaning about doing a press run that first week in November, so it better shine when I submit it or nobody gets paid. Cost me my left nut to get that late a delivery."

"What's this, your fifth nut?"

Max chuckled in spite of himself. "I'll have my intern book your flight. And I'll have a place set up for you. Okay? I'll have the kid get back to you with the flight details."

"And Max? Isabel! I'll need Isabel there too. And we need to start on the first."

"That's a Sunday! You want to leave New York on a Saturday? My assistant doesn't—"

"If you want a book, make it happen. I'm just a couple hours north of the city, not in Alaska." He disconnected the call without waiting for his agent's response.

Max spun his chair away from his desk and reached into the credenza. Finding his pink bottle of Pepto, he took a long draw and called

Isabel. When she didn't pick up on her cell phone, he left a short, scattered message.

Isabel looked at the phone with annoyance and continued working at her computer.

Max took a second swig from his pink bottle before he called the landline. When her home phone rang, Isabel listened to the caller ID and shouted to her daughter. "Eileen? Can you get that? It's Max, and I'm in the middle of..." Isabel glanced out the window of her office in the upstairs bedroom and saw that Eileen had started her long run. Headphones in, wearing her new Nike neon green top and tights, she would be out for at least an hour and a half. She watched her daughter slide into her pace with ease. Isabel shook her head wondering how the young woman she was watching had grown up so fast and knew how proud her father would have been.

Eileen quickly sped past several other saltbox houses like hers with two stories on its flat-faced front and one story in the rear. The steeply pitched rear roof resisted any snow build-up in winter or rain pooling in summer. She passed an empty lot where Hurricane Sandy had leveled a home. Although Sandy stripped off a good part of the roof of their house and forced immediate repairs, their home had survived. Few would guess that her unimposing house also held her home office for her translation and editing work as well as her mother's. Max had already linked Eileen to several established French authors. Now she was translating emerging American authors into French as well.

Isabel returned to her editing as Max left a long message on the answering machine. The breeze off the ocean had the faintest hint of fall and ruffled her auburn hair. The salted air carried a smoky memory of the summer's beach parties. She finished the edits to the last chapter of an interesting political history that loomed on her large monitor. Once she had saved the file, she stretched and walked downstairs to the living room. At fifty-five, her shoulder-length hair had yet to show any suggestion of gray. She was limber and started each day with her yoga routine, but her edges had rounded a bit after she gave up tennis and quit the club. Still dressed in her comfortable yoga pants and a sweater, she tapped the silver boxy message machine on the sofa's end table. She chuckled as the relic that her daughter hated buzzed before playing back the message. Then she listened to Max on her ancient flip phone.

After enduring Max's frantic whine in both messages, Isabel made a cup of green tea, plopped down on the sofa beside the machine, and paused to consider his tone. Max was excitable, but never this dramatic. She had made a good living from editing Jack's books. Editing his annual outpouring had paid off the mortgage and put her daughter through school. More than that, it had let her be a stay-at-home mom, running her business from her back bedroom. Only recently had she migrated to the large bedroom on the second floor, which had the space to hold her monitors, magnifiers, computers, and other equipment that she referred to as "mission control." The smaller ground-floor bedroom was more convenient, but change was inevitable. She let her tea cool, took a sip, and then left it untouched on the walnut coffee table. She waited for her daughter to come back from her long run on the bike path along the shoreline.

Just after two, Eileen came through the kitchen door, tapping the Nike fitness app on her Apple watch and shouted, "Hey! I'm back."

"Honey? Can you come in here before you shower?"

Although in her mid-twenties, Eileen was routinely carded at bars. She attributed this to her religious use of sunscreen, eating well, yoga, and running on the beach or her treadmill daily. Others saw her petite frame, short rusty curls, freckles, and inquisitive manner. On her way to the living room, Eileen grabbed a kitchen towel from the oven handle and mopped her face. Her bright Nike running attire was a sharp contrast to the conservative beiges and creams of the living room. Still catching her breath, she asked, "What's up?"

"Max called. You need to listen to his messages before you shower." Isabel pointed to the recorder.

Eileen tapped the button on the answering machine and listened to Max's whining, the gist of which was that Isabel needed to go to Paris and shepherd Jack's latest thriller with spies and lengthy sex scenes that he thought were romantic, into a presentable form before November first. Eileen glanced at her mother and frowned. "What's that all about?"

She handed her daughter the flip cell phone. "That's nothing. Listen to this."

Eileen stared at her mother's cell phone while the message played back on the speaker, then she closed the phone. "He's losing it," the young woman said. "That's about as close to a panic attack as I ever want to hear. Paris? He wants *you* to fly to Paris?" She handed the phone back to Isabel, draped the towel over her shoulder, and put her hands on both hips. "You never told Max, did you?"

"Why should I worry him? Macular degeneration sounds so dramatic, so final. I still have one good eye and the condition is progressing slower than they thought it would. Besides, mission control lets me keep working. You never told him why you wouldn't take long trips, did you?"

Ignoring her mother's comment, Eileen continued. "You're managing it and making accommodations that are fantastic, but..."

"Oh, we work so well together. I'll just call him back and say I can't go, but *you* can since you worked on his last two books."

"Are you kidding me? I have the workshop. Remember? Whidbey Island? I'm taking a month to work on my own novel? Come on, this is..."

"Think how much you can learn from just being there with Jack. Wouldn't that..."

"I've waited six months to get into the—"

"This is important for both of us. You need to go."

Eileen huffed. "Max just thinks of me as a translator, not an editor, besides..."

"This is your chance to get your draft in front of Jack. To use our connections to..."

"I can't. It's not ready. Besides—"

"You have to go."

"No. I don't."

Isabel took a deep breath and paused. "If he doesn't make his deadline, we won't be editing his next two books, because there won't be any."

"Shit."

"Then you're going?"

"I really don't want to. It's a whole month."

"In Paris! All expense paid. Even if you finish early."

Eileen cast her mother a side-glance. "Shouldn't that be *expenses?* And toss in a verb?"

"No. I was using an advertising phrase. Colloquial noun usage, but standard."

"Substandard."

"Fine! Edit my conversation. I don't blame you for being upset, but it doesn't change two facts..."

"We live in a post-fact era. Hadn't you heard?"

Isabel shook her head. "Well fact check this! I can't go, and we need the money."

"What if Jack doesn't want my help?"

"Tough beans. He's up the same creek we are if he doesn't get it in on time."

"*Merde!*"

"Glad all that tuition money was well spent so you learned to swear in French. I'll call Max and tell him that you're going."

Chapter № 2

September 30, 2017
Saturday

Two weeks later, Jack loaded his turtlenecks, two pairs of khakis, and his underwear into the old Maytag. Then he discovered that he was out of Tide. Hadn't he put it on the Costco list so he wouldn't have to buy it again for another year? He grabbed his clothes out of the washer, dropped them on his unmade bed, and started the shower. After rinsing off, he turned the valve tighter than usual. Didn't need it dripping for a month. He took one step out of the shower and swiped his hand across the steamed mirror in the cramped bathroom. He sighed and acknowledged that he no longer looked like the back-cover photo that his publisher had used on his books for the last decade. Then he rolled the word *decade* around on his tongue until "decade" slid into "decayed." He shrugged and thought how those PR photos were the cliché for thriller covers. Black turtleneck, tweedy jacket, chestnut hair slicked back, and tortoise-shell glasses. There was something professorial yet dangerous at the same time. Now, the black turtleneck had frayed at the cuffs and the neck had gone saggy. That jacket was at least one size too large. The steel gray at his temples had spread so his hair now looked sandy in the fogged mirror.

He brushed his teeth and wondered if the word cliché could apply to a style of photograph and figured Isabel would know. By the time he had finished, the mirror had cleared. When he stood, his wet hair fell over his eyes. He grabbed scissors from the drawer and trimmed the offenders back to mid-forehead. For a moment he considered getting a real haircut before the trip, but unless he found a barbershop at the airport, it would wait.

Besides, who was there to impress? Fans? Nobody had asked for his autograph in years, except at book signings. But still, his cookie-cutter spy-thrillers paid the co-op assessment on Marie's Manhattan apartment. After all that, he still had cash to pay for scotch to drink in his shitty, but paid-for, fishing cabin on Candlewood Lake. He chuckled when he thought of how that photographer from *Vanity Fair* had pimped it up with props and special lighting before calling it his lakeside retreat. Hell, his was just an old stone cabin built in the thirties by a savvy real estate guy who figured that summer people from New York would want to vacation at Candlewood Lake and ignore the fact that it was created by a hydroelectric dam in 1926, not God. He toweled off and pulled on his khaki cargo pants and the better of the two black turtlenecks from the pile on the bed. He grabbed his brown tweed jacket off its hanger and tossed it on the rumpled covers.

He sipped slowly on the coffee he had brought from the kitchen and looked around. The cluttered cabin was the only thing that was really his anymore, not counting the rusting Volvo that wouldn't die and the two insurance policies that sucked funds from his bank account every month. And maybe his creativity. Maybe he would find it again in Paris. Maybe that's where he'd left it with the first book. Maybe he was just retelling the same story over and over in his subsequent novels. Maybe he really was just a one-hit wonder who had stretched his lucky streak as far as it would go. At least he'd see his City of Lights again before his eighth decade. Wasn't that when it was supposed to start falling apart? Wasn't this too early?

As he snapped the scuffed cover on his Smith Corona Skyriter, he wondered if he'd need a new ribbon if he actually tried to write something during this effort to delay his inevitable humiliation. Rooting through his desk, he located a new spool, still neatly boxed from that typewriter shop in Hollywood. The one his wife found for him several years ago. The one he wrote to every March and ordered two ribbons— what he usually went through in his drafts. Now he had spares. He tossed a boxed ribbon into his battered briefcase. Paper? He could buy it there, if Max hadn't already stocked the place. A ream weighed about five pounds, and that was just 500 pages. The calculation was simple, a pound for each hundred pages. As he took the typewriter to the front door he chuckled thinking of how many tons of paper he must have used over his career, even with his lack of margins and jamming in every word as tight as possible during the first draft.

Nightfall went through eight revisions before it escaped into print last year. The critics were not kind, but the readers were. Sales were sufficient. He thought he must remember to thank Isabel, who had performed literary CPR on the pile of words he had vomited on paper in the middle of "the split," as Max called it. The split? As if any breakup were a thing of equal portions.

The turquoise hard-shell Samsonite had collected a film of dust on its exterior after a year in the closet. He swiped it off with his hand and dropped the suitcase on the bed. He inventoried as he packed. Indoors stuff: jeans, green cords, a couple of concert T-shirts, the blue work shirt, and the other turtleneck. Go-out stuff: a white shirt, tie, and the black funeral suit, if something formal came up or someone dropped dead. Underwear stuff: Skivvies, socks. He pulled his old leather Dopp kit out of the suitcase, went into the bathroom, and threw his essentials into it. He looked at the smudged glasses in the case and wondered how old that prescription was. He tried on the wireframes and decided they still would serve as an emergency pair. Suitcase loaded, he hoisted it with both hands and carried it to the door. He smiled as he thought that he would have the kid Max was sending lug it to the car.

Finally, he finished loading his leather briefcase. He checked to be sure his passport was still there, as though it could have somehow transported itself to some remote location. He tossed in two cheap high school composition books with splotchy covers that he bought on sale at Staples and a couple of new blue gel pens. He pulled the paperback of Haruki Murakami's short stories off his bedside table and dropped it into the briefcase wondering why he could not finish even one story. He loved *1Q84* and that ran more than a thousand pages. For a moment he reflected on Murakami's fitness instructor moonlighting as an assassin of abusive men and wondered how one reconciles such extremes or comes up with such an original character.

He took the briefcase to the kitchen, added four granola bars for the flight, and buckled it shut. He smugly congratulated himself on his pantry. Some scotch, several boxes of chardonnay, a couple cases of ramen, cans of tuna, and a big sack of rice from Costco every few months meant he didn't need to go to town nearly as often as when they had summered at the lake, as a family. Shutting the pantry door, he noticed the Costco shopping list pinned to the refrigerator under a magnet left by some realtor. He squinted and saw that he had put Tide on the list and shrugged.

After dropping the briefcase beside his typewriter on the porch, he locked the gun safe, unplugged his iPhone from its charger, and slid it into the side cargo pocket of his khakis. He noticed the brass cartridge in the ashtray, slipped it into his small watch pocket, and locked the front door. Bored, he walked to the end of the dock as he slipped on his tweed jacket. Fall had definitely arrived. The lake was now his. He pulled the cartridge from his pocket, flung it into the lake, and watched the ripples as he unzipped his khakis and took a leak.

The Saturday traffic toward JFK was light. Once the intern had armed Jack with his paper itinerary and checked the Samsonite bag at the curb, the young man fled. Jack hoisted the briefcase and typewriter and followed the crowd into the gaping terminal. He eventually found the long TSA line. Jack had his paper ticket verification sticking out of the chest pocket of his tweed jacket as though it were a pocket square. Bored after several minutes in a line that appeared to have cemented itself to the floor, he turned to look behind him and reassure himself that he was not the last person in the queue. As he turned, he came nose to nose with a slim black man wearing a bright blue Duke sweatshirt. "Oh. Excuse me. I didn't mean…"

"No worries. I had to check out the line too. Looks like it's a mile long."

Pointing to the sweatshirt, Jack asked, "You go to Duke?"

"Yes."

Jack nodded. "Good school."

The young man searched Jack's craggy face and then discounted his sloppy attire. He gathered his courage. "Excuse me, but may I ask you something, sir?"

"Sure."

"Are you that *Star Wars...Blade Runner 2049* guy? I saw the preview on YouTube and can't wait to see 'Twenty-Forty-Nine'..." He scrunched up his face then found the name. He spit it out like he was on *Jeopardy* and pointed at him. "Harrison Ford! That's it."

Jack laughed. "Well, that's a compliment, but no."

"But I think I've seen you somewhere, but not like in person. Like you're a celebrity, you know."

"Might have seen my face on a book jacket. I'm a good airplane read, I'm told."

He grinned and pumped his finger at him. "That's it. Jack... Jack..."

"Forrester."

"Yeah! The thrillers my dad's always reading. Oh man, he's such a fan. Once we pass TSA, if I bought your book would you sign it for him?"

"Sure. Happy to. What's your name?"

"Sam. Sam Greene. What gate are you flying from, so I can find you?"

"Not sure. Going to Paris."

"Oh man! That's my dream. To get there before med school."

Jack stood taller. "Every man needs to have Paris in him before he settles into whatever he must do."

"Really?"

"Really! Best time of my life, and I've had a few really great times."

"Wow. That big a deal?"

"Bigger. I'm pleased to be going back, even if it is for work."

"Cool, but out of what gate?"

"What do you mean?"

"Every plane has a gate it leaves from. Let me see your boarding pass."

Jack pulled the paper flight confirmation out of his pocket and handed it to Sam. "Oh, man. This is a ticket confirmation, not a boarding pass."

"They used to be the same thing, right?"

"No more. You're on Delta. Got its app on your phone?"

Jack dug out his scratched iPhone 4 from his side cargo pocket and handed it to Sam. "Do I?"

Sam clicked the home screen open and thumbed through the apps, then queried for it. Finding nothing, he gave Jack a weak smile. "Sir? You don't have a passcode on your phone."

"Didn't need one."

"Look, we're going to be chillin' in this line for another twenty minutes at best. Want me to get the app and set up your security?"

"Could you?"

"Sure. It will just take a second."

Jack shoved his briefcase and typewriter forward with the toe of his scuffed hiking boot.

Sam looked up from the screen and spoke softly. "What do you want your code to be? Four numbers you'll always remember."

"How about my birthday?"

"Pretty easy to guess." He tapped into his phone and then reported Jack's birthdate.

"How'd you..."

"Wikipedia biography. Is there another date or set of numbers?"

"Naw. Let's just leave it open. There's nothing on there for anyone to take."

"Okay, if that's what you want."

While Sam fiddled with the phone, Jack realized that he had not flown alone since September 11th, a date that he had started thinking of as nine-one-one recently. He frowned and tried to pull up the year. Stumped, he asked Sam. "What year was September 11th, the World Trade Center?"

Sam pressed the button on Jack's phone until Siri activated. "Ask her yourself."

Jack skeptically asked, "What year was September11th?" When Siri answered, Jack stared at the phone as if it were going to continue speaking. He looked at Sam. "Two thousand and one. My God. Sixteen years ago. A kid born that day might be driving now. How old are you?"

Sam looked at him. "I was three when it happened. So I don't remember much other than my mom being really sad for a long time."

Jack nodded and turned back to the line, which had moved again. He looked ahead to the TSA people checking identifications and past them to the screening machines. He felt a haze of separation between the day when the towers fell and today. They were out of the city when it happened. Their apartment wasn't damaged. It was a beautiful bright day for a one-day family outing before his book tour. Now travel confused him. In the past, Marie or someone from the publisher's PR department did all the arrangements, smoothed out the details, and went with him. Now he was alone.

When the public address system announced something, Jack frowned, turned, and asked, "What did it say?"

"No biggie. It was just announcing an arrival."

"Thanks." The amber haze of too much scotch, too little ink, and a family that had fallen apart weighed on him. He dug his passport out of his jacket's inner pocket and fumbled with his phone. Sam took Jack's phone, pulled up Jack's flight information on the app, and handed it to the TSA agent. Once cleared, Jack lugged his Skyriter in one hand and his briefcase in the other toward the screening machine.

Without looking at him, the screener asked him to open the case and turn on his computer. Jack smiled and rotated back the cover of the typewriter. Sam was motioned on by security while they examined the typewriter. Sam laughed. "Man! That's so old school." He hurried past Jack to the bookstore and asked if they had any Jack Forrester books. They had two titles. He bought both.

Jack asked the screener where the Delta lounge was and found it easily. Once there, he hid in a quiet corner. He sipped a crisp sauvignon blanc and tried to remember the last time he flew alone.

How had he forgotten how large the world was? How kind strangers could be? On tour, there was always a helper, someone to do these things, manage tickets and passes and luggage, find the gate, book a car, get the hotel, and make it easy. There was always some fan or paid somebody to meet him at a train station and lug the bag or fetch a meal or a drink. He had wrenched his back hauling the Samsonite to the front porch earlier that morning. The wine was not helping. This was crap.

At least the Spawn of Satan had booked business class and there was only one seat next to him. With takeoff at around five in the afternoon and arrival the next morning, he ought to be able to get dinner on board and get some sleep. Maybe dig into his briefcase for the Murakami and get in one short story. Just a snooze and he'd be back in Paris. Twenty years the wiser. Richer in many ways. But still 400 pages short of a man-uscript for a thriller.

He reached down and hauled his battered leather briefcase onto his lap. Most would take it for a professor's briefcase or a salesman's compan-ion. God it was heavy. Why hadn't he brought that new one his daughter gave him Christmas before last, the one made of microfiber and spider webs that weighed nothing and could stop a bullet? No. This old relic seemed somehow right for the outing. Fold-over top, cinched down by a belt across the middle. The brass on the buckle had gone green on the edges, seemingly overnight. *Must buff it up.* Jack had bought it in Paris while in his twenties when he decided that whatever he had to do to pay the bills, he would be a writer—and a writer needed a sturdy briefcase, a portable safe for his paper and pens and drafts, a place to keep a journal of thoughts and ideas. Lugged it to class during a lifetime of teaching. Had it when he met her and they lived together in Paris. The burn mark on the handle from when he used to smoke had almost vanished into the darkening patina. The wine stain on the back was now lost to a hundred other insults over the years.

He pulled open the flap, removed a black-and-white mottled composition book, dug out a new gel writer, and cracked the back of the notebook. He clicked the pen and rubbed off the blob of goo at the tip. Now it was ready to write. Granted it wasn't one of his leather-bound journals, but this was lighter. He stared at the lined page and the scribble left from the goo removal before he let his eyes drift out of focus.

He was startled when a poised attendant said, "Mister Forrester? There is a gentleman to see you at the reception desk. Something about a signing."

Struggling to his feet, he nodded and followed her to the entrance.

Sam grinned at him and placed an open hardback of his latest thriller on the granite counter beside an orchid arrangement. Sam had the foresight to offer a good rollerball to Jack to sign it.

"What's your dad's name?"

"It's Frank. Frank Greene, with an 'e' on the end."

Jack smiled and nudged him. "Funny way to spell Frank."

Sam started to correct him before he found the humor in the remark. Jack signed it with a flourish and closed the book. "There you go, Sam. Thanks for your help."

Sam reached into his backpack and offered a paperback copy of the older book. "And this one is for me."

Jack signed it: *To my travel pal, Sam. Hope you enjoy Paris as much as I did. Jack Forrester.* "There you go. Thanks again."

"My pleasure, sir. Have a good flight."

"You too. Enjoy Paris."

Jack watched the young man sling his backpack on as though it were weightless. He turned to the lounge and looked at his watch.

Three hours to kill. He turned back toward the kid. "Sam? Can I buy you a drink?"

"I'm not twenty-one yet."

"Ah...Ah..." He noticed a Starbucks far down the seating area. "Coffee?"

"Sure. I'd like that."

Jack turned to the woman. "Can you watch my briefcase and type-writer?" He motioned to the two cases by the chair.

She smiled. "Certainly. I'll move them up to the desk for you to claim when you return, Mister Forrester."

"Thanks."

He followed Sam to the long line at Starbucks. Not wanting to kill the mild buzz, he saw the "lemonade" sign and smiled. He pointed to it. "Had their lemonade?"

"Sure. I like it after a workout. Most of the team likes the peach and white tea lemonade."

"Sounds like you don't."

"I like the shaken black tea lemonade. It's kinda like an Arnold Palmer."

"A what?"

"Iced tea and lemonade. Very refreshing. I think that sounds better than coffee right now."

"Don't they just have a lemonade?"

"I don't think so. But you could ask."

Jack scanned the menu board as he reached for his wallet. "What do you want?"

"Venti London Fog."

"A what?"

"I'll order it. It's a big spiced iced tea."

When it was their turn at the counter, Jack motioned for Sam to order then asked for plain lemonade. Upon being told that no such drink existed, he asked Sam to remind him of one his teammates liked. Sam ordered for him. Jack raised his eyebrows when he saw the amount due and handed the barista his credit card.

Once they had their drinks, Sam motioned to a table near the window overlooking the runway.

Jack took a sip. "Not bad."

"I'm glad you like it."

Jack laughed. And almost choked on his next pull on the straw then grinned.

Sam looked at him and smiled. "What's so funny?"

He lifted his plastic cup in a mock toast. "This. I guess I just promoted myself to old fart."

"What?"

"All I really wanted was a lemonade. If the sign says lemonade, I want a fucking lemonade. And I don't know why they can't have small, medium, and large on stuff anymore either. It's worked since...uh, forever."

Sam laughed. "Not if you want to buy olives. Giant, jumbo, or extra large."

"Good point. You fly international a lot?"

He shook his head. "Going to LA. Terminal four is also Delta's long-haul domestic terminal. Had a few days off, so I came here to visit a friend in the city, then to LA for a fast family visit since I worked all summer. Then back to Duke."

"Good school."

Sam wondered why Jack had repeated himself. Maybe he was at a loss for words or maybe that was just cocktail party chatter that filled the silence. "Yes. I wanted to spend my junior year in Paris, but my dad wouldn't go for it."

"What's your major? They still have majors?"

Sam laughed. "Yes, they do. Program One covers all the standard majors. I'm in Program Two so I designed my coursework with an advisor. That way I can fast-track it to med school with more math."

"Sounds rough."

"It's a grind, but I'm already a junior, so I could be in med school before a lot of my buddies who are keggers and perpetual students are just getting their B.A.'s."

"Then what? Be a doctor?"

Sam shook his head. "Genomics or molecular genetics and microbiology. I got to be a research assistant in a lab all summer. Awesome time."

"Wow. When I was your age all I wanted to do was get laid."

"That too. I won't lie."

"Been to Europe, at all?"

"Not yet. Paris is top on my bucket list. Gotta see it."

"Don't see it, Sam. Live it, even if it's for just a week in one of those BB things. Hang out in the same café or bar to meet locals. Get a sense of the pulse of their day. Don't go to a McDonald's. Or do and see how it is different. It will change your life, or at least your perspective."

"Did it change your life?"

"Yup. Sure did. I hope you'll be as lucky."

"Thank you, sir." He checked his cell phone and motioned that he had to go.

Jack stood, smiled, shook his hand, and tried to remember a time when he wasn't "sir" to some kid. "Sure. Hey Sam? I got turned around. The Delta lounge..."

He pointed. "No worries. It's kinda hidden by gate B 32."

Jack retrieved his typewriter and briefcase. He found a comfortable spot and decided that he had time for another glass of wine, since that shitty assistant got him to the airport four hours early.

Chapter № 3

September 30, 2017
Saturday

Eileen slammed her bag onto the bed and pulled out flannel shirts and jeans and returned them to hangers in the closet. She opened her top dresser drawer, took out her packing list for business travel, her always-packed cosmetic bag, and her passport. While she scanned the list, she thought of her agreement with Max that he would not give her projects requiring travel of more than a week at a time. He acceded to her requirement and made her assignments work smoothly. But now, Jack's demand had thrown her schedule into turmoil. She had carefully planned a month away from home, for herself and her book. If she were honest, she wanted to get lost in her project at the writer's retreat and blot out Biarritz.

The writing workshop was Eileen's first long trip since her mother's early diagnosis of macular degeneration. Isabel's sister had stayed with her during the shorter trips, but had planned her cruise for over a year. Having finally been accepted to the writing workshop, Eileen scheduled the month away, cleared her work calendar, and arranged for an in-home care service to cook, clean, drive her mother to shop or to any appointments, and assist her as needed.

This had become a working trip. Eileen was packing city clothes not the comfortable flannel, fleece, and jeans she had planned for the workshop. Editing a rough draft and cajoling the reclusive Jack Forrester to tighten up his novel might be more challenging than just translating novels and nonfiction works of French authors into English or American novels into French. In translation, there was a precision. The structure was set, just a quibble here and there on context or the precise word. French was so much more predictable, stable, and reliable than English. But this was a different job altogether.

Isabel came to the doorway. "Thank you, dear. I know this is not what—"

She jerked a hanger from her closet. "No! It's not!"

"Max said it should only take a couple of weeks at most, so maybe you could still go..."

"No. I can't. The retreat is an all-or-nothing deal. And no refunds!"

"He promised you the whole month in Paris, 'just in case.' So, if you finish early, maybe you could work on your draft there."

Folding a pair of black slacks, she asked, "What makes you think I can just jam through it?"

"You know his style."

She ripped a blue and white flannel shirt from its hanger and slam-dunked it into her suitcase. "But—"

"Honey! You have to go. Can't you just make the best of it?" Eileen nodded as her mother turned from the doorway. She was right. It was crunch time. She knew his style. It was smoother than Ian Fleming's James Bond series but equally sexist. Fortunately, she had toned that down in his last book before the explosion of harassment claims filled the news. His work was intricately plotted, almost like John le Carré. His pace was almost as good as Lee Child's. In spite of the almosts, his style was his own blend of the thriller and spy genres. The sooner she finished the job, the more Paris time she would have to herself, if all was well at home. She paused, pulled out her phone, found the Find My Friends app, and then clicked the phone off.

As she packed she reluctantly decided that she was the best one to go. She grew up hearing her mother's side of lengthy conversations with Jack about whatever novel she was editing. Over the years, her mother's editing became more collaborative with Jack as they discussed plot twists and alternative scenes. He welcomed her additions to his work. Eileen also heard her mother talk about her other editing jobs, but none were as important or paid as well as Jack's books.

After Eileen's graduation from college, she moved to New York City and found work as a translator for an international law firm specializing in import and export issues and contracts related to France. She discovered that the challenges of translating were more interesting than the repetition of the legal matters, and so started a master's program. Soon she was translating for a series of French authors after Max recommended her to Jack's publisher. Eileen completed her master's degree in French, escaped the city for her childhood home, and started her own translation business.

Two years ago, Isabel thought her glasses were scratched and went to her optometrist to have the lens polished. It was then that testing revealed the blur was the start of macular degeneration in her right eye. Shortly thereafter, Eileen began helping her mother with the mechanics of editing more and more of his writing, until she almost worked alone on his last novel, reading passages to her mother for approval.

Isabel could still see well enough for most household things, but fine detail and the intensive reading that her work required was impossible without her new assistive devices. She refused to get a new cell phone, as their tiny apps were useless. At the start, there was just a blur in the center of her vision. Her doctor said it was early onset, but not genetic. It had no cure, but eating well, not smoking, and controlling her overall health might delay its progression. He was right. Fish at least once a week, spinach, Brussels sprouts and other vegetables high in lutein, and exercise all slowed the progression in her right eye and so far the vision in her left had not changed.

The small void in the middle of the text that looked like a blur was an annoyance that she initially overcame by glancing off-center. But as it grew, sneaking a glance at the type now failed to yield anything but frustration as the words refused to form, and reading with only her good eye was impossible. Once Eileen found an assistive reading system that let her mother continue editing, her office was converted from a small desk for marking paper pages of a draft by hand to a computer-assisted technology center requiring Eileen to relinquish her large bedroom with the ocean view. After struggling with Jack's poorly typed manuscript for his first book, Isabel had required all subsequent drafts to be submitted to her in a digital form, which made the transition to the command center seamless for her and invisible to Max, who had imposed this requirement on all of his authors whom she edited.

By using the massive magnified screen, she was able to mark sections for correction by using a footnote system, dictating corrections, and having Eileen proof her comments. She was back in business, but several of her clients wanted their drafts corrected and returned, not just notes where correction was needed. That's when Eileen started helping as a full partner. From late in grammar school, Eileen had watched as her mother worked over drafts, smoothed the rough edges, plastered over gaps in plot, and corrected character inconsistencies so that a reader would never know that the girlfriend's blue eyes in chapter eight somehow became hazel in chapter eleven. Beyond listening to her mother's half of the long conversations with Jack, Eileen diligently studied his published novels to understand the application of her mother's editing skills and his style.

Eileen's translations won critical approval immediately. Now book reviews noted that the work was "translated by I. E. Ross" as a mark of distinction. When her mother had made note of her using her initials not her name, Eileen explained that it removed any gender identification and got her more jobs. She never mentioned the happy coincidence of her father's insistence in naming her Isabel Eileen. Then she had teased her mother that it was good she did not want acknowledgments or use her initials, as they were not grammatically correct. When she said, "Isabel Rutherford Ross. So that's I. R. Ross," Isabel laughed.

Eileen reviewed the contents of her wheeled Costco black drag-a-bag. She needed just a pair of black slacks, her black pencil skirt, comfortable flats, a beige cotton turtleneck, the no-wrinkle white blouse, and a garnet cashmere turtleneck. She shoved the blue and white flannel shirt into the corner of the bag to make room for her Nikes, running tights, and the matching jacket. She tossed in her pre-packed underthings, the oversized *Hamilton* sweatshirt to sleep in, and her cosmetics bag that she hadn't used since her last trip to France. Seeing that there was room in the suitcase, she added a simple black dress for when she planned to shop at the Galleries Lafayette. The baggie with the plug converter and charging cords went in last. Her new noise-cancelling ear buds with the improved microphone was in her small purse, which was safely nested in the snap pocket of her huge charcoal messenger bag. Once she added her iPad and new MacBook in their foam sleeves, she was ready. Set to go an hour early, Eileen dressed in comfortable Wranglers, knee-high black boots, and a light gray cashmere turtleneck for the flight. She carried her lined black trench coat and let it drop on her suitcase after she pulled the bag into the living room and left it by the front door.

Isabel pointed at the suitcase. "How long?"

"I'll be there a month, maybe less, if the manuscript is halfway decent."

"No, dear. To pack."

"It took twenty-three minutes."

"Not your best time."

"I lost a charger cord and had to unpack my casual clothes. What color scarf can I get you this time?"

"Autumn hues, gold or amber."

"Good. That gives me something to look for."

Isabel smiled at her daughter. "Go on. No need to wait once you are ready."

"You sure?"

"Go! Call your Uber and give me a hug. I'll be fine. I still think that house cleaner you arranged is excessive."

"It's a home service, not a cleaner. They'll shop for you, make meals, and vacuum. They'll drive you places, fix the remote if you screw it up again...whatever you want. They can even read to you."

Isabel snapped, "That reader machine does just fine, unless it's a scribbled letter or postcard."

"That's the stuff you should have them read to you. You are impossible."

"You too, that's why I love you so much."

"Do you think he'll have a workable manuscript?"

"Who knows? It's been a long dry spell. He's pushing the deadline, so I hope that means it is polished."

"It is just weird that I'm going to meet him, not you. He's been your client for—"

"*Our client* for his last two books."

Eileen chuckled. "Not that he would know it. Still..."

"A little nervous?"

"Perhaps."

"Why? Hero worship?"

"Maybe. And maybe I'm just the slightest bit intimidated, since he's been our bread and butter for...forever."

Isabel asked softly, "You going to see Greg?"

Eileen leaned over and fiddled with a luggage tag that was securely fastened to the bag's handle. "I doubt it!"

"Why'd you say that? I thought you liked him. The selfie you sent on the beach looked like you two were having fun. He's handsome. Tanned, great smile, dark eyes, black hair. I like the way his hair made kind of a comma over his eye, like George Clooney in that movie, what was it?"

"Look. He's five years older than I am, knee deep in his work, and hasn't bothered to e-mail or call since I got back. What are the odds?"

"Why don't you call?"

Eileen gave her mother a withering look and pulled her iPhone from her pocket.

"Texting him now?"

She frowned at her mother. "Hey Siri! Open the Uber app." She tapped in her destination of JFK airport and slid her phone into her jeans pocket. "Five minutes away." She picked up her coat and hugged her mother. "Bye."

Once Eileen passed through security in the expedited TSA line, she wandered into the bookstore. She found two of Jack's thrillers on the paperback rack. She smiled as she picked up the latest and noticed it had the same author photo as the prior two books. He was rugged in a lean, rawboned, western way. The paperback had the old photo. A black turtleneck and a biker black leather jacket had completed the stereotypical portrait for thriller authors on his first few books. But there was always something about his eyes. They were pale, almost mountain stream blue against a good outdoorsman's tan. Walnut brown hair was gracefully receding into a widow's peak with a dusting of gray at the temples. High cheekbones and a lanky pose leaning against a silvered fencepost somewhere, gazing into the distance. His Ray-Ban aviators were pushed up on top of his head. He looked like a jet jock spy.

The hardback of his newest book carried his most recent photo. He had exchanged the leather jacket for tweed and tortoise-shell glasses with clear lenses for the Ray-Bans. He was the professor whom coeds signed up for whether or not they cared about writing a novel or short story. She chuckled when she recalled he had taught both. She guessed the picture was at least five years old. But those cheekbones were distinctive and those eyes were inviting.

She bought a pack of mints and walked directly to the Delta lounge. She looked over the moderately full lounge and spotted a tall man seated on a sofa. From the back, it might be Jack, but with much more gray in his hair. She hesitated when she approached him and sat in a chair to his right. He looked just a step away from homelessness. His jacket hung on him as if he were a scarecrow. His hair needed cutting as desperately as he needed a bath. She cleared her throat and said, "Are you..."

He glanced at her and went back to doodling in his composition book.

"Excuse me, aren't you the writer, Jack..."

"No."

"Forrester?"

"I used to be. Sorry, no more autographs." He reached down and tugged the heavy typewriter case up to the space next to him. Then he stood, clutching it with both hands, and shuffled to a chair facing the window, where he planted himself and watched the planes being serviced. Eileen viewed his disappearance with amusement and then confusion. She had him. She knew that he was the best-selling author. But he didn't know her. Yet. He had no idea that Max had sent her to edit. He was expecting her mother. But they had never met.

She shrugged and was about to return to reading on the Kindle app on her iPad and delay her introduction when she noticed that he had forgotten his briefcase, a stained leather fold-over that once was tan. Now scuffed at the corners and sweat stained on the handle, it was an appendage he had inadvertently abandoned. Summoning her courage, she picked up her carry-on messenger bag and his briefcase. She walked over to the window and stood in front of him. He tried looking past her by leaning to his left. She moved to block his view again and held up the briefcase. "You forgot this."

He reached for it. "Thank you."

She pulled it back. "Jack? It's time we talked."

"Who are you to intrude on...?"

"Max sent me. I'm your editor."

He stood and looked her over while frowning. "You can't be Isabel. You're what? About my daughter's age. Twenty-two?"

She smiled. "Close enough."

He squinted at her and shook his head. "You can't be Isabel. She's been editing my stuff for almost twenty years." He frowned. "Who the hell are you? And where is Isabel?"

"She's home. I'm her daughter. Didn't Max tell you that—"

"Lotta good that's gonna do me. I need Isabel."

"Calm down, Mister—"

"Jack. Just Jack."

"Okay, Jack. Here is how it is. Max sent me to edit your draft while you do some fill-in work in Paris."

"I still don't know how I'm supposed to trust you..."

She leaned forward and in a low, deliberate voice said, "I helped her edit your last two books."

"What?"

"Really. I did."

"Did what?" He leaned toward her, squinted, and pushed his glasses back.

She spoke louder and directly at him. "I helped her on your last two books."

"Why can't she come?"

"It doesn't matter. She can't and you have me instead."

"Swell. You're an editor too?"

"Yes. But I mainly do translations: French to English. English to French."

He slumped into a chair and was motionless. She stood in front of him, waiting for him to say something. Suddenly, his face assumed the expression of rigid terror common to hostage pictures on the evening news. His mouth moved soundlessly. Gaping like a fish. Then he said, "What am I going to do without Isabel?"

She slid into the chair beside him and put her hand on his arm to reassure him. "It's going to be fine. I know how to edit your work."

He looked at her and tried to think of what to say. Finally he decided to ask about her work. "So, you translate? How'd you get into that?"

"In a way, I have you to thank, seeing your books in translation at home. I was good at languages in school and French in particular. Did the usual undergrad stuff then decided to continue."

He fell back on his old cocktail party trick of just echoing what someone had said to him. "Continue, did you?"

"Yes. For my thesis, I did a comparative analysis of the key English
translations of *Swann's Way*. That's the first book of the seven that make
up *À la Recherche du Temps Perdu*. The stylistic differences and word
choices in translations, not the novel itself."

"Didn't I hear somewhere that they changed the title?"

"Yes. That's what gave me the idea for a comparative analysis, and to
do my own translation. It used to be called *Remembrance of Things Past*.
Now it's usually *In Search of Lost Time*."

"And which do you like?"

"Neither. Remembrance feels more like *souvenir*. But titles are usually
the provenance of the publisher so I'll let that go."

"Didn't he translate some novel from English to French?"

She laughed. "Ruskin's! His command of English was marginal. He actually had friends helping with the translation, including his mother, who
was an excellent linguist. When challenged, he had the best PR answer
ever. 'I may not know English but I know Ruskin.' How's that for brass?"

"Not bad."

"He was an odd duck. Lived at home until he was thirty-four, then left
home because his parents died and he got an inheritance. I still can't figure
if he was just a dilettante or really sickly."

"Couldn't he have been both?"

"Of course. Academics like to find neater answers."

"So, have you published your dissertation?"

"Thesis. I wouldn't expose anyone to that dreariness and navel gazing.
I barely remember it. You fall down this insular rabbit hole in academia.
I began with a project that was insane by proposing to compare Scott
Moncrieff's first six volumes, published in the thirties, to the translations
by Terence Kilmartin and later still by Enright."

"I'm confused, I thought you said there were seven volumes."

"He died before he finished translating the seventh, so it seemed unfair. Anyway, I had a sane advisor who reduced the thesis to a comparative of only the first volume, adding in the Penguin translation published in 2002, and requiring my own partial translation."

"Which one came in second after yours?"

"Actually, they all have merit. But I think the Penguin edition is the best, but then they had several minds working on it and new material to amplify some of the text. Christopher Prendergast used his knowledge and a team of seven other translators."

"Oh," he said before he stood, walked to the bar, and poured another glass of wine for himself at the courtesy bar.

She read and he dozed until the flight was ready to board. He made a dash for the restroom prior to boarding. Once buckled in, he took advantage of a glass of wine before and with his dinner then slipped into a comfortable sleep until their arrival at the Charles de Gaulle International Airport was announced.

Chapter № 4

October 1, 2017
Sunday

As the plane approached Paris, Eileen took out her mirror and surveyed the damage. Red eyes got drops. Her auburn hair was a tangle of curls that she smoothed by running her fingers through them. After a mint and the application of some lipstick, she was ready for Paris. She nudged Jack and offered him a mint. "Landing in a few minutes." She checked her watch. Almost eight in the morning. This was the perfect overnight flight. It arrived at a decent hour, allowed time for passport checks, baggage retrieval, customs, and finding the driver Max would have arranged. They would miss the weekday commuter traffic into Paris.

The line at customs was longer than usual and security elevated after a minor incident the prior day. Jack started fussing and frowned. "How long is this going to..."

"It's moving at least."

"I gotta go to the men's room."

"We passed it back there. I'll pull out of line and wait for you if I get close."

He slapped his pocket. "Got money for the attendant. Found a few francs from my last trip in my desk."

She handed him an envelope with several bills and coins. "Here are some Euros. They don't use francs any more. The coins are worth about a buck, if you need them. Just hurry."

Passing through each of the checkpoints in due order, they arrived at the exit door. Eileen had strapped his briefcase to her drag-a-bag.

He listed significantly to the right under the weight of the turquoise Samsonite suitcase.

There was a bank of limo drivers, all in black suits, each holding a board with their passenger's name on it. She spotted a sign with their names, and pointed to it. They made their way to the edge of the surging crowd.

The sky was overcast and colors muted. As they got closer, they saw a slim woman in her early twenties holding a sign for them and being jostled in the scrum of male drivers. The driver's hat, black slacks, and jacket made her appear similar to the other chauffeurs. But upon getting closer, they saw that her hat had obscured her fine features, delicate make-up, and multiple piercings.

She saw them walking toward her sign and stepped forward. "I'm Adele."

He scowled. "You're our driver?"

"Among other things. Here, let me take the suitcase, Mister Forrester." Jack felt his back pull as he handed it to her. "It's heavy."

"I bench one-twenty."

Jack stopped for a moment to reconcile her statement with her elfin appearance. "What are you, about five foot two?"

"Five one, actually. If you'll wait at the curb, I'll bring the car up. New limo rules here are a pain." She looked over her shoulder as a cloud of diesel exhaust floated past them. "Whatever you do, don't step into the street. They'll mow you down in a second." She moved the turquoise suitcase to the curb beside Eileen and nodded to it. "Easy to find you. Bet they haven't seen one like that since..."

Within a few minutes, a silver Mercedes sedan arrived, and the trunk unlatched. Adele ran around, opened the rear door. She grabbed the suitcase and slid it easily into the trunk. Eileen handed her the briefcase and her roller bag. Jack, after being stared into submission by Adele, relinquished his scuffed vinyl case. She almost dropped it. "Jeeze, what's in there, a bowling ball?"

"Typewriter. I need it to finish my book. Be careful." Eileen slipped into the car and slid across the rear seat. Jack folded into the seat beside her and fumbled with the seatbelt. Before he had clicked in, Adele had eased into the traffic crawling out of the loading area.

As the Mercedes left the Avenue de Paris and merged into traffic on the A 106, Adele tossed her billed cap onto the passenger seat and ruffled the spiked front of her hair. The shaggy ponytail fell to her shoulders after being released from the cap. She glanced back at them and said, "There are bottled waters in the center armrest if you are thirsty."

Jack tugged down the armrest and removed two bottles of Evian. "Thanks, I am dust dry after that flight." He handed Eileen one, which she put in the cup holder.

"The chefs always want water in the car. Got a special filter thing on the fridge. It's their thing."

"Chefs?"

"Didn't Max tell you where you were going?"

"You know Max?"

"Well, I've never met him, but I've talked to him several times. We text all the time. He's a mensch."

Jack laughed. "A mensch? You sound just like a New Yorker."

"I am. Max knows my dad and got me an internship with the chefs. Mostly I'm a go-fer for them. But I'm doing some of the shoots for his new book. They are on tour now so they let Max have their place in town for you to finish your book."

He frowned. "Who are these people?"

She chuckled. "You musta heard of 'em. Real ballers." When she saw Jack's look of discomfort, she continued, "Ballers! You know, like basketball rich guys who order a case of Cristal Champagne to make mimosas. Ya know?"

He cleared his throat. "I'm pleased you clarified that."

"No problem. They're really nice people. You musta heard of

Georgina and George. GG Cuisine. Or maybe you've seen their line of pans and cookware at Sur La Table. Google them!"

Eileen pulled out her iPad and did a quick search as Adele continued her overview.

"Georgina and George. She's a Georgia peach right out of central casting complete with lots of 'y'all' and 'sugar-pie.' She's something. Mangles both French and English, but then she has a laugh that makes you think you've known her all your life and she's your favorite aunt. George is, of course, French. He cornered the artisanal sausage market before most people knew there was one. She calls him 'shorsh' and no one corrects her."

Jack leaned forward. "What was that?"

"She just over-Frenched his name so it got smashed down to 'shorsh,' and sometimes it sounded like she was telling him to 'sush.' Max was brilliant in touring them together as he staged their annual cookbook releases every October. Got them both to be bigger than life, real show-stoppers. This year they both had spawned monstrous coffee table books. Max joked that they were actually the size of a coffee table, in addition to the one they did together. Check out the link to *Maison-Retro*."

As Eileen scrolled through their web page she found a link to *Maison-Retro*, the French version of *Architectural Digest*. Clicking the link, she brought up a picture of a pale building in a classic style. The caption explained that it was the façade of a slate-topped six-story stone building on the Left Bank, the tallest allowed in the Haussmann-era, which literally was on the bank of the Seine facing the elegant cathedral, Notre-Dame de Paris. The apartment was covered in Lutetian limestone, as were its neighboring buildings. Their connected balconies ran the length of the block and offered a unified appearance. She clicked the interior photo page. She gasped. "Jack, look at this!"

Adele glanced at them in the rearview mirror. "Yup. That's where you're staying. Chez Chef, as she calls the penthouse."

Jack looked up and pointed at the screen. "That's a mansion!"

"Pretty much. If you read the whole article, you'll see that it was originally two penthouse apartments: one facing the courtyard and the other facing Notre-Dame. He owned the river view. She bought the other one when they became an item. Then they bought the whole building. They're planning a massive renovation. Nothing outside can be changed from the original look from the eighteen hundreds. But inside!" She whistled. "Electronics are like it's a mission to Mars. There used to be four large residences on the top floor. They put their entrance at the end of the hall, next to the elevator, blew out walls in the other two apartments to make a huge open living, dining, and kitchen space on the view side and a walk-in wine cellar, pantry, guest bath, and two junior guest suites on the courtyard side. Installed a full chef's kitchen with studio lighting. They do most of the book photos there. I mean it's like at the Ritz. And the kitchen's probably better than the one at the Ritz."

"An office?"

"Of course. Interior, soundproofed, no view, like his suite. Max had me restock it to be sure you had new toner and ink in the printers and a carton of paper. Computers are set up with a guest password just for you. Left them on stickies."

Jack began, "This is so much...I don't know if it is—"

Adele interrupted him. "It's really a livable space. You'll see."

Jack was not convinced. "Interesting."

"They both love your books, Mister Forrester, and stocked the wine fridge in the kitchen just for you. You said in some interview that you really liked French whites. I hope that's still the case."

"Love 'em. But I'm confused. If there is a wine cellar..."

"That is *their* wine cellar. Trophies and library wines from some of the best houses. Gifts from other chefs. It's locked."

"Oh. I get it."

During the remaining twenty minutes of the drive into the heart of the city, Jack stared out the window as though he were searching for a lost friend. When Adele crossed the Seine, the water was running high. Where light through the scattered clouds painted the river, it looked like moss on slate. The stone buildings were still wet and dark from the morning rain.

On arrival, Eileen knew exactly which entrance was the chefs' from the picture on the cover of *The Blue Door Cookbook*. The faded blue on the curbside door and the massive door leading to the courtyard blended perfectly with the old stone. Rather than stopping at the curb, Adele pulled the front bumper close to a tall arched door and pressed a button beside the sun visor of the Mercedes. As both doors folded back, she inched the car into the bricked courtyard. She easily parked between a classic 1969 black Citröen DS 21 sedan and a new flame-red Mini.

After popping the trunk, she handed Eileen's light bag to her and carried the Samsonite. Jack, with his briefcase and typewriter, followed the women through a small garden. The benches and chairs were covered in canvas against the fall weather. Amber leaves had already started to gather on them. Tapping a number pad on the door to the lobby, Adele said, "Same key pad on the outside blue door and upstairs." Then she motioned back to the cars. "Guess who owns which?"

Jack chuckled. "She's gotta drive the Mini."

"Ya think? He let me drive the old Citröen a few months ago. We were going out to photograph a pig killing and do portraits of some truffle-hunting dogs. Made the cover of a French cooking magazine. My first big credit. Anyway, its suspension is as soft as a baby's butt. He said they built it for the post-war roads that were wrecked or were still cobblestones. It actually goes up and down to allow clearance of more than a foot. He says it's a fussy car to maintain now, but I've never heard of anything like it and my dad was a car dealer always bringing home something weird. If George is back before you leave, ask for a ride. He loves to show it off."

Once in the lobby, Jack put down his briefcase and typewriter at the foot of the polished brass birdcage elevator. Beside it was a gleaming brass rack for coats and a brass umbrella stand holding a dozen perfectly matched umbrellas. He waited for Adele to slide back the elevator's gate. It echoed against the black and white veined marble covering the floor and walls. Eileen sniffed the air. Fresh, a lavender scent mixed with clean oil from the elevator's exposed cables. It had the scent of a summer day near the sea.

Jack looked up. "Who else lives here?"

As the elevator rose smoothly, Adele pointed to the carved doors on each floor. "Just them. Imagine! Six huge apartments below their penthouse in the heart of Paris! They are planning to convert them into a cooking school, an art school, and make a ground-floor exhibit and event space. She says it's going to take forever to get approval, but even if they don't, they can still do a VRBO deal for high-end short-term rentals. This is a goldmine, even if they never publish another book."

When the elevator stopped, a massive carved door that looked like it had been purloined from a cathedral blocked their way. Adele slid a wood panel aside to expose a keypad like the one at the lobby entrance, tapped in some numbers, and the imposing door swung open.

"That's some trick," Jack said.

"Yeah. Got a battery backup the size of a couple of refrigerators in the basement. A prototype from Tesla."

Eileen stopped a few steps into the huge living room. "It looks almost like the article. The pictures..."

Adele pointed to a cluster of family photos on the wall. "*Almost.* The magazine staged some prop Rembrant-ish oils there. I think their photos are better. Drop your stuff for a minute while I get my gear, then I'll show you around."

They left their bags by the original fireplace that was framed with a cream-colored marble. The side pilasters were carved with delicate vines that formed a heart on the center tablet under the scalloped mantel. Eileen glanced at the dozen antique wine openers that were displayed on the top of the mantel, which was almost at her shoulder level. A brass screen covered the lower half of the tall firebox.

She turned and stared at the massive living, dining, and kitchen expanse. A mix of occasional chairs from several French eras dotted the edges of the room while a sleek three-seat sofa in ebony leather with a bright chrome exoskeleton faced the fireplace. A two-person version of the same sofa was backed against it facing toward a large granite-topped island with several high stools allowing guests to observe the chefs in action or dine informally. Beyond the island was a commercial-grade kitchen. The ovens and refrigerators were of buffed stainless. Between the island and the window was a small walnut table.

A contemporary glass dining table with a dozen chairs ran parallel to the bank of windows, leaving a large open space between the sofas and kitchen's massive island.

Jack nodded at the sofas. "Interesting putting modern pieces there."

Eileen chuckled. "Modern? I saw those sofas in a museum! Le Corbusier designed in the late nineteen twenties. Almost a hundred years ago."

"No kidding. Looks like they invented it...tomorrow." He looked around the room. "Think this is their stuff or they just paid somebody to make it look cool?"

"Look at these." Eileen pointed to the small wall to the left of the fireplace containing amateurish oils and watercolors of seascapes sprinkled among well-framed snapshots of family pictures. This was an eclectic collection of framed black and white pictures of the chefs from their youth to their current fame. Scanning the photos, it was evident that they led very different lives until they met in middle age.

The photos were clearly personal. In one, she was twelve, in a canoe, splashing water on a younger girl. The droplets from the paddle sparkled in the light. Another showed Georgina at twenty in baking school with three other women. Each wore a checked apron, held a certificate, and had that self-conscious smile common to mandatory class photographs.

Another snapshot was of her in the back of a bakery, elbow-deep in dough. Her hair was in a net and her grin genuine.

George at twenty, whip thin, wearing a bulky field jacket that had flown open, was racing after a truffle dog toward a dark forest. George standing over a dead boar with a rifle in his hand. Bare-chested George sailing a twenty-footer over glass-clear water, possibly in Greece. Their wedding picture was informal, taken on a cliff at sunset, and joyous. She leaned closer to a small photo. "I think these are the real them. But the rest of the artwork? I wonder if they collected it or if they used a decorator."

He walked over to the wall closer to the door that was a solid mass of frames of all sizes mere inches apart. All of the artwork was suspended by thin wires from a sturdy molding. Everything was themed to their profession. In the center of the mass was a large Picasso lithograph in shades of blue and cream showing a smeared plate melting off the edge of a table, a deformed basket of bread, and a bottle of wine that listed to one side. Surrounding it were eight other individual pencil drawings or etchings of specific fruits or vegetables, all framed alike yet scattered in the collection.

Miscellaneous modern oils of wheat fields or forests suggested a farm-to-table theme. Two prints of Audubon's birds anchored the left and right edges of the collection. A print of a wild turkey faced right. A print of a willow grouse faced left, each in deep shades of brown and cream. Both birds eyed the Picasso.

Above the fireplace was a large, dark oil painting, suggestive of the Dutch painters of the seventeen hundreds. A table was laden with a dead rabbit, a pheasant, apples, and cabbages. Dew on them glistened against a background of dark ruby velvet. Eileen moved closer. Every hair of the rabbit's pelt was distinguishable, every shimmering feather its own thing. Each dewdrop held a rainbow. She shook her head. "Wow. The detail is—"

"Detailed!" Jack chuckled. "Think it's real?"

"Who knows, but I love it. Here in a chef's home, it's perfect."

He leaned so close to it that she thought his nose would touch it. "You know, there was a Dutch painter. A guy that did still life like this, but he really was a flower guy. Once he told his patron that he had to wait a year longer to complete his commissioned painting because he needed to wait for a yellow rose to bloom before he could finish it."

"Is that true?"

"Who knows? Some stories just sound right. It was either Jan van Huysum or Vermeer. But I don't think Vermeer did many flower paintings."

"Think Max could use the 'yellow rose' ploy?"

"Doubt it."

Adele returned and dropped her backpack by the door. "Okay. You gotta choose which suite you want."

"Suite?"

"His and hers, officially, but they sleep together in the 'His.' Hers overlooks the Seine. His is deadly quiet facing the courtyard. Zip view. I put all their personal stuff away so you'd have the top drawers. And I put out guest robes in both bathrooms."

He stared at Adele again and wondered if she left the safety pins in her earlobes at night and how she could blow her nose with that ring in it.

"Lemme show you the suites." Their shoes clicked on the buffed parquet flooring as they followed her. At the end of the hall Adele opened two richly carved doors that faced each other flanking a large armoire. "Take your pick. They just installed new windows that open in both suites. Hers looks over the city. With the window open, it can be as noisy as she is. But you can see Notre-Dame and the kestrels when they circle above that tower."

"Really? In the city?"

Adele nodded. "There's a nest. I've been photographing the nesting pair from the roof. There's a bird guy that is going to pay big when I get the right shot." She laughed. "So I'm kind of a bird paparazzi for him. He says there are thirty nests in the city, but he can't get a good shot of any of them."

The master suites were almost identical. In spite of the use of the French provincial furnishings, white-painted wood with gold accents and the ivory velvet-tufted side chairs, both suites had the sterility of a hotel. They were distinguished only by minor variations on the color palette the interior decorator had selected. Hers had Degas ballerina sketches. His had dark oils of hunting scenes. The artwork looked original. Her suite emphasized soothing lavenders and creams while his used shades of chocolate and beige.

The bathrooms, which were as large as Eileen's living room at home, were identical in their oak flooring, heated stainless towel racks, beige toilet and bidet, pale granite countertops with black and oxblood flecks, a glass circular shower that had a steam feature, and a massive soaking tub against the far wall. They were distinguished only by the color of the huge tubs, his being onyx and hers being the same oxblood porphyry as Napoléon's Tomb.

Jack pointed to the window facing the cathedral. "Take it, I like quiet."

They followed Adele back to the living room. "Any questions before I grab my stuff?"

Eileen raised her hand to stop Adele. "Is there a market nearby?"

"Oh. I've stocked the fridge and the freezer. Eileen, Max said you liked a vodka martini on the rocks, but didn't know if you preferred Ketel One or Tito's. Chefs aren't into the hard stuff so I put both in the freezer door. Vermouth's in the fridge door. There's a corner bodega a few blocks that way if I missed anything. Bread and smokes. The usual Seven-Eleven stuff."

"Impressive. That's the *épicerie* we passed on the way in?"

"Yes. It's great. And there's a big Monoprix just over on Boul San Miche if you need anything—sort of a Target on crack. You can find it on your Google map."

"On Saint-Michel. Thanks. Oh, is there a good running path nearby?"

"There's a full gym in the basement. I'd recommend using it rather than a street run."

"Keys or codes?"

"Oh. You don't need a key for the penthouse or the outer doors from the courtyard or street. Max told me your birthdates. I entered them both as separate access codes. There's a buzzer by the street door. You can answer it at the phone by the penthouse door or look at the visitor by tapping the screen. Neat hidden camera. Okay? Four numbers to the code. Month and day, like in the States, not the year, not flipped like here, followed by the hashtag."

Jack frowned. "The what?"

"Hashtag?"

Eileen chuckled. "The number sign."

Adele said, "Look, Max said you needed the place to power through some editing, so I'm going to be at a friend's loft in the Marais shooting my own stuff for travel magazines. I cover the bar scene, the street markets, touristy stuff for commissions. My cell number is on the counter if you need me."

Eileen followed her. "Before you go, let me be sure I can do the lock. Okay?"

Adele nodded as she swung the large backpack over one shoulder and a scuffed Nikon camera bag from the eighties over the other and marched into the hallway. Eileen followed her and closed the door. As she started to tap in her birthdate, Adele touched her arm and spoke softly. "Is he okay?"

"What do you mean?"

"He seems kinda spacey."

"I'm feeling some jet lag, and he's so...he's older."

"Maybe that's it. Anyway, good luck on your project."

"Thank you for all your help."

"No biggie. I'll check in toward the end of the month and see when it'll be convenient for me to come back. If you leave early, call my cell. Okay?"

Eileen and Adele entered each other's numbers into their contacts on their phones.

Adele watched until the lock opened successfully. Eileen waited until the whine of the elevator stopped, and the outer door closed.

When Eileen returned, Jack looked at her and shook his head. "She looked like that tattoo girl."

"*The Girl with the Dragon Tattoo?* Lisbeth Salander?"

"Yeah. How can you stick pins in your ears? That's just weird. And the nose ring? Had a bull once that…" He shuddered. "Never mind." He looked around. "Let's get settled in."

Eileen reached her hand toward him. "Hey, give me your phone for a minute. I'll put in our numbers so if we need…"

He dug his iPhone out of his pocket and handed it to her. "What's your code?"

"Code?"

"Yeah. Your code to open the phone."

"You just push that button there."

She tapped it. His screen showed the low battery warning. "When did you charge it last?"

"Beats me. Back at the cabin, I guess."

"I'll set up a charging station in the office and get my computer set up."

After she entered his number into her contacts, she left both their phones on the desk in the office. He lugged his suitcase into the room, and opened it on the floor under the window. She called after him, "Hey! You have an international plan?"

He yelled back, "A what?"

She shrugged and just called her phone from his. It rang. She reversed the procedure so her number was at the top of his recently called list and added her number to his contacts. She rolled her suitcase into her room and then carried her laptop and a baggie of cords, adapters, and chargers into the office. She nearly ran into Jack, who was retrieving his typewriter. She pointed to the massive partners' desk in the large office. "There's plenty of room for both of us." The wall of bookshelves held cookbooks authored by the chefs as well as the work of several contemporary fiction writers, including Jack's full collection. Each side of the desk held a laptop with the password written on a stickie. The shelf that was level with the desktop held an inkjet color printer, a dedicated photo printer, and a black and white laserjet printer.

"That's okay. There's a small desk in my bedroom. I'll set up in there."

"Fine. Let me know when I can load your thumb drive so I can get an early start tomorrow."

As he left, he called over his shoulder, "Sure thing."

She crawled under the desk, plugged in all the chargers, and snaked the wires up to the surface of the desk. As she plugged his phone and her MacBook in to charge, she heard Jack come to the doorway again. "Getting all set up?"

"Yeah. I can load the thumb drive now."

"The what?"

She spoke louder. "Thumb drive. That little thing you have the draft saved on."

He shrugged.

"Did you burn it to a CD? Old school?"

He shook his head.

"The cloud? Dropbox?"

When he failed to respond, she stood as tall as possible. "You didn't bring it on paper, did you?" He looked away. "You told Max that..."

"I don't know why I did..."

She put both palms against the embossed leather blotter and let her head drop. She took a deep breath, sat hard into the ergonomic chair, and then glared at him. "You lied to Max!"

He spread his arms. "It's an old literary tradition. Fitzgerald lied to his Max."

"Maxwell Perkins was his editor, not his agent. Your Max—our

Max—is trying to help you meet your contractual obligations and put money in your pocket! Why lie to him?"

"I lied to myself."

"Why?"

He pulled out the matching chair and slouched into it. "I'm stuck."

"So it's a messy manuscript?"

"Nope. Not a word on paper."

Eileen crossed her arms and scowled at him. "But you told Max my mother had to come here to edit it."

"She'd never been to Paris. I thought she'd enjoy it. Sort of a thank you or a last hurrah, I guess."

She stared at him, gripping the arms of the chair, and breathing hard. Finally she asked, "Are you drinking, like Fitzgerald? Opioids? If that's what you are saying, there are interventions…"

"No meds. A snort of scotch every now and again, but no. I haven't crawled into the bottle like Hem and Fitz did. Not yet at least."

"Hem? Hemingway?"

"The *Post* compared my last book to his work. Said it had 'all the vigor of Hemingway at his peak but in the complex modern world of espionage and terror' and some other garbage."

"It was a good book. I expected you to build on your continuing characters."

"That's what I was thinking, but I don't have a plot to hang it on. Not a thought in the world. I guess I could do one of those magical thinking books that make no sense but have people seeing ghosts and ice storms in the middle of summer. When a bite of snow reminds them of their grandmother's cookies." He laughed. "But Proust beat them to it with his madeleine. One taste of that little cookie cake and he spewed out his memories for a billion pages. What a bitch that must to have been to edit or translate."

"You think it was really edited? Not to my standards! Look, I told you that I translated the first hundred pages and contrasted that to the significant prior translations as a part of my master's thesis and…" She noticed he was staring past her into the living room. "What I'm trying to say is that I can work hard and we can get something..."

Jack ground his palms against his eyes. "It just ain't there anymore. I lay down some words then I gotta polish them. I was raised plainspoken and still think that way. That's why I was a good teacher. I know my stuff, but I cut through the crap. I'm clear. Or I was. That's why my plots could do a loop-de-loop and still come out right-side-up. But now. I can rub on 'em all day long and they just sit there like dull pennies."

"Is that how you work, reworking over and over?"

"Hell yes. First draft is just to slam it down. Get a big mug of coffee and type until I had to pee. Blast it out, get the flow. That's writing. The next is cleanup. Shine it up. Putty over the holes. Build up the suspense. Get it balanced. Read it out loud in my cabin at full volume like that French guy."

"Flaubert. *La guelade* is what he called it. Shouting. He'd frighten his neighbors."

Jack chuckled. "Benefit of living in a cabin off-season. No neighbors to frighten after Labor Day."

She watched him carefully as his eyes sparkled with tears. "Do you think we can write something fast enough to meet the most minimal contract compliance?"

"Hell if I know. I usually run through eight to ten spit-and-polish sessions after I have a good plot line down..." He stalled and she waited for him to collect his thoughts. "You know, people think you just have this stuff dripping off your fingers, as if typing were writing. They don't expect poets to go to the market and ask the butcher for a cut of meat in iambic pentameter, but no one ever thinks that prose has to get tamed and shaped just like poetry, 'cept it's a damn sight longer."

She looked at him, trying to find something to say or suggest or offer, but she was stunned. She had that same feeling when she had lost her phone a few years back. A numb denial.

Jack stood, wobbled, and leaned against the desk. "Don't need to sugarcoat it. I know I'm slipping. I just don't know how far or how fast or what I can do about it, 'cause I'm way up shit creek and I lost my paddle." He shuffled to his suite and slammed the door. Eileen clasped her hands behind her neck, leaned back as far as she could, and stared at the ceiling.

By noon, she had showered and changed into black slacks and her garnet turtleneck sweater. She put away her clothes and was hungry. She knocked on his door and heard him groan. He opened the door and blinked at her. "Just resting my eyes." His turtleneck drooped over his khakis, which were even more wrinkled.

"I heard the best way to beat jet lag is to stay up the day of arrival."

He ran his hand through his mussed hair. "That so?"

"Let's get some lunch and a walk."

"Sure, give me a minute to pee and grab my jacket."

When they had walked less than a block, he pointed to a café and motioned for her to enter. They paused at the chalkboard with the daily specials under the heavy block letters, *Le Menu*. He nodded, "Looks good."

Once seated, she ordered a wedge of mushroom quiche and a salad. He ordered a bottle of a mid-priced Chablis and a ham and cheese sandwich on a crackling baguette. He silently hurried through his first glass while waiting for his food to arrive. He poured himself two more glasses as he wolfed down his sandwich, with crust flying like shrapnel across the small table. He excused himself and seemed to spend a protracted time in the men's room. She had a glass that she nursed throughout the meal. When he returned, he gave only the most minimal replies to her effort to have a neutral conversation. He killed the remainder of the bottle while waiting for the bill.

Once back at the penthouse, he said he wanted to rest. Within a few minutes, she heard him snoring. Still, she closed his bedroom door and hers before sitting on the edge of her bed and unlocking her iPhone to pull up the world clock. It was two in the afternoon in Paris, early

morning in New York. She'd catch her mother before she started editing. She paused a moment, sighed, and called home.

Isabel answered on the third ring. "Hi. How's Paris treating you?"

"Paris is grand, as always. This is a spectacular apartment that
Max got for us. The chefs he represents own it and are on tour. I'll
send a link to their website with pictures. I can see gargoyles from my
window. Nice café just down the block. Had quiche and Chablis for
lunch."

"Wonderful. I figured you and Jack would be unpacking, getting
your office set up, and planning what nice restaurant you'd be going
to tonight after a good day of editing and revision. All on Max." She
giggled at the thought. When Eileen didn't answer immediately, Isabel
continued. "What is it? What's wrong? Is the draft a mess?"

"Mom. There is no draft. He's blocked."

"Shit! Have you told Max?"

"No. I'm trying to figure a way to save him from blowing his contract. Even if I can get him to crank out something, anything..."

"Nothing?"

"He says he's blocked. How do I get him unblocked?"

"Well, you know some people actually do write a novel, at least a
first draft, in that November deal. What's it called? Nan A something?"

"NaNoWriMo. National Novel Writing Month. It's just a way
to get people writing. It's an Internet thing. It's not going to work
for Jack. If somebody writes fifty thousand words by the end of the
month, they get some badge. People plan ahead for months, write
something, and then they have the sense to work it over until..."

"Fifty thousand words. That's about a third of Jack's usual novels.
He wrote some real doorstops. What seems to be his problem? He's
got solid continuing characters to build on."

"That's what I'm trying to understand. He drank too much
at lunch, but I'll give him a pass—I'm jet lagged too. But I swear, I
thought he was a homeless man at the airport. Shuffling along, skinny

as a scarecrow, and in need of a shower. Seriously, he was a mess. At lunch he seemed better. But he got blitzed and is taking a nap now."

"How's the office there? Set up to work, if he gets going?"

"It is a great office. Mom, he brought a typewriter!"

"Wow. I only had to edit *The Titans* and *The Collusion* as paper drafts. Then I put my foot down. Told Max I needed an electronic file. Remember the first ones were on those floppy disks, then the little blue plastic diskettes? I thought Jack would be using a computer by now. Should I ask Max if he had them transcribed before he sent them to me?"

"No. That doesn't matter, besides, you know how Max worries. Let me see what I can do here."

"Is it quiet enough there to work?"

"Yes. But if he doesn't have pages for me to edit, I'm not going to get paid. The plane ticket and free room and board here isn't going to pay the bills."

"Good point."

"How can I light a fire under him? You've talked other writers through a dry spell. How?"

"Think of it like sex. Start with foreplay. Small successes lead to great—"

"Mom!"

"You're a grown-up, Eileen, be frank. Not every encounter is skyrockets. So trust technique and don't get fancy. Go back to basics. Can you talk him into a plotting session, then build characters?"

"Like I've been trying to do on my novel?"

"Exactly, except don't self-edit as you write; that is what's slowing you down. Stop coloring inside the lines—be messy. Get him back on the bicycle again, even if it is only writing descriptions of what your snazzy apartment looks like. Once his pen gets moving again, the rest should kick in."

"Sort of a Viagra moment?"

Isabel laughed. "Exactly. Sorry. I'm editing what Max hopes will be the next *Shades of Grey*, and I'm getting a little randy."

"Do you have any other ideas?"

"Once he gets writing, optimize your time. If he writes while you sleep, and then you edit while he sleeps, you can pull more productive hours out of the day. Eat in. Drink less, him not you. I don't worry about you."

"Mom? Can you check in with his family and see if..."

"Estranged. Wife and he split a year ago, maybe it was two. There's a lover in the mix, according to Max, but I don't have more than that. Fractured family."

"So we're it?"

"Yup. Rather, you are his parachute."

"Thanks, Mom. Good ideas. You doing okay?"

"You've only been gone a few hours. How far astray could I go?"

"The lady who the agency sent—"

"She got sick. They sent the nicest man yesterday. Which is fine as I can tend to all my personal matters just fine. He'll be here at about one to straighten up and plan dinner. So don't worry about me, just focus on getting him to write something, anything. I'm sure you'll find a way to get it done."

"I hope so."

Isabel laughed. "Just think of yourself as his little blue pill."

"Well, go back to your lurid reading."

"Love you."

"You too."

Chapter № 5

October 2, 2017
Monday

At six, the alarm on her iPhone played "Flight of the Bumblebee." She swatted it and stumbled toward the shower. She had not slept well, but smiled when she remembered that his typewriter clattering away in the other room had interrupted her sleep before she had closed her door. She slid into her Wranglers and blue and white plaid flannel shirt and toweled her hair dry as she walked to the kitchen. After she turned the electric kettle to boil, ground coffee beans by hand in a Japanese mill, and loaded the French press, she noticed the stack of eleven typed pages in the center of the table. In blue ink at the top of the first page was scrawled *Story #1*.

She decided to start the coffee before she got lost in reading his first story. She paced and wondered why the kettle was taking so long to boil. She started to reach for the pages as the kettle whistled. She laughed at herself and poured the water into the glass press. Setting the timer on her iPhone for the mandatory three minutes, she sat at the table and turned over the title page.

The typed page was sloppy. The margins were minimal. The type was smudged. She read quickly and finished the first page. There was a flow, a familiarity of style. Characters were quickly sketched and full of promise. Tension. Good setting. By page three, she had fallen in love with the story and was skimming. Soon, her excitement turned to frustration. By page six, she had clenched her jaw and knew why she loved the story.

When her phone buzzed, she jumped and stood to press the plunger of the French press. Distracted by what she had read, she leaned heavily on the plunger. It skidded sideways on the granite counter and crashed to the floor. The glass shattered on the tile. She grabbed the whole roll of paper towels from the holder under the counter and played them out like fishing line to sop up the steaming water. Grounds had splattered against the cabinets and her jeans. She was kneeling, slamming hot wet towels into the garbage can as Jack wandered in, barefoot and wearing a luxurious robe. He pulled his glasses from the pocket and stared at her.

"You okay?" he asked. "I heard..."

"Stay back. I broke the damn coffee maker and there's glass everywhere. I'll go out for a couple take-away cups as soon as I change."

"I'm up. I'll go."

She stood and slammed a sopping towel into the trash. "No you won't. You'll sit your ass down and write another short story. Something I can edit this time."

He plopped in the spindle-back chair as though slapped. He picked up the draft that she had dropped on the breakfast table. "What's wrong with this one? Why can't you edit it?"

She grabbed another roll of towels from the cupboard. "It's not what's there so much as what you left out."

"Short stories always leave out stuff. That's why they are short." He grinned at his humor while still groggy.

Her head bobbed up from the mound of towels on the wet floor to stare at him. "Really? You're giving me that shit?" She dropped her head in frustration before standing and putting her fists into her hips. "We're trying to salvage your career here! Do you understand that?"

"What? What'd I leave out? Plot gap? Character flaw?"

She reached down and threw the wad of dripping towels into the trash. "The fucking leopard."

"You want a leopard?"

"Hemingway put one in. A frozen one when he wrote *The Snows of Kilimanjaro*."

"Then why would I put one in mine?"

She grabbed the pages with her wet hands. "This is *his* story! You've used his story."

"Have not!"

"Have!"

He spread his arms to explain. "This is about the AIDS crisis in the 1980s, when all the gay writers were dying—"

"Gangrene!"

"And they escape to Fire Island—"

"Camping in a tent on the side of Kilimanjaro..."

He spread his arms wider. "And the dying writer has these flashbacks on his life..."

"It was nice of you to put them in italics, just like Papa did..."

"But Adam Nicklaus is..."

She shook the wet pages at him. "Nick Adams! Nick Adams keeps popping up in Hemingway's stories. He's his recurring character."

His shoulders slumped. "Really?"

"Really! Haven't you read them recently?"

"Not for years. Maybe I'm on to something, thinking like the old man."

She dropped the pages onto the table. "Jack? Did you intend to copy it? Use the style as a springboard?"

His eyes sparkled bright blue. Tears ran down his cheeks when he shook his head. "Why are you so mad at me? I'm doing the best I can."

She quickly rinsed her hands and dried them on her shirt. "Oh, Jack. I'm not mad at you. I'm scared." She pulled out her chair slowly and sat across from him. She put her hand over his. "What's going on, Jack?"

"I don't know. Maybe I could write a more intimate dialogue between a man and his lover, she is about to have an abortion and what is left unsaid between them..."

"*Hills Like White Elephants*. Hemingway."

"Or an existential angst when three men confront the emptiness of their life."

"How about in a bar in Spain?"

"Good setting."

"Papa thought so when he wrote *A Clean Well-Lighted Place*. Are you messing with me? Trying to channel Hemingway?"

He shook his head slowly. "Not on purpose. Maybe my subconscious..."

"Were you drinking when you wrote it?"

"No. I read a while and fell asleep. Then I woke up with this fire in my belly, like I used to have."

"Jack, if I were teaching, I'd look at it as plagiarism."

He sat straight and slapped the table. "I never have stolen—"

"Maybe not on purpose. Regardless, this won't work."

He looked like a lost boy when he asked, "What do we do now?"

"Let's start the day over. Can you go for coffee and a couple crois-sants? The café across the street should be open by now. This is going to take a while to clean up. Damn coffee grounds are everywhere. On the cabinets. And I need to change."

"Sure." He dressed quickly in baggy green cords and the faded turtle-neck. He grabbed his wallet and left, without his phone or coat.

Jack walked past the elevator and down the stairs, holding the rail. By the time he reached the ground floor, he had limbered enough to make the slow walk across the street easier. Soon, he found himself in the small café where they had lunched the day before. But instead of ordering "*deux cafés* to go," he drifted to the bar at the rear of the café while trying to recall how to say "to go" in French. He stood at the end of the short counter. Three stocky workmen in blue denim coats and dark trousers huddled at its center. Jack understood enough of their conversation to know that they were vendors from the nearby street market who had set up their stalls and now sought a break before the market opened.

Each was nursing a small brandy. Jack motioned the barman for the same, "*Moi aussi, s'il vous plaît.*" When the workmen were served their coffees afterward, so was Jack. While he nursed the brandy, he stared at his reflection in the fogged mirror behind the bar. The clatter of the cups against the saucers when the men finished made him jump.

They paid and exchanged jests with the barman. When Jack finished he left a twenty-euro note and turned to leave. The man called after him. "*Attendez*. Stop, you have too much paid."

Jack waited at the door for the man and looked surprised when he brought his change to him. When he pocketed it, the man asked. "*Et où*...where is your daughter today? A lovely woman with the excellent French?"

"My daughter? Her? Oh, yes. A cold, nothing serious. Could you give me two croissants and two coffees to take away? *À porté*."

He ignored the fact that the American had actually said "wore" instead of his intended 'take away'. Even this oddly dressed man wouldn't want to wear his two cups of coffee. He shrugged. "*Certainement*. Tell her...keep a scarf on her neck and the infirmity will depart three days less."

"I will tell her." He balanced a handful of one-euro coins and crumpled bills in his open palm. The barkeeper picked the payment from his extended hand and nodded at him as he dropped two euro coins on the counter.

Jack had to try the entrance code three times before the lobby door opened. Once inside the penthouse, he called for Eileen. He put the small paper bag on the center of the table, pulled a couple of paper towels from the rack, and sat staring at the two tall paper cups of coffee. Not that he wanted any more coffee, but he wondered why it took him so long to get them, and why he slipped into the drink at the bar. Was it a drink or the men or interest in getting some material for a story that he was seeking, or did he just drift?

He was startled when she came into the kitchen, having changed into her black slacks and beige turtleneck.

She put plates on the table and took a bite of her croissant. "Thanks. Just what I needed. Were they busy?"

"Why?"

"It just seemed to take a long time. Maybe because I am hungry. Want a scrambled egg with that?"

"Sure. Couple of 'em would be nice."

While she whipped eggs in a bowl and started the pan heating, he took the lid off his cup and poured it into a tall ceramic mug. "Want a mug?"

"No. This is fine." She slid the eggs onto his plate, handed him a fork, and sat across from him.

He smiled. "Some of Paris seems so familiar from when we lived here, but sometimes it is like being on Mars."

"When were you here?"

"Last time I *lived* here was ninety-three. Snowed the day I got here in January, just days after Bill Clinton was sworn in. I had a year-long fellowship." He chuckled. "Funny, I can't even remember who gave me the money for the year. I'd been getting fellowships for a couple years, patching them together while I was still teaching so I could cover the summers." He paused and peeled a layer off his croissant and recalled that was how his wife always ate them. He took a deep breath. "My short stories were selling well, but you can't make a living off them. I'd put in my twenty at the university and got a decent enough salary. Worked on my book during summers. I lived light. 'Cheap,' Elizabeth used to say." He looked at the croissant and peeled off another layer. "Anyway, I salted enough away to retire early. Took the fellowship, finished my novel, found Max, made the *Times*' list. 'Overnight success,' they said."

"That was *The Titans*, right? Mom said when Max hired her she made him promise to pay her whether or not he found a publisher for the book. He said it was the best damn story he'd ever read, but so sloppy that it needed editing, and retyping, before he could even submit it anywhere. Did you know that?"

He ignored her. "Well, that fellowship really didn't stretch as far as they said it would. Wrote my ass off when she was in class and...God...

our nights. It was all adrenaline and sex. Then I was back in the States, with my first novel a success and a wife."

She was having difficulty following him. "Elizabeth?"

"No. We'd lived together on and off for years while we both taught. No. Marie. My wife is Marie. Love of my life. I never really understood what love was...until...." He looked startled to see his coffee in front of him and paused to take a sip.

"You met here?"

He nodded.

"Is she French?"

He shook his head. "Old line Boston. Her mom was DAR. Banker dad. She was doing a late junior year abroad. Feeling her oats. She loved it here. Or more likely loved not being in America that year."

"Why?"

"She wanted Bush, again. I didn't. We called a truce on that. It was not a good year back in the States. Branch Davidian standoff and burning down the place. The Unabomber. Some nut with a gun on the subway. The French thought we were a bunch of homegrown anarchists and barbarians. And some of us were."

She pinched off a bite and held it as she asked, "What did you most like here?"

"The freedom. The illusion of freedom you get when you don't have a clue about the culture or the local laws or customs. Fortunately, the French have a well-developed sense of humor about good-natured bumbling as long as you are not driving bad or ordering cheese incorrectly. Or insulting their dogs."

She grinned. "You're right. I remember my first time here alone—"

Jack glanced out the window. "When I was her age, that is when I was twenty, I backpacked through Europe. That was in seventy-three. Fresh out of school with a job waiting. Had this book I'd got second-hand telling you where to stay and eat on five bucks a day. Of course it was more. Glorious." She chuckled at the interruption. He ripped his remaining croissant into thirds and stuffed a tail end into his mouth. He sprayed crumbs as he spoke. "I think that's why she hooked me. I saw in her what I had been. Free, twenty, in Paris. Adventuresome. She made me brave again. Bought me that Skyriter off one of her classmates. It was old even then. She moved in after a week. Went by her dorm room once a week to call mommy in America and do our laundry."

"Did she drop out of class?"

"Her? Hell no. She's like a dog on a bone if she has a task. Finished her senior year in six months. Straight to law school. Pregnant that first year. Took the baby to class with her most days so I could work on *The Collusion* in peace. Can't imagine how she finagled it. That's what makes her such a great trial lawyer. God damn pit bull."

"Have you been back since then?"

"A couple times, alone. Quick trips. She had her law practice by then. And our daughter. I'd do short speaking engagements, one or two signings of translated editions. Mostly lectures at universities. They thought me something of an icebreaker. No, I mean groundbreaker— by combining spy and thriller genres into something fresh. 'The pivotal transitioning from the spy novels into something as cerebral and complexly plotted but with the glisten of sweat on its brow of a thriller.' Their words, not mine."

"When I was a kid, I saw your books on Mom's special shelf of the bookcase, high where I couldn't just snatch one. They were her trophies. I saw your titles in other languages. That's how I discovered that someone had to translate them. I thought that must be a fun thing to do."

"Is it?"

"At times. There is a precision, a joy, to finding the author's voice so it has the same resonance in the second language. Idioms can be a bother, but fortunately your writing is quite straightforward, so yours would have been a delight."

"What's the last job you did? Good book? Should I read it?"

She laughed and jostled her coffee. Wiping up the spill, she said.

"No. It was a medical research paper for a scientific journal. Just over a hundred pages, but very technical. I thought I'd pull my hair out. Fortunately, Greg, the doctor who wrote it here, is bilingual and was a great help."

He drained his mug. "Where do you want to go today? Café de Flore or the Musée d'Orsay or the—"

"You've got to write something, anything, for me to edit."

He stood. "What?"

"Maybe just a description of getting coffee this morning at that café. It's action that—"

He turned to go. She called after him. "Jack? I'm doing a wash after I clean up the dishes. Do you want me to throw in anything for you?"

"No. I'm good. Just gonna plant my ass at the desk. See you later."

Eileen stared at him as he shuffled toward his suite. After straightening the kitchen and starting a wash, she retreated to her room and closed the door. Without checking the time on her world clock app, she called home.

"Mom?"

"Who'd you expect?"

"Funny."

"Is he writing?"

Eileen paused. "Well..."

"Simple enough question. Is he writing?"

"Well...he is. But the problem is that he is echoing Hemingway."

"That style, short and crisp should be easy..."

"Mom! He is parroting back Hemingway's storylines. It's like he is a high school kid thinking plagiarism is such a big word that no one would know what it means."

"On purpose?"

Eileen paused. "I don't know. I really don't."

"Think he may be slipping a cog? Just blocked?"

Eileen paused. "Have to think about it. Is your helper still okay?"

"He made scallops last night."

"Yum."

"Honey? Jack used to give lectures on writing. See if you can find one on Google or YouTube. Maybe there's an idea there for him to use."

"Okay. Call ya soon."

Chapter № 6

October 2, 2017
Monday

Eileen grabbed her laptop, curled up in the velvet-tufted side chair, and typed in his name. Wikipedia gave an excellent overview of his career and works. There were a few newspaper and magazine reviews, links to buy his books, and a video on YouTube of a lecture and question-and-answer session at the University of Dublin. The video was hand held, possibly from someone's phone. He was fit, handsome, and at the top of his game. The film was amateurish and jerky; however, the audio was clear.

In a honeyed voice, Jack began his lecture with a recap of how his life in rural Montana gave him the freedom to think, uninterrupted by the close rules of a city, or judgment of others, or any of today's electronic distractions. That got a chuckle. He said he knew from early on that he needed to live a life larger than his small town, and found it in the town's library, which could order anything in the state's entire system.

Jack grinned. "I discovered almost all about sex that way before...you know, girls would have me. And I discovered that there were worlds I wanted to know. I studied hard at school and at my college. I knew that that was my ticket to a larger universe. A state school, not nearly as prestigious as yours, but a good one. I had good teachers who cared about their subjects and their students and in that way I share a gifted legacy and good fortune with you."

He concluded the lecture with a brief summary of the thread of his novels emerging from the Cold War into the current muddle and ambiguity in almost all areas of society. He then exhibited a gentle patience in answering the typical asinine undergraduate questions on how do you write—not inquiring about overarching philosophy, style, or gestalt, but what kind of pen did he use. Jack said he used a Dixon Ticonderoga B-1 or a Palomino Blackwing because by using the darkest and softest lead in editing his work, he could read it the next day. He paused while the audience chuckled. From the chair beside his lectern, a stout man cleared his throat and stood. Eileen reached for the trackpad to end the video, but hesitated.

The moderator used a theatrically important tone. "Now that the students have had a go at you, I must inquire on a matter that has always puzzled me about your dialogue. I want to know how it is that you, an American, can write your British characters so convincingly."

"It's in the ear." He tugged at his right earlobe like a bashful suitor and grinned. "It's all before you but, 'You gotta listen' is how my uncle in Billings, that's in Montana, might have said it. He's a plainspoken man. In New York at my publisher, they might answer you..." He paused and changed the tone and pitch of his voice as well as the speed of his delivery. "You must listen, eavesdrop, be an aggressive listener, never let a phrase slip past you without taking its measure."

The moderator nodded at the clever shifts. Jack gave a quick side-eye to the man. "Now, I think you have embedded in your question the notion that being plainspoken is a sign of inferior intelligence." He raised his hand to stop the man's denial. "But I know that's not the case. If it were, I wouldn't have had to buy a new black suit to have your honorary degree bestowed on me tomorrow. But what you asked me is what we all ask ourselves when we listen to another. Who is he? Where is he from? Is he friend or foe? Is she my type? Is she really telling me the truth? In writing my British characters, those in the service of the Crown at least, I make assumptions about them as well. I assume they went to a top-tier school. I assume they all took the mandatory Latin coursework, not for a year but for several and read Latin and possibly Greek as well, still, for pleasure. Well, you see in Latin there is a form of construction called the ablative absolute."

She hit the pause button and backed up the video as she wrote "ablative absolute" on her notepad on the computer. She replayed it and watched the moderator's puzzled expression.

Jack continued confidently. "I'll save your trying to recall it. It's the special use of the present and perfect participles. It's a Latin construction that consists of a noun and participle or adjective in the ablative case that is syntactically independent of the rest of the sentence. In English, it looks like a hanging clause that's off meter. But it isn't. It's an echo of the ordering in Latin that these men have carried into their own language. English, upper class, well educated, British English. If you know your character, really know him, down to the color of his underwear, you can find his voice. So in conclusion, I thank you and say to you in the ablative absolute form...weather permitting, we will have a lovely ceremony tomorrow. Thank you."

His grin was impish as he shook the moderator's hand and clapped him on the shoulder, like a cowboy might in greeting a long-lost friend. Eileen clicked off the video. *Who was this man?* Erudite, wry. Fast on his feet. She looked at the date on the banner behind the lectern, five years ago. He looked fit, agile, and downright handsome. Explaining how a Latin structure echoed in English! Where the hell did that come from? How did he make such a steep slide from then to now?

She did a search on "writer's block" on the off-chance that there might be a hint of how to unstick him. One of the threads left her staring at the screen. "Memory loss from disease or injury." Shaking her head, she wanted to disabuse herself of the notion that this could be a factor in his lack of productivity. She took her laptop to the kitchen, made a cup of tea, and worked on her novel at the kitchen table for an hour before Jack's situation intruded on her concentration. Maybe it was worth considering.

Opening her web browser, she Googled "Alzheim..." and the screen loaded before she completed her entry. She looked at the results but then Googled the broader term, "dementia." Recalling something of the medical work she had translated, she looked for the quick indicator test. Scrolling down, she found it. A list of ten indicators of dementia, with the helpful caveat to seek medical determination, that some symptoms are not dementia at all, but another medical problem too subtle for the ten-question quiz.

She ran through it slowly, trying to find other reasons for Jack's behavior. After twenty more minutes of searching the web for guidance, she folded down the screen on her laptop and returned to her suite. She shut the door, picked up her phone, and called her house.

After the fifth ring, there was a muffled sound. "Mom?"

"What? Hold on I dropped my glasses." Her tangled pink flannel nightgown impeded her reach. Eileen heard the rustle of the covers being tossed aside and a small groan.

"Did I interrupt your reading?"

"Be serious! It's still the middle of the night here."

Eileen paused. "Sorry, I can call later."

"Hold on a minute. I need the toilet." After a brief pause during which Eileen wondered how much the silence was costing her, her mother returned. "I know it must be important for you to call again, so what's up?"

"I think it might be dementia."

"That's a bit rash, isn't it? Jet lag and—"

"We've been here long enough to... I Googled dementia."

"That's just a big sack of information, some good and some loony. You know how I feel about unverified sources."

"Of course, so I used good sources. Hospitals and legit association websites, not the chatter of web-monkeys."

"And? Something is wrong or you wouldn't be calling without looking at my time zone first. I know you."

"Mom? Did you know that poor vision is associated with poor cognition?"

"Makes sense," she giggled. "But I'm still making sense. I'm editing well and see my doctors regularly."

"But the article also said that hearing loss when accompanied by vision loss is a significant contributor to dementia. It's an early study, but the idea is that if your brain is struggling to see and hear, it can't do some of its other jobs."

Isabel sat up straighter, her tone changed. "Just where is this going?"

"It said that everyone ought to get their hearing checked professionally every decade and every three years when they reach your age."

"You didn't wake me up just to recommend that I schedule a hearing test, did you?"

"I didn't know that about vision and hearing impacts—and wanted you to know. But then I looked up the ten warning signs."

"If you are going to give me some test from the Sunday paper's supplement, next to the meatloaf recipe, I'm going to hang up on—"

"He got a ninety percent. And not in a good way. I gave him a pass on the question about 'recent changes' since I really don't know where he started."

After a pause, Isabel's tone changed to one of concern. "Run them by me, will you?"

"Lemme get my notes." A rustling of papers caused static on the iPhone "First, a memory loss that interrupts daily life. Check, he is chaotic. Confused. Almost panicky at times."

"That's understandable. He is under extreme duress given the deadline and the lack of production. And he's away from home."

"Two. Challenges in planning or solving problems. He can't get anything going. Really, he was a mess at the airport and here. He's at a loss on how to even start his writing. Seemed confused about the menu on the plane, like he couldn't decide between the two crappy meals they offered."

"Next."

"Three. Difficulty completing tasks at work or home. His work is nonexistent and he barely got milk from the fridge into his coffee, then said he liked it black."

"Oh."

"Four. Time or place confusion. Got a timeline all messed up telling me he lived in Paris in the sixties with his wife."

"So?"

"In the sixties she would have been ten years old, if he told me right that she was a decade younger than him. Seems to think he's at his cabin until he stumbles around for a bit and has some coffee."

She stifled a laugh. "Next."

"Five. Spacial relations and visual images. He doesn't seem to see what I see when we walk down the street. It's like he intentionally doesn't see what I'm pointing out."

"Are you being bossy? Maybe he's ignoring your comments because he doesn't like know-it-all women."

Eileen huffed and continued. "Problems in words or writing! Bingo. He scribbles and wads up paper. I opened some of what he left wadded up on the kitchen table. It's like a kid wrote it. Nice penmanship but simplistic. Seven, misplaced things. Check. Eight, poor judgment. Probably why we are here."

"Perhaps."

"Nine. Withdrawal from work or social stuff. He lives in a cabin on a lake in Connecticut. I've seen his pictures of it on his iPhone. It's tiny, not at all the glamorous lakeside place that we saw a couple years ago in that architectural magazine. And ten is that recent changes question. Changes in mood or personality. As I said, I gave him a pass on that as I didn't know him in the past and he seems to have no personality at all now."

"Look, if you are..."

"And he isn't taking care of himself. He looked...disheveled at the airport. I'll send you the selfie I took of us when we landed."

"I'll call Max in the morning and get his take on your concerns. If you are right, this is more important than a missed deadline."

"Mom?"

"Yes?"

"Maybe we should wait. You know how Max worries."

"Okay, but just for a while longer."

"Sorry. I didn't mean to wake you, but I am really worried for him. And I guess it carried over to worrying about you."

"And us? This is more than an editing job now, it's his survival."

"I guess I'm as much concerned as pissed off. I passed on the retreat to do this."

"Well, just remember what your grannie used to say."

"That 'Don't put too much vermouth in my martini'?"

Isabel laughed. "No. Grow where you are planted."

"I'm not planted here or with him."

"No. But if you can make his life better, wouldn't that be a good thing, whatever else happens?"

"I'll think about it."

"Promise?"

"Sure. Mom? He doesn't look at all like his book jacket or website picture. He looks...frail."

"Really? His latest bio says he runs three miles before breakfast every day."

"Bogus. He can barely shuffle out for coffee in the morning."

"Max might know if there is a health problem or—"

"Let's wait, okay? Talk soon. Actually, e-mail me. I don't want to add more to his worry list right now."

"Good idea. And honey?"

"Mom?"

"Greg is there still, isn't he?"

She took a deep breath and paused before answering. "I don't know."

"You should find out. Wasn't his paper something about memory?"

"Thanks. Bye, Mom." She turned off her phone and sat still, trying to push past her pride to consider calling Greg. After plugging her phone into the battery charger, she opened her Kindle app, hit the documents tab, and opened her final translation of Doctor Gregory K. Patel's research paper on cognition and aging. She thumbed past the title and introductory material, then stopped when she came to the abstract. She read it slowly. The pithy three paragraphs at the start were the most critical to translate. She had to find the balance between informing the lay reader and explaining the superstructure of thought on which the complex research findings were hung. The balance between educating and informing, he said she hit perfectly. Praise from Greg was not common but welcome. After she had finished the translation, he invited her to go to the Atlantic coast for a week. Just them. It was a celebration of accomplishment and an opportunity to get to know each other. Two rooms.

After two days, she gave up her room. He was a pragmatist about his work and silly during their week in Biarritz when he tried to get her to rent a Vespa and zoom around town with him. That was before she got crazy.

She opened her Find My Friends app and saw that he was at his apartment. She tapped "contacts." All of his Paris numbers were still on her phone: Office (shorter than The Institute for the Study of Cognition), Desk (for his private backline), and Home (his cell phone really, for his small apartment near the Institute, which was painted lemon-drop yellow and smelled like curry from a nearby restaurant).

She took a deep breath and hit the number beside "Home."

The male voice mumbled, "*Oui?*"

"Greg?"

He looked at the caller ID on his cell phone. "Eileen?"

"Yes. Sorry to call so early, but I needed to talk to you. I hoped I could catch you at home." She heard a pan clatter.

"Sure, what time is it there?"

She paused, listening for another voice, and was embarrassed that she did. "I'm in Paris."

"Really? Hold on a sec." He checked the calendar on his phone. "Got time for dinner tomorrow? I'll get reservations at that Italian place."

"I'm not alone." She frowned. That had not come out like she wanted. "Oh."

"I'm with a writer." She shook her head. "It's a job, not..."

"Okay, I get it. I'd still like to—"

"I need your help."

"Are you okay?"

"Me? Yeah. But I'm still trying to get a grip on what's going on with the guy I'm supposed to be editing. Famous guy. About sixty. Seems to be in the middle of writer's block or depression or..."

"Dementia? Is that why you called me?"

"In part. I don't want to jump too fast. Maybe if you met him?"

"Hang on a sec." He moved the teakettle off the burner. "I can book a clinical appointment in a couple weeks at the Institute."

"We don't have a couple weeks. He's got to get a draft cranked out by November first or his life as a writer goes down in flames."

"Isn't that a bit over the top?"

"No. You have no idea how screwed up his life is right now or how cutthroat publishing has become. He's about to blow his contract. That breach is more than just bad publicity. It messes up his on-the-rocks relationship with his family, if he even has one."

"A family?"

"A relationship with his wife. Here's the deal. If he's not slipping a cog, maybe he is depressed. I'm no expert, but I did pay attention to the substance of your paper."

"I know you did. You were superb."

"Enough for a favor?"

"What?"

"Dinner tomorrow with both of us? We ought to be unjetlagged by then. My treat. Café de Flore."

"It's touristy."

"That's where he wants to go. If you can just let me know if I'm over-reacting or if he needs some medical or psychological intervention."

"Symptoms?"

She stalled, wondering if she should share her concerns. "I'd rather you discover for yourself."

"Fair enough. Have reservations yet?"

"No."

"You'll never get in calling cold. I'll make them for eight."

"I can't thank you enough, this man..."

"Does he have a name I might recognize?"

"He's a big deal. Would that make a difference, if I told you?"

"Probably not. Unless it's the guy who wrote *The English Patient*. Then all bets are off, he's a freaking genius. I'd just sit there in awe of whatever he did." She laughed. "Eileen, you were right. I don't know how I missed reading it when it came out. Just read it again. Every time there's something new..."

"I know! I just love Michael Ondaatje."

"You know him? You didn't tell me you knew him when you gave me the book."

"Just his work, not the guy. I'd be so...so, flustered. I don't think I could make it through a dinner with him either." She laughed again. "I can see it now, two fans just drooling, staring, and trying to think of something to say."

"So? It's not him?"

"No."

"Okay. I'll have a 'diagnostic dinner' with you and your mystery man on one condition."

"Which is?"

She could hear the smile in his voice. "Promise me a lunch. Just the two of us."

She grinned. "That's a deal."

"Tomorrow at eight. I'll call if there's a hitch. Can I ask you something?"

"Sure."

"What if he can't get the draft out in time? What's that mean for you?"

She straightened her shoulders and tried to focus on his question. "I get paid by the page, and there are no pages. But, it's more than…" There was a catch in her voice.

"Hey. Hang on. So you're not going to get paid if he doesn't have something for you to edit? Did I get that right?"

She sniffed. "That's not why I got upset. It's about him losing himself."

"I thought you said he had some contract date to meet or his life was going to crash around him."

"I probably did. But it's more than that. Contracts don't make you who you are—your mind does."

"But if he blows the contract, you're…"

"It's not about me, Greg. I thought you could help, or point me to someone who could."

His tone sharpened. "Is this how you are with all your clients? Pamper them. Flatter them so they fall for you?"

"What? I just met the man on the plane ride over. And he slept through most of that. Besides, he's old enough to be my father."

He ran his hand through his ebony black hair. "Sorry. I don't know where that came from. Dinner tomorrow."

"Thanks, Greg."

"Eileen? I'm glad you called. I've missed you."

"Me too. Bye."

Chapter № 7

October 3, 2017
Tuesday

She checked the time. Jack had been in his suite for over an hour since she heard the shower start. She listened at the open door and heard snoring. She paused for a moment wondering how she could intrude. She tapped on the door. "Jack? I'm making coffee now, if you want to take a break."

"Uhh. Sure. I'll be out in a minute."

She was pouring the steaming water from the electric carafe over the grounds nesting in the filter paper of a Chemex carafe when Jack ambled out of his room and crawled up onto one of the high barstools in front of the massive kitchen counter. She looked up. He was still wearing the faded turtleneck and rumpled green cords. He hadn't shaved or showered. "I heard you typing last night."

He ran his hands over his face and blinked hard. "Just limbering up my fingers."

The last of the water dripped through the filter, which she discarded in the pullout garbage compactor. She poured coffee into a stoneware mug. "Good." She handed the mug to him, poured another one for herself, and leaned her elbows on the counter.

"Maybe I should write about the Paris *intelligencia* with a party overtone, or a year-long drunk with several notables."

"That's *A Movable Feast*. Hemingway did it."

"Maybe I should write about Hemingway's wife? What's her name?"

"That's *A Paris Wife*. Paula McLain did it. The wife was his first, Hadley Richardson."

"No. The reporter one. Mary Gilbert? Wellborn?"

"Martha Gellhorn."

He blew on the steaming coffee. "Yeah, that one."

"She wrote her own book and they even made a movie about them, surprisingly titled *Hemingway and Gellhorn*. Love the second billing, even though I think she wrote more than he did. Better journalism, different styles in their novels. I thought after reading her collected war stories she was as good as they got."

"But his work, the front-line stuff, under fire and all..."

"She was a war correspondent, front line in a helmet, in wars he never even read about." She flushed at contradicting him but failed to stop herself. "Ferchristsake, Jack! Hadn't you even heard of her?"

Jack ignored this. "That guy was something. War, running with the bulls. A man's man."

"Stop drinking that macho Kool-Aid. It's more bullshit than bulls, if you ask me."

"He had balls!"

"Her balls were twice as big as his!"

Jack laughed. "That didn't make any sense."

"Of course not to you, you're a man. You surprise me, being so dismissive of women in literature. I wouldn't have thought that after reading your novels. Your women characters were rounded and complex, even if most of your guys still are sexist."

She placed the steaming coffee carafe on a cork coaster on the table. They moved to the table and sat across from each other. He wrapped his bony fingers around the mug. He frowned and seemed hurt by her criticism. "Sexist? Dismissive? Really?"

"Name three current writers who are women that you have read in the last three years. Just three. I'll give you one a year."

Jack opened his mouth, but nothing came to his brain. "Three years?"

"Okay. How about five, maybe ten."

He frowned then shrugged.

She folded her arms. "That went well. How about foreign authors?"

"In translation or original?"

"What do you read in another language?"

"Nothing."

"In translation?"

"Well." He stopped and glanced out the window.

"What are you reading now?"

He shrugged, not wanting to offer up the Murakami that he couldn't seem to penetrate. "What would you suggest?"

"Nothing now. We don't have time for a modern lit course. We need a manuscript in..." She looked at her watch. "Four weeks from today or we both are screwed."

"We?"

"Look, I gave up a huge opportunity for this job. Max sold it to my mother as a last pass on a fully formed draft of your next spy-thriller. She's always worked from home. You know that. But what you don't know is that I helped her on your last two books—"

"You told me that at the airport."

"Yeah I did, didn't I?"

"Why'd you come?"

"Her vision is failing."

"She's going blind?"

Eileen closed her eyes and took a breath before answering. "Macular degeneration. There's a blank hole in the middle of anything she looks at."

Jack let his hands drop to his knees. "Oh my God! How can she read?"

"It's at the early stage now, and only one eye is involved. But it won't get better. We have a reader machine with an oversize computer monitor. Converts text to speech, which is easier than her trying to read everything. Works about ninety-five percent of the time. I set it up to read the punctuation as well. When she hits a problem, or even thinks there is a glitch in the plot or some technical issue, she flags it and dictates potential corrections. Then I make them and try to catch anything she missed. Which is about never."

"So you are a team?"

"By default. She still does almost all the brainwork on her projects. I come in at the bottom of the ninth to bat cleanup."

He was quiet for a moment. His shoulders slumped. "I had no idea. I am so sorry."

"Glad she didn't hear you say that or she'd kick your ass, figuratively. But if you even suggest writing about some blind guy..."

"Hemingway probably did it already."

"Did he? Most of his guys catch it in the knee or nuts. If so, he is surely bested by recent works. *All the Light We Cannot See*. Teenagers with cancer in *The Fault is in Our Stars*. Come on! Have you been in a cave? Don't you have Internet and a Kindle or at least the app on your phone?"

"Well..."

"And what's with the typewriter?"

"That's how I write."

"Oh my God. You are a dinosaur."

"Thanks. Just the ego boost I needed." Then he continued, "Maybe I should write a travel narrative about dissolute friends escaping Paris?"

"That's *The Sun Also Rises*. Hemingway did it."

"See! I told you he had a gift for story."

She shook her head. "That's retrograde thinking. You just participated in time travel, Jack. You are stealing his plots then giving him credit for being forward thinking. Is this part of the men's club secret handshake?"

"No! I'm dying here. I can't get a storyline to save my ass."

"Keep going. Brainstorm."

"Maybe I should write about soldiers in Paris. Three guys on leave who have a special bond?"

She choked on her coffee. "That's *The Three Musketeers*. Alexandre Dumas! Have you forgotten everything you ever read?"

"It does tend to blur."

She looked at him and left the room. She escaped to the bathroom and stared at her reflection. "Oh, fuck." She flushed the toilet unnecessarily and wondered what she would say to him when she returned. Taking a deep breath, she walked back to the kitchen and poured more coffee into each mug. "Does Max know you are blocked?"

"What do you mean by blocked? All those were really old books. What if I modernized them? Like making the Musketeers gay, or one of 'em bi? Or the other thing...transm... trans..."

"Still stealing."

"Stealing? There are only so many plots in the world! And they all have been taken! What am I supposed to do? Invent something new?"

"Yes. That's exactly what you're supposed to do, Jack. Surprise your readers. Invite them to a place they have never been. That's exactly what you've done in each of your books."

"Maybe I should start a murder series."

"Why? You have a fan base for your spy-dude-thriller series already."

"I'm tired of him."

"He's your meal ticket. You should write on..."

"I can't." He paused and she wondered if he was going to cry. He rested his head in his hands for what seemed minutes. Then smiled and took a deep breath. "Murders. I could start a series of murder books, here. Do it by tourist spot."

"Claude Izner did it."

"Okay, I could do them by *arrondissement*. There are what, fifteen or so of the municipal districts, each with its own...?"

"Twenty. There are twenty, and Cara Black has it covered."

"Black! That's not a French name."

"American. Lived in San Francisco, last I heard. I like her stuff. But back to your strategy. Before you could write a series, you need to get the first one in front of the reader— and so far you have what?"

"I..."

"So, you have exactly what you came with right? Zippo. Nothing for me to edit at all. Right?"

"In actual fact..."

Eileen pressed him for an answer. "Right?"

"Well, if you—"

"Right!"

"Maybe I should write about my time in Paris in the seventies. Sexual discovery. Culture clash."

"That's *The Dud Avocado* from the fifties. Elaine Dundy. An eternally optimistic American girl, eternally 'green' plunged into madcap hijinks..."

"You sound like a book-cover blurb. You read it?"

"I *borrowed* it from my mother's bookcase. First book that I read that explored female orgasm in fiction, well before Erica Jong changed everything in *Fear of Flying*."

He almost blushed and then managed a crooked grin. "I don't think I could 'move that needle,' but maybe from a male perspective..."

"*Portnoy's Complaint.* Been done. Don't even consider it. It's too far from your genre. You'd lose what readers you still have."

"I *still* have?"

"It's been a dry spell for them, too. You'd usually have your latest on the market by now and..."

"Them? What about me? Do you have any idea what it's like when the sophomore slump hits?"

"That only refers to a dip in sales of the second book, after a wow debut. You've published too many bestsellers to use that excuse. You have shown mastery of the novel. You moved a commercial genre into real literature that is convertible into film. Three or four made it into movies? You've done it all. You just need one more now to meet your contract. And then get your next advance and the next deal."

"And if I don't?"

"You have to pay back your advance on this book. And everyone gets to hear how you've dried up."

He laughed. "I can't pay back the advance."

"Why not?"

"I've spent it. Marie kept the apartment. I paid it off. Couldn't down-size her."

"Really? I thought you were...well, rich."

"Was once. But I left. Had to. Told her to keep it all. Walked away. My cabin's paid for, and I live simply. Figure I could lecture when I get strapped. You know I taught writing for years?"

"Yes. I wish I could have taken your classes. You were quite the item. Refused to join the Iowa writers."

"I fit in Montana. Taught what I knew. This novel was going to get me back on my feet. But I seem to have no..." He looked away searching for something that was lost. "I can't weave a plot. You know I usually have three or four themes running..."

"At least."

"But I can't follow one now. I'm adrift in my work so I used to go for walks, and now my legs are going to shit as well."

"It's a Hemingway problem."

He half-smiled. "Limp dick?"

She laughed. "Wouldn't know about that. I mean it's probably just the pressure of the deadline and your...breakup causing a block. Insecurity. Paralysis."

"Good call. Dick's fine, but I can't get my brain working."

"Grab your coat."

He scowled. "It's been raining."

"So what? Are you a snowflake, or made of sugar? Don't you walk in the rain?"

"I didn't bring a raincoat."

"There are umbrellas in the lobby, if you hadn't noticed."

"But..."

"Let's get a new experience. Some exercise. Your narratives have always been strong, physical, and vivid. Let's just get you writing about what we see on this soggy outing."

"So you think writing a narrative of a wet Paris or a café setting is going to prime my pump?"

"Get your coat. Now!"

After three blocks in a driving rain, she relented and followed him into a small crowded café. He pointed to an empty table under the awning. They hung their umbrellas on the back of a third chair at the table. He brushed rainwater off his tweed jacket and shivered. She unbuttoned her trench coat but left it on. In silence, they stared at the traffic through the heavy plastic that shielded them from the rain but rippled with each gust of wind.

When the waiter arrived, Jack ordered a brandy. She revised the order to two coffees and a basket of croissants. She slid her chair around to face him, putting her back to the street. The plastic wall held some of the warmth from the heaters. He tried to look past her but she moved the chair again so he could not avoid her. "Can we talk about something other than my non-novel for a bit?"

"Sure. I'm curious about how you teach. You still do the occasional class, right?"

"Correct. Usually I find a place I want to visit, and call them or have Max arrange it, so they pay my travel costs and provide some dough."

"Writers conferences or just schools?"

"Both."

She shrugged. "I don't get it. How can you teach a novel in a couple weeks?"

"You can't. But what you can do is work on character or scene structure or the balance between narrative and dialogue."

"You have time to read their stuff?"

"Yes. I get a writing sample before if possible and work on the weaknesses by contrasts."

She frowned. "Contrasts?"

"I use strengths as examples and love to watch the baby writers puff up when one of their sentences is used as an example."

"Do they all get a gold ring from your carrousel ride?"

"Damn straight they do. Praise in public. Corrections in private, my scribbles on a page were for them alone. The whole game is so subjective, unless they just take a dump on the paper, I give them some credit."

"And?"

"And what?"

"How do you manage writing assignments? Aren't most conferences just a couple of days long?"

"I give them a prompt. They write for an hour, free writing. Then half an hour for editing. Then they read aloud what they've just written. Mutual combat ensues. I play United Nations peacekeeper, and we all go for a drink in the hotel bar and continue talking about what worked."

"And the semester courses? Can they write enough then to get a feel for if they really can produce a novel?"

"For some, yes. But in that format, I have them do a short story a week. Treat it like a scene in their novel. I read and comment on every submission. Then in class we discuss my comments, the ones that the students want to discuss. No mutual sharking." He saw Eileen's confusion and clarified. "Fighting. Attacking each other. I tell 'em that they might need each other in the future. A couple of them published their work as short story collections, but there's not a writer I know who can make a living off their short stories."

"Really? This month, a collection by Jeffery Eugeneides is coming out. And there's a complete Vonnegut collection, almost a hundred some early unpublished..."

"Yeah. *Unpublished.* See! That's why I tell 'em how to get started in the business. Getting their stories in lit mags is one way. Publishers stalk the magazines for fresh blood. Or used to, anyway. Now they need a platform, not just being a hell of a writer."

"Like what?"

"Some shit that makes you different. That makes you the circus freak who will get people to your readings and buy your book on

Amazon. Like sawing off your own leg after a lion gnawed it to shreds on a photography safari, or going around the world in a tramp steamer, or inventing Uber. That might give you enough publicity push to get noticed. But for regular writers, they're going to need each other. They'll need to write jacket blurbs for each other's stuff, refer a buddy to their agent, that sort of thing, so I stress positive relations."

"Yet you live like a hermit."

"Ironic isn't it?" He muttered as he fussed with his coffee, adding sugar and putting all his concentration into stirring it.

She finished half of her coffee. "You like baseball?"

Jack looked up from his cup. "Yeah, late in the season."

"Why not earlier?"

"Nothing on the line. I don't have a home team."

"What if you did?"

"Then the stakes are higher. I might be interested."

"My dad was a Cubs fan, like his dad."

"Bet that sucked, until last year or was it the year before?"

"November 2, 2016. Game seven. Tied. In extra innings. Rain delay of seventeen minutes at the start of the tenth."

"Is this going somewhere?"

She nodded quickly. "Maddon, the coach, called in his second pitcher, Mike Montgomery, for relief. This guy had never thrown a game-saver in his career, and here he is on the mound. This Cincinnati player, think it was Martinez, yeah Mike Martinez, gets an infield grounder off him, But it is fielded by Bryant out on the soggy turf. He throws to Rizzo to win the game and series. Bam! A hundred-and-eight-year drought is over."

He pointed at her cup. "Want another?" When she ignored his question, he asked, "Why the Cubs?"

"They were my dad's team. Now you're supposed to ask me what this has to do with anything."

"Okay. What's..."

"This is a lesson learned. I'm your Jason Heyward, except I'm not a guy who is a leftie who works right field like he owns it."

"Huh?"

"He was the guy who gave them a rah-rah speech during the rain delay. They go back on the field and Bob Zobrist connects for a tie-breaking double that put it all home."

He leaned forward and frowned. "Was that before or after that Rizzo catch?"

"Never mind. Look, what I'm trying to get into your skull is that they had a long drought. They had all the talent, conditioning, and guts to win it."

"And I do?"

"Not with your current shitty attitude. But they did something we *can* do."

"What's that?"

"They worked as a team, went back to basics, strengthened every part of the game, maxed out every player's talents, and got guys with a passion for the game. They *built* a perfect outcome together."

He chuckled. "And you think we could make the deadline?"

"Yes!"

He leaned forward. "How?"

"I'm no longer your editor since there is nothing to edit. I'm your coach."

"Okay." He sounded tentative.

"Today you rest. Tomorrow night, we have a great dinner out. But starting tomorrow morning, we are going back to basics." She reached for her purse, which she had dangled off her knee, and pulled out a small notepad with a pen shoved into its wire spiral binding. She slapped it on the table in front of him.

"You want me to just start writing here?"

"Yes. I want you to write twenty prompts for short stories. If you can write just one a day, that could make a legit book. Use the same ones as when you were teaching. We are through playing *their* game. We need to take a second look at the rules. The contract doesn't require a *novel*, it requires a *literary work*."

"And?"

"We're bringing them to *our* game. If your students can knock out a short story in a couple hours, you sure as hell can in a day. You've seen every permutation on those prompts and should be able to write a reasonable short story during the day—*your own story*—that I can edit that night. I still see a way out if we double-team it. Ready?"

"Sure."

She put her hand on his briefly. "Good. Now about the camaraderie part…"

"Another Cubs story?"

"Short one. You know the Cubs lost their first six games that year."

"Of course not. I don't know a thing about them."

"Well, on the plane on the way to the seventh game, the coach breaks out a really good bottle of something. Poured a shot for everybody and raised his glass. 'To the best zero and six team in all baseball' or something like that. They thought they could do it, and they did."

"Are you proposing a shot of whiskey?"

"How about we launch this with a bottle of Champagne tonight after you've written all the prompts. By seven tomorrow morning, you need to be showered and at your desk grinding out your first short story. We can work non-stop."

"We'll starve!"

"I can cook while you write. Or bring in something. Besides, we have dinner plans for tomorrow."

"Wine with dinner?"

"On my terms."

Chapter № 8

October 3, 2017
Tuesday

After lunch, Jack disappeared into his suite with the scribbled list of prompts. He sat at the desk, rolled a page into the typewriter, and stared at it. He placed the list of prompts beside the typewriter, smoothed the paper, and read them all, twice. He thought the first one: "Retell a family story of loss and redemption in a modern way," might work. He put his hands on the keys and waited.

And waited.

Blinking, he thought that any typing might loosen up the muscle memory and get him thinking of a story, so he typed out each of the prompts.

And when Eileen heard him starting to type, she smiled and went to her suite to work on her novel.

Jack looked at his output. Each one of the prompts was perfectly numbered, two blank lines were inserted between them, margins had been set correctly, and the list typed without any errors. Then he rolled out the typed prompts and laid the page over the handwritten prompts, adjusting the corners so they matched perfectly. The page that he rolled into the typewriter next remained blank in spite of his sitting, staring at it, hands on the keys, for twenty minutes. He stood, his legs trembling. With the ferocity of a bear after a salmon, he swiped the typed prompts and the handwritten page off the table, scattering the pages across the room with an anger that frightened him. He walked over to the bed and fell on it, watching the ceiling for any inspiration until he drifted off to sleep.

When she brought him a large cup of coffee in the midafternoon, she mentioned the eight o'clock dinner reservations. At seven that evening, she tapped on his door. He opened it, still dressed in his turtleneck and cords. Both of which had new coffee stains.

He looked at her little black dress and the small gold chain at her neck and smiled. "You look nice. Have a date?"

"Yes, with you for dinner."

"Oh. Is that tonight? I've been working on a story. Musta lost track of time."

She glanced past him into the room and saw the usual clutter of clothes crawling out of his suitcase onto the floor. The typewriter had a page in it that seemed new. The rumpled bed had a fresh dent in the down duvet. "Can you change and put on a tie? If you hurry we still can walk to the café and won't need an Uber. The weather's cleared."

"A tie? I think I brought one. I'll look, if not, the turtleneck…"

She closed the door to hurry his transformation. A few minutes later he appeared. As requested, he had dressed in his black suit pants. His tie was knotted loosely at the neck of his creased denim work shirt. His brown tweed jacket was over his arm. His hair was still tousled in a way that shouted bed-head. She sighed as she noticed he was still wearing his hiking boots.

They walked the few blocks down Rue Dauphine, then past Le Procope where she had dined with Greg months before, to Boulevard Saint-Germain. In a few minutes, they passed the cathedral, Église de Saint-Germain-des-Prés. Lost in gazing at the lights on the church, she was surprised when they arrived at Rue Saint Benoit and the café. Even in the chill of the evening, the sidewalk tables were filled and the chatter of those enjoying a glass of something invited them to a good evening. They were a few minutes early. As they approached the door, Jack looked worried. "We should have made reservations. It's crowded."

"My friend Greg did. He's joining us for dinner. You'll like him."

Once inside, he looked over the dark wood-paneled walls and recently reupholstered long banquette seating. He grinned. "Yeah. I remember this place. I saw Brigitte Bardot in here one night. God she was beautiful. Not in a movie star phony way, but so sure of herself. Like you. Maybe that was even more attractive than how really pretty, physically pretty, she was."

"Visiting?"

"Lived here a year with Marie. My wife. My soon to be ex-wife, I guess. Saw Jane Fonda here. She and Roger Vadim were on the edge of their breakup. It was in all the papers then. Belmondo. All the New Wave movie people came here. And the clothing designers. Yves Saint-Laurent in his turtleneck..."

"That must have been a special time."

"Was." He fiddled with the loose knot of his tie, making it even more off-center. "She was in her twenties and I was in my thirties and she made me feel like I could do anything. Write anything."

"You still can. In fact, you are even better now than your earlier work."

"Really?" He laughed. "Pen's dry."

"Let's get a good dinner, relax, and get to work in the morning. No more work talk tonight, I promise."

At the entrance, she smiled at the slim waiter with the perfectly starched apron that brushed the tips of his well-polished shoes and explained they were meeting a friend. He nodded and let her look into the restaurant. She grinned when she saw Greg at a table near the window. He stood. His closely tailored dark blue suit was both formal and stylish. His light blue shirt had a flared collar setting off a perfectly centered white silk tie with a wide Windsor knot. The waiter escorted them to the table. Greg gave Eileen a hug, and helped her remove her coat. He stood close enough for her to smell the lime in his aftershave and feel his warmth. He extended his hand to Jack. "Greg Patel."

"Jack."

Greg gave the coat to the waiter and held his chair to the side allowing Eileen and Jack to slide into the padded banquette. Eileen took the end seat, next to Greg's chair, while Jack took the seat facing Greg.

"Eileen! You look wonderful. I am so glad you called."

She felt a blush and cleared her throat. "We appreciate your getting reservations. Jack really wanted to come here."

Jack fiddled with the fork at his place. "Yeah. How'd you get us in? I heard it was a long wait."

"I live here, so I know some people who helped."

Jack looked around the room. "Nice. I've been here before. This is where the writers hung out."

Both Eileen and Greg offered stories about Hemingway and other writers who frequented the Café de Flore in the twenties hoping they would spark some conversation. Jack just smiled and nodded. His earlier enthusiasm for Hemingway seemed depleted, or perhaps he was embarrassed by his inadvertent appropriation of Hemingway's stories. Greg stopped and smiled at her and then at Jack. "I've placed you now. You are Jack Forrester, aren't you?"

Jack looked up from turning pages in the leather-bound wine list. "That's what my momma always called me."

"Sir, I am a big, no, a huge fan of your writing. It's a pleasure to meet you."

"How's your French, Greg?"

"Pretty good. Why?"

"See if you can get that boy's attention and get some drinks going."

Greg looked at Eileen, who rolled her eyes. "Jack? What about a Champagne and some appetizers while we talk, then we can order."

"Starters?" Jack turned to Eileen. "I like your friend already." He turned the wine list to Greg. "See that? Who'd imagine a bottle of Champagne could cost that much?"

Greg chuckled. "A vintage Krug is pricey."

Greg got the waiter's attention with a subtle glance and ordered a bottle of Champagne, which was priced for tourists. Once the ice bucket was placed and the bottle opened, with but a whisper, Greg motioned for Eileen to taste the wine. The waiter poured Eileen's glass first and waited for her approval. On her nod, he poured the flutes half full. She took a second sip while their glasses were being filled. "Crisp. Overtones of pear and apple. Really a nice choice."

Greg picked up his glass. "Welcome to France, Jack."

"Oh. I've been here before. Looks a lot the same. Maybe cleaner in this part, washed some of the grime off the buildings. But graffiti. Don't remember that much of it when I was here in the seventies."

Eileen turned her head quickly to see if he was joking. The political unrest in the late sixties and early seventies found expression through spray cans and tearing up the cobblestone streets to chuck stones at the police, who hid behind Plexiglas shields. It was almost a sport to see which street would be the next platform for free speech. She had translated a history of the movements and counter-movements of those turbulent decades and had also translated the captions under the photos that explained the spray-painted graffiti.

When the menu arrived they studied it in silence. Then Eileen took a deep breath. "I wonder if I could just order a plate of whatever that luscious aroma is." She sniffed again. "Garlic and toasting bread, rosemary, and roasting meats. It is so. So." She looked puzzled for a moment, searching for the exact word.

Greg chuckled. "So French?"

"Exactly!"

Jack shrugged and poked at his menu. "What's that by the price? Is that a new franc mark?"

"It's in euros now. Been using this currency since 2002."

"Ugly little symbol, isn't it? Looks like an embryonic something or an armadillo with a hard on." He laughed at his own joke and sputtered when he tried to take a drink. Returning his glass to the table, he asked Greg, "So! What's a euro?"

"What..."

"How many of 'em in a dollar?"

"Right now, one euro is worth about a dollar ten to fifteen. I usually just figure it at a buck and a quarter and never get a surprise when my Visa bill arrives."

Jack slammed the menu on the table, opened it, and jabbed it with his finger. "But this salad is twenty euros, that's..." He abandoned his calculation. "That's fucking ridiculous!"

She flipped back to the salad page. "Oh the Salad Colette, it's got a special lettuce and grapefruit as well as prawns..."

"Prawns? Gold-plated ones?"

She laughed. "Might be. Anyway, Max is paying, so enjoy yourself."

"Max is, is he? Really? You know he expenses me against my royalties before he forwards them to me?"

"I know that's customary, but he promised this trip was on him. His firm, not an expense to you or me. I asked."

He grinned. "In that case, did you see the cold buffet plates? That's what I'm thinking could be a great appetizer."

Greg asked, "What else strikes your fancy, Jack?"

"Looking at the terrine of duck foie gras with toasts, since Max is paying."

Greg nodded to Eileen who said, "That and the caviar with a supplement of the blinis, so we could share them. What do you think?"

Greg grinned at her. "Your wish is my command." He motioned to the waiter and ordered.

Jack looked shocked. "That's it? Aren't we gonna have a steak or some duck?"

Eileen patted his arm. "He's just taking the order for appetizers. He'll be back when we finish them."

"Oh, okay."

Greg noticed that Jack was finishing his Champagne rapidly and asked, "Anyone want water?"

Eileen nodded. "Yes. Still, please."

Greg ordered a bottle of still spring water. The waiter provided stemmed wine glasses.

When the waiter started to pour for Jack, he reached for the man's wrist. "None for me, son. I'll be up all night peeing as it is."

To Eileen's relief, the waiter was one of the few who did not have a complete grasp of English. Greg interceded and told the waiter to leave the water bottle and he'd pour it as needed. Greg turned to Jack. "If I remember right, you used this café as a meeting place for a microfilm hand-off in *The Capricorn Affair.*"

"Might have. You know, I never really picked the titles. I just wrote the books, then the marketing geniuses at the house slapped a title on the cover."

"Well, I've loved your titles. But what really hooked me as a reader is the complexity of the plots. You seemed to have several stories going at once, and never got the characters doing something wrong..."

"Oh, there were plenty of bad guys, and gals."

"I mean out-of-character."

"Sure. Hard work that. Spent most of the year just getting names and locations right. Then the action line got drawn in under it."

"Drawn in? How do you mean?"

"Drawn! With a black grease pencil on butcher paper that I stapled to the wall in my office. Some books took up the whole wall. My wife hated that. Made me close the door when company came over. Messy, she said. But it paid the bills."

"Do you write start to end, or by sections, or how does it work?"

"Fuck if I know. But it did. Twenty books is a pretty good run."

Eileen watched Greg, who did not flinch at Jack's loud outburst. Greg smiled. "I can't wait for your next one."

Jack chuckled. "Me either."

"How'd you decide to put the hand-off here?"

"Easy. Everyone can imagine it. Been described in a ton of books—Hemingway, Fitzgerald, even guidebooks. So all I had to do was give the outline and let readers color inside those lines. The hard part was inventing a new location. That took too much time. That's why I like to use places I've been. Like here."

"Makes sense."

"Yeah, took my bride here a couple times in the seventies. We'd see famous people, mostly from fashion. Yves Saint-Laurent. Saw Bardot here." Jack grinned. "Ever tell you about the time I saw Jack Kerouac in here? Boozing it up with some French avant-garde types."

Greg leaned forward and rested his elbows on the table, long past the American notion of holding his hands in his lap during dinner. "Loved his stuff when I was in college. Wish I could have…"

"You know he wrote in French? Read one of his manuscripts. Used a phonetic writing of the French-Canadian. He called it Canuk-French. I guess that's not politically correct to say anymore, but that's what he called it. Phonetic, ignored grammar. Son of a bitch wrote his novella, *La Nuit Est Ma Femme*, in just five days in Mexico, probably on a bender at that."

"Really? I never knew he wrote in French."

"Parents were French-Canadians. Came by it naturally. But those novels, novellas really, were still unpublished when he died. Published now, if you can find a copy."

Jack turned to Eileen. "Ever read *Maggie Cassidy?*"

"Sure."

"Wrote most of it in French. When he figured out he was barking up the wrong tree, he did it all over in English. Guess he wouldn't have needed you."

Greg came to her defense. "Not unless he wanted it to be readable."

Jack laughed loud enough to turn heads. "Touché. Got me there, pal."

The waiter arrived to remove the empty plates and took their main course orders.

Greg asked, "What's your fancy?"

Jack smiled. "Maybe just a dessert?"

"How about something more substantial first. Look about two pages back in the menu."

"That all sounds too heavy."

Eileen offered, "I'm having an omelet with fresh herbs. Maybe you'd like that or the omelet with mushrooms. Or a quiche."

"Oh, alright. With mushrooms. You order it while I see where the men's room is. Gotta see a man about a horse."

Greg watched him walk away then turned to Eileen. "I'm glad you called."

"Even for a favor?"

"Even for a favor. Remember, you owe me a lunch after we see what's going on with him, if anything." She smiled as he leaned forward and took her hand. "He seemed confused about time just now. I know that Kerouac died in sixty-nine, so his appearance here in the seventies is impossible."

She looked skeptical. "How'd you know that?"

"Term paper in high school. I remember weird stuff. Is he confused about other chronologies?"

"Some things he has said in our short time together didn't match things he's said just hours before. I don't know if he was here alone in the seventies or with his wife, I don't know how old she is, but he said she was twenty when they met, and he was either thirty or forty."

"He said, 'either thirty or forty'?"

"No. Once he said one and later he said the other."

When the waiter returned, Greg sat back in his chair and ordered. She ordered for Jack and added a mid-range Champagne just as he returned from the restroom and said, "And a bottle or two of Krug to wash it down."

Greg looked at her. She frowned. Greg held up his hand to stop him. "How about I surprise you with a grower Champagne."

"What's that?"

"A small producer that does everything from tending the vines to pasting the label on the bottle. Not like the big commercial houses."

"Sure, if you're buying."

Eileen reminded him that Max was funding the evening and Jack grinned. "Make it a good one."

On several occasions during the conversation, Jack disrupted things by adding something unrelated to the discussion. He finished his omelet quickly. When he noticed that Eileen had not finished her omelet, he suggested another bottle of Champagne, a vintage Krug off the wine list.

The waiter paused and looked to her for confirmation. She smiled and let him leave. Jack again visited the restroom.

Greg looked at her. "Mind if I sub in some sparkling water and see if he notices?"

"Can you? He keeps trying to order that six-hundred-dollar bottle of Krug. Maybe it's to spite Max. Maybe as a last hurrah, like he said."

Greg stood, and approaching the waiter, placed his hand on the server's arm. "I regret," he said, "that my uncle's health does not allow more wine, but if you would be so kind to bring a bottle of Pellegrino sparkling water well wrapped in a napkin and treat it as Champagne, it would mean a great deal to me. I so do not want to embarrass him."

At first, the waiter raised an eyebrow at having his substantial gratuity reduced as the bottled water was five hundred euros less than the Krug, then he gave a shy smile and nodded. "I am so sorry he is…drifting."

Greg handed the waiter a fifty-euro note. "It would be even better if it arrived in a Champagne bottle."

The waiter at first declined, then agreed. In a few minutes, the server faked uncorking it, presented the cork and cage to Greg, who nodded approval. He then showed the bottle's label to the table and poured the sparkling water into their empty Champagne glasses with style. Eileen sighed with relief that Jack had not noticed the sham opening ceremony or that tasting had been omitted. He sipped and paused. She held her breath until he announced, "Not bad, but the ninety-four had a lot more body. That was my favorite. The year Grace was born."

Greg asked, "Your daughter?"

"Yup. Only one. Won't talk to me now."

"Grandkids?"

He seemed surprised by the question, drained the glass, and searched for the waiter. "Uh. Just had a boy." He seemed distressed by his empty glass.

She quickly pushed her glass over to him, past his three dessert plates now smeared with chocolate smudges. "Here. I've had enough."

He drained the glass and pulled his napkin across his face with a grand sweeping motion. "That was pretty good. Any more?"

"Nope. Afraid that was the last of the Krug."

She asked, "A coffee?"

"Naw, I think I'm ready to call it a night."

She nodded to the waiter, who had been watching them closely. He took her credit card and smiled.

The chill in the night air was startling and welcome after the warmth of the noisy café, the richness of the food, and the tension she felt from not knowing what Jack was going to do next. Greg stopped just outside the restaurant. She saw his hesitation and smiled. "Why don't you come back to our place for a nightcap?"

Jack clapped him on the shoulder. "Sure. Good idea. But I'll let you two catch up. I'm bushed."

Greg laughed. "I'd love to come in for a minute."

When they reached the building, Jack had the staggers and decided to hang on Greg's shoulder as though they were best friends out on the town. As soon as the elevator opened to the top floor, he hurried to the door, and as soon as she unlocked it, he scurried to his suite without pausing to close the door. In a moment the flush of the toilet echoed in the quiet living room. He came back, trousers zipped but with his belt flapping loose. "I need some water. Some nights I get a dry throat." He partially filled a glass from the tap on the refrigerator door and shuffled back to his room.

When he heard the door to Jack's suite shut, Greg looked at Eileen and raised his eyebrows. "Got a laptop we can use out here?"

"Sure." She retrieved it from her suite, sat at the kitchen table, flipped up the screen, and powered it on. "What do you have in mind?"

He stood behind her and leaned down to whisper. "Some fact checking. And let him get to sleep."

He pulled the chair from the end of the table and sat beside her. In a few taps she had brought up a comprehensive biography on Jack. Born in fifty-one, married in ninety-three. Photo of the wedding. City hall in Paris, a windy spring day. Jack squinted into the sun. Gazing at the picture, Eileen whispered, "His tweed suit looks like something Fitzgerald might have worn. Quite writerly."

He pointed. "What's with her suit? Its shoulder pads are…"

"*Sleepless in Seattle*. I think that's what Meg Ryan wore in the movie. Stylish then."

"Yeah but look at that *Pretty Woman* set of curls. Damn."

Eileen chuckled. "That's a lot of hair."

He frowned. "Okay, he said they married in the seventies, so she'd have been what?"

"One or two years old."

Greg grinned. "That's one full 'growed-up woman,' there. I know. I'm a doctor. You can trust me on that."

She punched his shoulder. "So that's a flub. What's with the bathroom runs? That's been going on since I met him at JFK."

"It could be several things. Don't focus on that. How about inappropriate language, missed conversation cues, and swearing?"

She shrugged. "I'm saturated, having spent the past few days with him. He blurts out stuff. We were talking about Hemingway and he says something like, 'At least, I don't have a limp dick.' But, I'm getting numb to it all, the time gaps, the swearing, and the vacant looks. How off was it?"

"Off. But that's not my biggest worry. It's his gait."

"He's an old guy, cut him some slack. Says he has bad knees."

"No. He's fine up and down curbs. It's his side-to-side motion that worries me."

She nodded. "He does sway."

"And he walks like his feet weigh a hundred pounds each."

She sat straight and looked at him. "Is it the triad?"

"You read my paper again?"

"How could I translate it if I didn't understand it?"

"He's got all three! Confusion, gait difficulty, and possibly incontinence, at least frequency or urgency. Did he mention a prostate problem? You know if he's using a pad? Like Depends?"

She pulled back. "Jesus, how would I know any of that?"

"You said he told you that he didn't have any 'limp dick' issues. Why wouldn't he tell you if he had a bladder issue?"

"God! I'm not his mom. He just says things. I don't even know if they are true."

He laughed. "I guess that's good news."

"I missed your laugh. I'm so scared for him."

He touched her hand. "One step at a time."

"He misses cues. Doesn't answer, I don't..."

"Eileen! He's deaf as a stone in his right ear. You did notice that, didn't you?"

"No. But if I think on it, he did seem to be more focused when I sat across from him than when I was beside him."

"Or at least to his left."

"I feel so bad for all he's got on his plate."

"Which is what, exactly? What's the emotional pressure?"

"He has a book due in..." She looked at the calendar on her iPhone, and said, "Four weeks from today. By Halloween night. If he doesn't cough something up, he'll be in default."

"So what? That's business."

"It's also who he is. So, then he is a 'blocked writer.' He'll have to return his advance, which he's already spent, and he'll get a shitstorm of publicity that'll kill his next deal. Oh, yeah, his wife left him and his daughter won't talk to him, and he's never met his grandkid, because all the women important to him hate him. And maybe he knows he's losing his mind. And if anyone gets a whiff of any of this, the rumors in the tabloids will push him over the edge. Really! I've got to get him writing."

"Is it really that bad?"

"Yes!"

"What are you doing at noon tomorrow?"

"Buying a cattle prod."

Greg touched her arm. "Seriously."

"Working to get anything on paper."

"Come see me."

Eileen frowned. "Greg, I said..."

He reached into his wallet and pulled out a card. He wrote on the back of it and handed it to her. "Bring him at noon."

"I know where the Institute is, remember? We worked there."

"This is the address for my apartment."

"I remember that, too."

He smiled. "Good. But I didn't know if you still had the street address. I can do most of the tests there without anyone knowing."

"Could you?"

"Didn't you call me to help the guy?"

"Yes. He needs more than just an editor right now."

"It looks like he's got a friend, one he didn't know he needed."

"Thanks. You think he'll come?"

Greg nodded. "Yes. He senses how deep a hole he is in. I don't think you need to recount the many areas of concern—just say I might be able to help with his writer's block."

He stood and grabbed his coat off the chair. "Let him sleep in. Don't prompt him on showering or dressing. Take Uber. I don't want him exhausted for the tests."

She walked him to the door. He hugged her again. This time, it was longer.

She showered, threw on her boy shorts and *Hamilton* sweatshirt, crawled into bed, and started *Y is for Yesterday*. She started blinking away tears, not at Kinsey Millhone's problems or the tragedies befalling the residents of Santa Teresa, but at Sue Grafton's battle with cancer that had stopped her writing. Eileen had devoured the entirety of the alphabet of mysteries and loved the groundbreaking female detective. She imagined Grafton as someone she would have enjoyed as a friend and wondered what the last book would have been. She Googled Grafton's website. It reported that *Z is for Zero* was the planned title for the last book that she was too ill to begin. She wiped her eyes with the sleeve of her sweatshirt, washed her face with cold water, and had a hard time falling asleep. She slept lightly and was awakened several times by Jack flushing his toilet. The third time, she closed her door. Once she was deeply asleep, a shrill beeping startled her. She swatted her phone on the bedside table. It fell to the floor. When she reached for it, she saw it was four in the morning and realized that the beeping was from the kitchen.

She bolted from her bed and opened her door. As she ran past his door, she shouted, "Jack! Wake up!" She recognized the smell of burning toast before she saw the pale patch of smoke that floated at the end of the hallway. She sprinted into the kitchen. Black smoke was billowing from the toaster oven. She yanked the power cord from the wall and put the stove's vent fan on high.

When she turned, she saw the white of Jack's robe through the dense smoke. He stood at the window looking at the river. Grabbing silicone mitts, she moved the smoking appliance from the counter to the stovetop directly under the industrial exhaust fan. She turned and shouted over the fan. "Jack! What..."

He turned and blinked before noticing the smoke. "The toast. Shit! I burned the toast."

She collapsed in a chair at the table, ripped off the mitts, ran her hands through her hair, and succeeded in not screaming at him. Her heart was still pounding when he sat down across from her.

"Sorry I made a mess of it. I just wanted something to..." He ground his fist into his stomach and grimaced. "Got kinda an acid stomach. Thought some toast...or crackers."

"I'll see what's in the cupboard. Okay?"

He tugged the tie of his robe tighter and watched her hunt for crackers. "Thanks."

She found several boxes intended for cheese boards. "English water biscuits, some kind of thin rice flour cracker, rye crisp, a dark cracker with apricots and hazelnuts, and pita chips."

"Don't they have normal food?"

"How about a slice of bread?"

"Fine."

She cut two thick slices, handed him one, and started nibbling on the other.

He nodded appreciation and stared at her sleep shirt. "What'd you think of the play? Or would you call it a musical? Wasn't that the one with the rapper songs in it?" When she realized that she was only wearing underwear and a sweatshirt, she retreated to her room.

Chapter № 9

October 4, 2017
Wednesday

It was still dark outside when she returned to the kitchen, rolled up the sleeves of her warm flannel shirt, and started the water kettle for coffee. Jack brought eleven typed pages from his room and put them at her place. Both were silent until the coffee was made and cups filled. Jack stirred his black coffee and looked past her at the clock above the stove while she read his pages and nodded. "This isn't bad. Original, at least to me. Your characters seem really developed, impressive for a short story. Your format is sort of, well, unusual."

"I always clean up the paragraphing later, this is just a first draft. Neater than I usually do so you could get the drift. This cut is just to get the plot and dialogue right."

She straightened the pages, put them beside her cup, and took a deep breath. "Jack? Greg and I talked last night. He thinks he might be able to help you with your writer's block. He could meet us at noon, if you're..."

He looked at the steam rising from his cup and tugged the belt on his robe tighter. He thought it was the grief. Wasn't it standard wisdom that grief has stages? If that is true, isn't it a scrim that shifts between dark and light? He closed his eyes and felt the loss of separation, of losing his family, of losing his memory. He compressed realization and denial and anger into an explosive mixture. His fist hit the table. The saltshaker jumped and tipped over. "I'm not losing my marbles! I can't! I write books, and I am here, aren't I? I'm writing again! It may be slow, but you can work with me, and it will be fine."

"Jack. I can't edit what you haven't written. And I've only got these few pages from you that are any good."

"It's the grief. I've lost my family as sure as if a hurricane blew them out to sea."

She wanted to say "tsunami swept," but just took a breath. "What if it's something simple that is fixable? Wouldn't you want to know?"

"What if it's not?"

"We'll cross that bridge when we—"

He scowled at her. "Or burn it. What if it isn't fine? What if things do seem harder? What are we gonna do about it? Nothing is gonna give me back my family—can't you see how I'm grieving?"

"Let's go see Greg today."

"The man we had dinner with last night?"

She nodded. "He's a doctor, and I trust him."

He paused then looked at her with a set jaw. "Why? There's nothing wrong with me that a good night's sleep won't fix. Maybe it's that jet lag thing and not just grief."

"How many days have we been here?"

He narrowed his eyes. "Why?"

"How many? Give me a number."

He frowned and narrowed his eyes. He shouted, "Two!" as if he were a toddler having a tantrum.

She shook her head and rolled out her fingers from her closed hand as she spoke. "We left JFK on Saturday, arrived here on Sunday. You wrote that Hemingway knock-off and..."

Jack nodded. "But I couldn't get it right, could I? Somehow Hemingway kept elbowing his way into my stories."

She got up and poured more coffee into each of their cups. She smiled and let her shoulders slump. "We had another plan. But it didn't work. That's when I called my friend."

He scratched the stubble on his jaw. "The guy we had dinner with at the Café de Flore."

"Right. Greg. So how many days have we been here?"

"More than I said."

"Right and it's getting worse not better."

"Why wouldn't it?" His voice rose. "You pestering me all the time. Write! Write! Like I am some galley slave." He laughed. "Get it? Galley as in rowing a long ship or reading a printer's proof."

"I got it. That's the first real joke you've made since we got here."

"So? Arriving to face the music has not exactly been a bundle of laughs. If I make more puns, will you work with me without this un-necessary interruption? This browbeating."

"I can't ignore what's happening, Jack. Greg can meet us at noon."

He puffed up and snarled at her. "You gonna tell the tabloids that I'm all dried up? Get some scoop. Make your money off me one way or another?"

She sat back as if slapped. "I don't follow—"

"Gonna get a check from those celebrity rags for the exclusive story for exposing..."

She pushed her chair away from the table, uncertain if his anger was going to escalate. "Stop it. You know better than that. I'm invested in your success, maybe more than you are." She restrained her emotion and then calmed her voice. "I'd never do anything to harm you or your reputation after all that you have been to my family. Listen, Greg will see us in private at his apartment so no one needs to know. He's my friend. I think he can get you out of your writer's block."

Jack snorted. "Does Max need a witness to tell him I'm slipping? Sign some papers? Is this about some insurance he has on me, so he gets paid if I can't work, like a disability policy or something? Am I go-ing to make him rich? Oh hell, I see it all falling apart. The lawyers..."

She leaned forward; close enough for him to feel her warm breath. "Stop it," she snapped. "You don't have any clue what's going on with you and neither do I." She slowed herself again. "I texted Max the selfie I took of us at the airport here just to show him we'd arrived. He texted back that he hadn't seen you for over a year. Said you looked like a scarecrow."

"So … you've told Max?"

"No. Maybe I should have, but I haven't. How much weight have you lost this last year?"

He shrugged.

"Okay. We have some forms to fill out before we see Greg at noon. He e-mailed them to me. Are you going to try and see what's going on or throw in the towel now?"

"I'm no quitter."

She went to the office and returned with a handful of pages. "Then show me. I printed these last night. Help me get these filled out before your meeting and—"

"Today?"

"Today! Noon today."

"That soon?"

"Yes. We'll fill them out right after I make breakfast."

"I'm not hungry anymore."

"Okay. I'll write the answers, but you need to tell me the truth. This is reality, not fiction you can bend and rework. You can't blow it off like it's some petty annoyance."

"Shoot." He pouted and leaned his elbows on the kitchen table.

She grabbed a small container of peach yogurt from the refrigerator. She asked for his passport and driver's license. She ate her yogurt while he retrieved the documents. After copying the information, she returned his passport and asked for his place of birth.

He stared at her. "Don't I even get to go through the stages of grief? That Ross-Klubber thing?"

"It's Kübler-Ross and Kessler. And no. You've already been around that track twice. Stop stalling. Just answer my questions so we can get this filled out."

"How'd you get an appointment so soon?"

"We're friends. I translated his work from French into English a while back. He's seeing you as a favor to me. Place of birth?"

"Saginaw. Michigan."

"Date of birth?"

"Easy. January 9, in 1951. Easy to remember, see, one is for January and nine is the day and put it together with fifty-one and it's nineteen-fifty-one."

She started to write the date and then remembered that in France the day comes before the month.

He made a face and challenged her in a singsong voice. "What's the matter, forget something?"

"No. Just want to do it right. They flip the numbers here."

"Aren't you going to ask me my address?"

"Got it off your passport. New York."

"Nope. Moved out right after I got it. Been at the cabin for the last six...eight months. Shit, close to a year, I guess. It's right on the license."

"Thanks."

She corrected it and handed the documents back to him. "Current medications?"

"None, unless you count a glass of wine for dinner and the occasional snort of a good hooch. Scotch preferably."

She looked at him. "None?"

"Fit as a fiddle."

"Your doctor's name and address."

"Nope."

"What do you mean 'nope'? Why aren't you going to give me that information? If he needs to review your records..."

"No records to review. Not for the past four or five years. I outlived my doc. Had a heart attack at his golf club. Too much rich food and too many rich friends. So I decided to hell with them. I'd just live out my life like God intended."

"Are you a Christian Scientist or have a belief that doctors are—"

"Hell no. Doctors are just fine for other people. Just too much fuss for me since I feel fine."

She dropped the pen on the questionnaire and stared at him. "You haven't had any medical attention for five years?"

"Got a cast on my left wrist maybe a year ago. Sidewalk iced over. I took a spill in town. Hairline fracture. Healed fast. I just had the hospital cut off the cast a few weeks later and went on my way."

"No PT?"

"What's that?"

"Physical therapy. It makes the healing go better and accelerates recovery."

"Nope. Just worked itself back to normal. Able to type at full speed again in a couple months."

She looked up from the printout. "Operations?"

"Appendix and vasectomy."

"When?"

"Appendix at seventeen. Vasectomy...not soon enough."

She started writing again. "I think they are looking for a year or your age."

"Right after Gracie was born. Marie had an ultimatum. No vasectomy. No sex. Guess which I chose."

"When was that?"

"Didn't you want to know the details?"

"Not really. When?"

"Nineteen forty-nine."

She stopped and looked at him. "How old were you when you decided to get snipped?"

"Thirty-seven. I mean seven or eight. I was close to forty but not quite."

Eileen put a question mark on the line, recalling that he was over forty when he married. She looked up from the questionnaire. "In case of emergency?"

"What?"

"Whom to notify in case of emergency?"

"You, I guess. My ex is really ex and my daughter hates me. You're here. Max, I guess if it's about money."

"Insurance?"

"Nope. Not for health. Got it if I drop dead or need a nursing home."

"Any of these ailments?" She handed a full page of diseases and conditions to him. He laughed. "Guess not since I can't read 'em in French."

She translated them. He said he did not have any of the listed medical conditions or concerns. Once the questionnaire was completed, he retreated to write. She went to her suite and debated between taking a long hot bath in the massive soaking tub or using the ultramodern steam shower that looked like the transporter in the early *Star Trek* movies. She elected the rain shower and stood under the tropical downpour longer then usual, trying to calm herself. As she thought of how very alone and afraid Jack was, she started to cry. Once she regained control, she wrapped herself in a warm bath sheet and then dressed for the day.

At ten he pulled on his turtleneck and green cords. At eleven-thirty she opened the Uber app and tapped in Greg's address.

His apartment building had survived two world wars with just a few nicks from small arms fire in the upper façade. The seedy bar on the ground floor was packed at a quarter to twelve. When they exited the Uber, Jack pointed to the bar. "We're early."

"Not that early. Come on."

He pouted as he tagged after her to a door that had been varnished shortly after the last armistice had been signed. The kick plate had dents in it and splinters at the edges. She looked over the names. Occupants had a key and guests had to be buzzed in. She ran her finger along the names. Paper slips that announced a psychic, a carpet cleaning business, and several individuals of the female persuasion were all faded.

G. Patel was the only freshly printed name card. She pressed the button beside it. Almost immediately, the door hissed as the electric lock opened. She held the door for Jack, who stopped inside and looked around the dim lobby. It smelled like cumin, browning naan, and tandoori spices from the nearby Indian restaurant. Black-and-white tiles floated in a grimy grout. He eyed the small, rickety elevator. She slid back the gate and nodded for him to enter.

"Think it'll hold both of us?"

"Come on, unless you want to hike up."

"Let's walk."

She followed him slowly up the carpeted stairs. A faint pattern was still recognizable along the edges of the tread.

He chuckled a nervous laugh. "So this is where he's gonna look under my hood and see how many cylinders are still working."

She laughed. "Something like that. Remember it's his apartment, so don't be surprised." Jack had stopped on the stairs and looked past her toward the lobby door. She smiled at him and said, "It's going to get better."

"My French isn't what it used to be."

"He speaks English. Remember, you liked him at dinner."

He took a deep breath. "Can you stay with me in there?"

"I'm not a relative..."

"Ask him. I've never been so scared in my life."

"You can trust him."

"It's not him I'm worried about. Please?"

"Sure, Jack."

A dark oak door, at least ten feet tall, opened. Greg stepped into the hall. He was wearing dark trousers and a blue button-down oxford cloth shirt. The cuffs were rolled up to the elbow. He held up his hand in greeting and grinned. "Eileen! Right on time. Hi, Jack. Come on in."

Greg turned and walked into a small living room of a shabby apartment. To the left was a wall of exposed pale stone and mortar. The plastered walls were of a smudged yellow. There were several amateurish landscapes in muddy tones hanging on the walls. A scuffed leather couch huddled against the far wall, a scarred coffee table was in front of it, and a small bentwood chair that leaned against the stone wall completed the random furnishings. To the right, two barstools were shoved against a high counter. Past that was a small sink, a two-burner electric stove, and a microwave barely large enough to heat a cup of coffee. A refrigerator covered with travel magnets was under the counter.

Jack looked down the two-step hall and saw two closed doors. "Nice place you got here."

Eileen wondered if he was being sarcastic or trying to be polite.

Greg laughed. "Rented it 'as is.' So I take no pride or blame for it. I'm rarely here, and it just lets me pay off my student loan faster."

"This your office? I thought you worked at the Institute."

"I do, but if I interview you here, we could meet today. And Eileen indicated that you are concerned about privacy."

"Thanks. Let's get to it."

"Please come with me. I'll interview you in my study. It's almost as glamorous as the living room, but it's private."

Jack looked back at Eileen. She dropped her messenger bag on the sofa and sat down beside it. "I'll be here if you need anything."

Greg opened the door to the left and entered, standing by it until Jack was inside and then he shut it with a loud click. He pointed to the folding chair in front of a desk made of a discarded door and sawhorses. "Relax. This is the easy part. Just going to ask you some questions. I think your writer's block might be coming from a cognitive impairment, but it could be a number of other things. By asking you a series of questions, I can get a better idea of what the trouble is and how we can help you feel better again. I'd like to know *why* you are having memory issues, so that if it can be fixed, we will get it fixed."

Jack settled into the hard chair and slouched slightly. "Shoot."

"Why are you here today?"

"Eileen says I'm slipping a cog or two. I can't write, and that's what I do for a living. I got a block. And she says I'm messing up on other stuff too. Not being neat. Forgetting stuff. Maybe it's Old Timer's Disease?" He chuckled at his joke but looked frightened.

"This isn't about Eileen, although you should thank her for noticing there might be an issue and taking action on it on your behalf. You know how many people just would have let you carry on like there was nothing wrong until it was too late for any help?"

Jack stared at him, unable to respond.

"First, let's find out where your memory and cognitive skills are and see if there is anything wrong before we jump ahead into the 'fixing' discussion. Any questions?"

"How much is this gonna cost? I don't have any insurance."

"Nothing. I have authority to evaluate a number of patients as a part of my ongoing research. With your permission, I will use your results, anonymously, as one random case history for a teaching tool. Agree? If so, I'll have you sign some papers at the end of today's session."

"Okay. One more question."

"Sure."

"How come your English is so good—and do I have to take the tests in French?"

"That's actually two questions. But here are the answers. I am American, born there. Raised in California and here. I'm here now on a joint research study that is a ten-year project. I wrote our first findings in French, because that is where we are based and who is sponsoring the research. Eileen translated it to English, which was a better use of my time than my rewriting it. That is how we met."

"Can she come in?"

"I find that the tests are better if there are no distractions, and I also want to do a physical exam, in private. But at any time if you are uncomfortable, I can stop. Clear?"

"Yes."

"So first. I'm going to get your height and weight. There's a bathroom scale I borrowed from my neighbor and a tape measure. Not fancy, but it'll get the job done. Then I'm going to do what we call a mental status tests. It's nothing more than me asking you questions or having you remember words or numbers to repeat them back to me. Really, it's just talking. There is also a computer-based test I'd like you to consider, if you would be comfortable doing it. You can decide that when we get to it. And finally, I want to ask you some questions on what is called the Beck identifier for depression; sometimes depression can interfere with our memory and our focus. Sound okay?"

"Yes."

Greg's manner was simple and direct as he sought to understand Jack's situation. Questions ranged from factual matters such as the name of the current U.S. president or what month it was, to questions about family history and historic events. Short-term recall was also tested; Jack listened to brief phrases and sets of numbers or letters, then Greg asked Jack to repeat them after answering other questions or doing a simple math problem. This frustrated Jack, who tried to reply immediately and not have his recall interrupted. He balked when Greg asked him to draw a clock with the hands of the clock at a set time. Jack laughed. "Nobody's gonna have a clock with hands on it in a couple years, what with phones and digital clocks. Kids today couldn't tell you the time of day looking at Big Ben."

"Regardless, I'd still like you to draw a clock face for me, with all the numbers on it and the hands pointing to the time I tell you. Okay?"

Jack chuckled then struggled to make a circle on the paper. Then he added the numbers to the oblong clock face, reversing the six and nine. Looking up with a smile, he asked, "What's next?"

An hour later, Greg returned to the living room and sat beside Eileen, who was dozing on the couch. When she woke, he said, "He's taking a computer Q and A. It's a simple program but helpful on some areas. Should take about ten to fifteen minutes."

She stretched. "Was he okay with using a computer?"

"Seemed to be. Just using a mouse. He's an interesting fellow, but from what you said and what I saw at the café, I was expecting more disorganization."

"Disorganization?"

"In his manner and attire. Did you help him get dressed or give him any hygiene suggestions?"

"I told him to smooth his hair, which got windblown on the way over. Had to bite my tongue not to tell him to shower and change from that damn turtleneck."

"Anything else to add since our phone call?"

"He almost set the kitchen on fire early this morning. I thought about texting you but thought that might skew your view of him, so I waited."

"What happened?"

"About four this morning, the kitchen smoke alarm goes off. I go out and he's looking out the window. Smoke's pouring out of the toaster oven. He'd set it on broil, not toast. Seemed startled by my appearance. I must have scared the hell out of him rushing in wearing just a sweatshirt and panties."

He held back a smile. "Three desserts might have been a bit much."

She nodded. "And drinks."

"Come on, we just shared a couple bottles of Champagne over a long dinner."

She nodded. "Still, it was a good idea to substitute the Pellegrino."

"I was really testing his senses of smell and taste. He never seemed to notice the difference. Was he being polite or did he say anything about it later?"

"Not a word."

"Anything else?"

"I think he's lost a lot of weight recently. His clothes just hang on him. His agent, Max, whom I work for as well, described what he looked like so we could meet up in the Delta lounge and chat on the plane during the flight over. Nobody looked like the man Max described. When I figured out who he was and asked him directly, he said 'no' and ignored me."

"Publicity shy? Could he have thought you were some fan?"

"I don't know what he thought. It took me aback so I didn't introduce myself just then. Probably should have. But I did a few minutes later."

"How'd he act on the plane?"

"Bored. Avoiding me."

"Haven't you done something like that to avoid someone? I know I have. Contact with any other passengers?"

"We had two seats, side by side. I had introduced myself by then."

"First class? How much are you charging him?"

"Business class. His agent paid."

"How about when you landed?"

"We just followed the crowd through customs and baggage. Nothing eventful."

"Anything else about the trip?"

She looked uncomfortable. "His...hygiene was..."

Greg said, "Stinky?"

"Exactly."

"Did he shower after you got here?"

"Once, I think, even though I've heard the shower start several times. We have separate bathrooms, but he keeps wearing the same clothes, until I suggested that he change."

"Anything else since we talked yesterday?"

"Other than trying to give me a heart attack? No." She sighed. "Mom has seen writer's block, and I've worked with some temperamental authors, but this is different. To be honest, I think he is sinking and there's no one in his life to toss him a life preserver, except you."

"Suicidal?"

"God, I hope not. He's just so sad. And alone."

"You've helped a lot already."

"I haven't done anything, really."

"You got him here. The fear of dementia stops so many people from getting a good evaluation. Some forms of mild confusion, even early dementia, can be reversed. Sometimes the patient misidentifies the problem, or their doctor incorrectly upgrades a diagnosis into the ir-reversible range. That's a tragic gap in our health care systems in the developed world, if you want to call it that. Fear, limited access, and incomplete diagnostic tools for the general practitioner. That's what I want to change, get better diagnostic tools validated and increase patient and doctor education. And this is not just a 'first world' problem. It's a human problem." He shook his head, more in anger than sorrow. "It's a real tragedy when people give up, fail to recover functionality when their problem is reversible." He looked at her and she saw the pain in his eyes. "It's throwing away a life."

The buzz at the apartment door startled her. Greg got up, hit the button, and thirty seconds later opened his door. A slim man arrived carrying a yellow plastic container that looked to Eileen like a large lunchbox. Greg motioned toward his makeshift office. "Excuse us." She heard the door shut. A few minutes later, the man left. Jack came out, carefully pulling his sleeve down over a fresh bandage. He sat on the sofa beside her and toyed with a thread on his frayed cuff.

She smiled at him and patted his wrist. "How you doing, Jack?"

"Fine. Just a lotta questions and talk, until that guy took some blood."

Greg returned and sat on the small chair. "That's it until I get the blood tests back."

Jack leaned forward putting his elbows on his knees. "How soon do you figure?"

"Should have some preliminary results by tomorrow or the next day and a full panel for the main indicators by the day after. A couple of the tests are going to take longer."

"So?"

"So. We wait until we know something before we start guessing and worrying."

Jack gave a small snort. "Easy for you to say."

"Okay. Here's my impression. If you were depressed, you aren't now. You've lost a lot of weight, and I want to know why. If this is just a thyroid issue, you can start feeling better in a matter of weeks with a simple morning pill and if..."

Greg stopped and glanced at the kitchen then back to Jack. "Could you go and sit at the bar? There is another test I want to try."

He laughed. "What? See if I fall off the stool 'cause I'm so wobbly?"

"That's the last thing I'd want. Eileen, can you come over here and stand behind him? Jack, what I want you to do is hold on to the bar, shut your eyes, and keep them shut. I'm going to pull a couple things out of the refrigerator and cupboards and want you to tell me what each one is based on the scent. I'll put a glass of water in the mix as well, so it's okay if you don't smell anything. Just say so."

"Okay."

Greg opened the small refrigerator door and pulled out a jar of peanut butter and a tightly wrapped wedge of Camembert cheese. He unscrewed the jar lid and unwrapped the cheese. He opened and shut a cupboard, turned on the tap, and filled a glass with water. "Ready?"

"Guess so."

Greg took a teaspoon and scooped a bit from the peanut butter jar and held it under Jack's nose. "Here's the first sample. Smell anything?"

"That's the glass of water. Smells kinda rubbery, like a chemical, maybe chlorine."

"Okay." He grabbed another spoon and scooped up some of the runny, overly ripe cheese. "How about this?"

"You mix something in that water, like some soap?"

Eileen grimaced and blinked when he waved the spoon under her nose. Greg searched the counter and grabbed a pencil with a new eraser. After rubbing it on a piece of paper, he held it under Jack's nose. He jerked his head back, almost slipping off the stool. "Shit! That smells like a burning tire. Man!"

Greg tossed the pencil back on the counter, returned the cheese and peanut butter to the fridge, and dropped the sample spoons into the glass of water with a squirt of dish soap. "That's all. You can open your eyes now, Jack."

"How'd I do?"

Frowning, Greg asked, "Can you take off your glasses for a minute? I want to check something."

"Sure, but I really need 'em."

Greg looked at Jack's face then ran his fingertip across the bridge of Jack's nose where it was dented by his glasses. "That a new scar?"

He chuckled. "How'd you notice that?"

"Recent?"

He looked embarrassed. "Got it last spring. Switching out the storm windows for screens."

"When I asked you earlier if you ever had a concussion or hit your head, you didn't mention this."

Jack slid his tortoise-shell glasses back on. "Wasn't anything to mention. I got in a hurry and set up a ladder in some mud. Taking down the storm windows, one came off easier than I thought, and the ladder shifted. Damn metal frame hit me smack on the nose." He paused and frowned. "No biggie other than a good nosebleed. Didn't even break my glasses."

"Black out?"

"No. Never fell off the ladder or dropped the window."

"Have a headache after?"

"Maybe. Probably, that was a heavy window. Double glazed."

He started nodding, and then a slow grin remerged. He rubbed the faint scar, which was usually hidden by the bridge of his glasses. "Now that I think of it, it was about that same time I thought things smelled funny in the cabin, like mold or burning rubber sometimes. Then everything sort of dulled down. Not normal, but I had real bad hay fever that spring and passed it off to allergies."

"Okay. That's something I want to follow up on. What are you doing tomorrow?"

Jack glanced at Eileen. "Writing? What'd you have in mind?"

"I'd like to get a MRI and see if you sustained more damage from that accident than you thought or if there is something else going on with your right ear besides just hearing loss."

"Can you do it that fast?" Eileen asked.

"Besides my research, I have an arrangement with the Institute. I volunteer my time in their clinic and in return, am granted access to testing equipment. It's not part of the longitudinal study but I make a side report on any clinical work that I am doing. If you can meet me there at eleven tomorrow, we should be able to slide you in. Eileen knows the place. Seventh floor."

Jack nodded. "Say, got a bathroom here?"

"Sure, through my messy bedroom."

Greg pulled out his phone after Jack had left the living room. "Can I order an Uber?"

"Thanks," Eileen said.

"I think I exhausted him. It's gotta be frightening."

She nodded. "But the way you are with him is comforting."

"I hope. It will be interesting to see what tomorrow's tests show."

"What are you thinking?"

He shrugged. "Let's wait and see."

He glanced at his phone. "Four minutes. Want me to go down and hold the car? I don't know how long he's going to be in there." Just then Jack returned and smiled at them.

Greg said, "Your Uber's almost here. I'll see you both tomorrow morning."

Jack smiled as he left. Eileen lingered and whispered, "Thanks."

The Uber driver was a stocky Algerian who spoke very British

English. After greeting them and verifying their destination, he asked, "So? You are just from America?"

Jack answered. "Yeah. Earlier this week. Flew in from New York."

"Could I ask you a question about Las Vegas?"

"Sure. You like gambling?"

"No, sir. My question is about the shooting that occurred there."

Eileen opened the news app on her phone. She gasped and turned to Jack. "Somebody in a hotel shot down into a crowd at an outdoor concert. More than fifty people dead and over five hundred in hospitals."

Jack muttered, "Fucker."

The driver glanced at her in the rearview mirror. "What I do not understand is how you Americans value your firearms over the lives of your children and neighbors. Can you explain?"

Jack grabbed the back of the driver's seat and pulled himself forward. "No! I can't! This isn't who we are. That was some sick son of a bitch. He does not define who we are. Clear?"

The driver was silent for the remainder of the trip. Once at their destination, Eileen handed him a five-euro note. "Thank you for asking. But no, we are not all savages."

Eileen punched in the lobby door code. They rode up in silence. When they arrived at the apartment, he slipped out of his jacket and stretched. "I'm flat tuckered out. And pissed! Think I'll try to write, okay?"

She nodded. They retreated to their rooms. She settled in to reading on her Kindle app, hoping that the last Grafton mystery would blot out the news from home. Her iPhone vibrated in her pocket. She saw it was Greg calling and smiled. "Hi."

"Hi, yourself. How's it going?"

She paused, thinking about the Uber driver and Vegas and wanting to see Greg. "He seems appreciative of your talk. Better but maybe a little nervous about the tests."

"I'd be too. Time for an early dinner? Just us. Pizza at my place? Just hang out? Super casual."

She relaxed and chuckled. "Did you buy an oven after we left?"

"Nobody has an oven in an apartment as small as mine. But there's a great take-out place just down the street. Just discovered it. Crazy selections. Meet me there at four?"

"Sure. Text me the address."

"As soon as I hang up. It's called the Pink Flamingo."

"At four. I'll phone if anything goes sideways."

"Perfect. Bye."

In less than a minute, her phone vibrated again. The text had the address on rue Bichat. She knocked on Jack's door. He mumbled something that she did not understand. She knocked again. This time he shouted, "Come on in! I'm decent."

She opened the door slowly and saw him propped up on his bed, writing in his small composition book. "Greg just asked me to an early dinner."

"Good! Go on."

"Want anything for lunch now?"

He shook his head. "I'm fine."

"How about I make you a big ham and cheese sandwich? *Jambon et fromage?* I'll leave it in the fridge?"

"That'd be nice."

"There's a half bottle of Chablis in there. Feel free."

"Have a good time. Thank him, will ya?"

She nodded. "I'll leave the kitchen light on in case it gets late. You sure you're gonna be okay?"

"Yup. No toast. Promise. Have fun."

After she made his sandwich and found some crackers he might like as a later snack, she showered, toweled dry, and stared into her cosmetic bag. She'd been ignoring it for days now. Why hadn't she taken that little bottle, the size of her ChapStick, out of her bag? He had surprised her with it. Locally made, lighter than cologne, almost lighter than an eau de toilette. The hand-painted bottle was wrapped with tendrils of green. The jasmine base had a hint of rose and the possibility of sandalwood. It was a light summer scent, easily overlooked from afar. She picked up the bottle and hesitated. Would it be too noticeable on her neck if he hugged her again, would he read too much longing into it if he even noticed it? She decided on a discrete dab between her breasts, just for herself. After dressing in her comfortable jeans, a beige cotton turtleneck and her blue-and-white plaid flannel shirt, she tried to read again.

Chapter № 10

October 4, 2017
Wednesday

The overcast had not cleared by the time she arrived at the Pink Flamingo on rue Bichat. He was waiting on the street under a black awning with pink lettering on it. The wind ruffled his hair. He had traded his blue shirt and black slacks for slim-cut black French jeans. The top of a rugby shirt with wide red and white stripes peeked out of his black leather jacket. The few outdoor tables were occupied, as were the black-and-white tables set along a black banquette. She smiled and kissed his smooth cheek. His lime aftershave was crisp. "Why doctor, you look so Euro. Collar up. French jeans?"

He put his arm around her and walked past the shockingly pink façade. Once inside the warm restaurant, he unzipped his jacket and helped her remove her trench coat, which he held. "Like the jeans? Somebody copped my Levis at the gym about a month ago. Had to run home in workout shorts and a jacket." She laughed. He looked at her turtleneck, flannel shirt, Wranglers and Nikes. He smiled. "Come on, American girl. I'm gonna introduce you to serious French pizza." They joined a line to order.

He pointed to the chalkboard behind the counter. "Crust is like... brittle thin with toppings like nothing you can imagine. Named their pies for famous people. The *Ho Chi Minh* has a green curry sauce. It's wild. *La Poulidor* is duck, apple, and chèvre. The *Basquiat* is Gorgonzola, figs, and cured ham. The *Almodovar* is basically paella on a pizza."

"Clever."

"Just discovered it. Each place is unique. Very hip and usually too crowded for me. One of their places has chairs from an old beauty salon with those things on top." He held his arms in an arch above his head. His hair fell forward in a dark comma touching his eyebrow. She swept it back in place.

"You look like a ballet dancer."

"Thanks. I try. What are those things called?"

"Dryer chairs?"

"I guess. These big clunky chairs with these huge helmets hovering over the pizza-eaters are really funny. I usually get a 'to go.' Want a quick drink here?"

"Sure. Surprise me."

"On the drinks or pizza?"

"Both."

He ordered *La Poulidor* pizza to go. The bar was small and crowded. He slipped in ahead of her, put his back close to a tall man in a dark suit, and pulled her into the space he made in front of him. With her back to the bar, he leaned close to her ear and pointed to the slate with the chalked bar options. "No martini, I'm afraid. Beer or that list. How about a Kir?"

She glanced at the smudged board. "Kir! Kir is fine."

He ordered a Kir Royal for her and a Jack Daniels with water for himself.

"A Royal?"

"Anytime is right for bubbles."

She grinned at him. "A Jack Daniels? In Paris?"

"Why not? It's exotic here."

She laughed.

Greg smiled. "So? Tell me about your book. How's it coming?"

"In fits and starts."

"You're worried about him, aren't you? All this for a client?"

"He's more than that."

"How so?"

"Mom started editing his novels right after my dad died. Working on Jack's first book let her start her own home-based editing business. So, I got to spend a lot more time with her while I was growing up."

The young woman in the tight black T-shirt and pink Dutch boy haircut mixed their drinks behind the bar. First pouring the whiskey into a stubby glass and a shot of Cassis liqueur into a tall Champagne flute. Then she reached down into a small refrigerator under the bar and pulled out an open bottle of Champagne with one hand and a pitcher of chilled water with the other. She added a splash of water to his whiskey before filling the flute to the rim with the Champagne. It overflowed. She balanced both with care as she pivoted and slid them over the bar top, ignoring the drips and pocketing the bills Greg held above the wet bar.

Once the slim woman returned to her duties delivering pizza to tables, Eileen asked, "Real or a wig?"

He shrugged. "I didn't really look."

She leaned over her full flute and took a sip. "Good call, Mister. This is perfect." It was warm and moist in the bar. The aromas of wet wool and blistering crusts fought for dominance. She turned and caught the scent of jasmine. She smiled at her longing.

The waitress bumped Eileen's drink while handing a glass to a customer behind Greg. Eileen grabbed her flute before it fell. He gave her a nod. "Nice catch." He leaned closer. "Shouldn't be long now." He put his arm around her to shield her from a woman wedging toward the bar. He lingered near her neck. "I get it, now. It's personal with Jack."

She smiled at him. "Yeah. It is odd to meet someone who has made a difference in your life, when he has no idea how important he has been."

Greg watched her as she frowned and looked away. He pulled her closer. "He's got a chance at getting better. Hold on for a while longer. Okay?"

She turned and buried her face into his shoulder. After a deep breath she took a sip. "The waiting is hard. Can you tell me what are you looking for in the blood test?"

"How about I give you a general overview and we don't talk about Jack in particular."

"I want to know about Jack."

"Wish I could, but he hasn't given me a written release."

"Did you ask him for one?"

Greg shrugged. "Okay, I'll keep it general until I do. A couple problems can be corrected by medication or supplements. Low thyroid or certain vitamin deficiencies will show up right away." He took a drink and paused to find the phrase.

Just then, the short man at the window to the kitchen called his name. Greg waved to him and the pizza was placed beside them on the bar.

They finished their drinks quickly. As they hurried to his apartment, he continued his overview. "Some other findings could be more difficult to reverse but could allow for improvement, such as advanced syphilis or heavy metal poisoning, both of which seem unlikely, but these are also results we can see pretty quickly. Other indicators such as bacterial infection require growing samples in media. Just growing the culture takes time, longer for some than others. Depending on what shows up, we might go on to added testing. Again, there are ways to manage these findings as well. At the far end, there is genetic testing and..."

"What?"

"I want to see the initial results tomorrow before I..." He pointed at a series of benches as they passed the Canal St. Martin. "End of summer, there was a warm spell. People would order at the Flamingo and get a pink helium balloon to carry down here. Then the delivery staff would find them and reclaim the balloon. Every now and then a kid refused to surrender the balloon. That's how I discovered it." He chuckled.

A gentle drizzle started. He looked at her and shrugged. "We can make a run for my place or grab a cab..."

"Run for it."

Once inside his apartment, the richness of the duck pizza overcame the residual curry smell. He dropped the pizza box on the center of the small bar that doubled as a dining table, took her coat, shook off his jacket, and ran his hand through his wet hair. They were breathless and smiling.

She kissed him quickly. The oaken warmth of whiskey on his breath welcomed her. "God, I'm glad to see you again, Greg."

He pulled back and joked, "Good to be seen." He pointed down the hall. "Clean towels in the bathroom."

As she went toward the bedroom, he called after her, "Wine?"

She returned wiping her hands then blotting her hair, making her short curls even tighter. "Yes. I'd like that."

He pointed to the counter. "An Italian red?"

"Sounds perfect for pizza."

Greg pulled two wineglasses from the open cupboard, turned, and put them on the bar. "Want me to warm the pie in the micro?"

She shook her head. "I'm sure it's fine."

She watched him deftly open the bottle and nodded as he poured her glass. After sniffing the wine, she took a sip. "Barolo?"

He nodded and opened the pizza box. "Plates?"

She chuckled. "Fingers are fine." He handed her a couple of paper towels from the rack on the wall, washed his hands, and sat beside her at the small bar. She took a slice, nipped off the point, and rolled her eyes. "This is obscene!"

"Thought you'd like it."

"You're right. You were right about Jack, too. I think he's feeling better already. Seriously."

He pushed a wayward chunk of duck toward the center of his slice and smiled. "He probably is. Just the worry of thinking you are... I work with it every day, and still I can't imagine that fear. 'The mind is like the sky...' She said it better than I could." He took a big bite.

"Who? One of your colleagues?"

He muttered, "Emily Dickinson." He stopped, chewed, and swallowed. "She's so tight with her words." He poked the air with his pizza for emphasis. "Every time I read her, there's a new layer. Thought you would have known that line."

She took another sip. "Didn't."

"I'm glad he's relaxing."

"Seriously, he's better already. I don't think you believe me."

"Sure I do." He took a sip and smiled.

Looking at her, he waited. Finally, he broke the silence. "What?"

"Is this our *Hills Like White Elephants* moment?"

He frowned as he held the brittle end of the pizza crust and snapped off a bite with his fingers. "Is that the Hemingway short story where this couple talks about everything but the elephant in the room?"

"Yup."

"What's our 'elephant'? Biarritz?"

She nodded. "I've been thinking about it—a lot."

"Me too. I didn't think you'd go with me. You wouldn't even have dinner with me while we were working together."

"You were a client then. But I'm glad you asked me once we'd finished."

"Really? I couldn't read you. I didn't want it to end like that. I didn't want it to end at all."

She looked away from him for a moment then searched his face. "But you seemed so...casual. Like it was your vacation, and I was a tag-along. You'd go surfing and I just felt...extra. I never knew where you were."

He pointed at their phones on the bar. "Even with that app that I put on our phones? I wanted you to know when I was in town in case you wanted me to pick up something, or when I was surfing, and the phone was in the car at the beach."

"I never knew *when* you were coming back. I just wanted to get to know you better. It was so much so fast." She shrugged and looked away.

He took her hand. "Some days I stayed out longer than I wanted to because I thought you were working on your book. I thought you wanted to focus on it. I felt like I was intruding."

She looked at the ceiling in frustration. "I was waiting for you to get back to the room so we could do things. Explore the town, go for lunch, not just have you arrive pooped out at four. I was spending the whole day waiting for you and then..."

He looked at her and sighed. "I'd just want to stay in, make a cheese plate, and have some wine with you. But our afternoons! How'd we... How'd *I* get it so wrong?"

"Why didn't we talk about it *then*? Were we too...accommodating, guessing what the other person wanted?"

He moved a random curl to behind her ear and kissed her. "Even so, our time together was spectacular." He chuckled. "Say it. We were great in bed." She recalled the jasmine scented breeze from the garden cooling them as they lay in a sweaty tangle. He watched her blush but continued. "I'm really glad you called. But I admit I was surprised."

"Really?"

"It's been three, almost four months since your e-mail..."

She dropped her crust and stared at him. "What e-mail? I never sent you any e-mail! I thought that you were going to contact me. That was the last thing you said. When you didn't, I figured you had moved on. I was too embarrassed to e-mail or call you, after all I said."

He stood, almost knocking the bar stool over. "Come on!" He rushed into the small office, sat, and turned on his laptop. While it loaded, she stood behind him, her hands on his shoulders. She leaned down to look at the screen. Once his e-mail had loaded, he went to a folder he called "Eileen" and opened the one e-mail in it that held a short chain of correspondence.

He left the cursor on the brief reply to a longer e-mail. "Look! I e-mailed you about ten minutes after your plane took off. This is your reply." He stood up and motioned for her to sit.

"You're kidding. I never..." She read the short message out loud, haltingly. "I really don't know who you are. Please don't write to me again." She squinted at the address on the e-mail. "It's not me. I didn't send it."

He grinned. "It wasn't? That's the address I had."

She pointed at the screen. "The first part of that address was right, but you sent it to a gmail.com account. I don't use gmail."

"So you never read it?" He reached past her and scrolled down so she could read his long message.

"Can I?" He nodded. She read the message twice. "Wow. You really said that? You said that you loved me?"

"Love you. Present tense." He shrugged. "Still do." She stood, pulled him to her, and kissed him. His kiss was slow and tender. She pressed into him and felt him inhale sharply. He held her closer and kissed her neck. "Jasmine? Is that?"

"That you bought…" He kissed her again. This time there was an urgency to his embrace.

She pulled back slightly and laughed. "Want any more pizza now?"

"Seriously?"

She grinned. "Then Maslow's wrong."

For a moment he frowned then laughed. "Hierarchy of needs, right? Food, shelter, sex. So sex is more important than food?"

"Sometimes." They crossed the hall to the bedroom. He kissed her and started to unbutton her shirt.

"I didn't think we'd be—"

He smiled as he moved to the bedside table, opened the drawer, pulled out a foil wrapped three-pack, and tossed it on the bed. He chuckled. "Leftovers from Biarritz."

She ran her eyes over him as he approached her. "Jeans a little tight?"

"Hmmm. Weren't when I bought them. Musta shrunk."

She undid his belt and slid the zipper. "Maybe I can help with that."

"Maybe you can." He laid her shirt on the chair near the door. She stripped off her turtleneck and turned for him to undo her bra. He did and cupped his hands over her breasts and kissed her neck. She turned and took the neck of his rugby shirt. She felt his heat as he slid out of it and grinned at her. She remembered everything about him: his broad shoulders, narrow waist, and fine chest hair. They both slid out of their jeans and underwear with their eyes locked on each other.

She pulled back the duvet and slid into bed. He sat on the edge, of the bed and ripped the foil open while she kissed his neck and let the tips of her nails lightly trace his spine. When he rolled backward into bed, she straddled his waist and looked at him. "Can we start over?"

He gently flipped her onto her back and laughed. "No way. There's too much I want to remember." He let his full weight fall on her for a moment, to catch her scent. Then he arched his back to look at her and kissed her neck. Then her shoulder, collarbone, and each breast. She moaned before he slid lower. His dark hair brushed her belly. She shivered. He looked up. "Cold?"

"Hardly."

His hands cradled her buttocks. She moaned again.

He looked at her, eager as a puppy to please her. "Take your time."

"Is it baseball scores you guys are supposed to think about?"

His chuckle was muffled. He ignored her question to proceed with more important priorities.

Soon he turned. His hands found her breasts, the small of her back, and then he was atop her, watching her. He moved easily and slowly, intending to prolong their reunion. She pulled him down to her, kissed him, and planted her heels into his buttocks. She clearly had other plans. He kissed her neck. "Baseball scores, my ass," he muttered just before he plunged deeply, and she let out a cry of delight.

She pushed his shoulder so he moved down and rolled across the bed onto his back. When she straddled him, he locked his arms behind his head and watched her lower herself slowly, teasing him, tempting him, her eyes searching his. She held his face in her hands as she began to move. His hands slid over her breasts and hips, lighting his desire.

Their breath soon came hard and fast and joined as time slid sideways. Spent, they fell back, panting, their legs tangled. Once his breath came normally, he kissed her forehead and rolled to the side. Cupping her in his arm, he said, "I've missed you. And not just this, which is pretty spectacular, but who you are. How you make me feel. I really missed you."

She sighed. "I can't believe we almost missed each other. If it weren't for Jack needing an editor."

"You can edit me anytime, my love!"

She chuckled. "Wouldn't change a thing. Seriously! There are no words for what *that* was. No words at all."

He propped up on one elbow and looked at her. "Seriously? Have you translated any sex scenes?" He gave her a sly smile.

"Sure!"

"So? Tell all!"

"Nothing to tell, either they are biology lessons with weird names for body parts and no emotion or so much emotion that there is no hint of real physical coupling."

"Weird names?"

"Do you have any idea how many names are there for a dick?" She laughed. "I translated a ship's log once from English to French for a maritime museum in France. He was an English captain of a French merchant ship who had a wench in every port and recorded his conquests ashore with even more detail than the weather, or the cargo manifests. He referred to his uh *member* as a 'yard.' My first impression was he was referring to a unit of measure." She giggled. "Some masculine illusion of grandeur. Then I decided he was referring to the cross bar on a mast that holds the sail up."

He chuckled. "At least he didn't call it his 'mast'!"

She curled against his chest and ran her finger down his treasure line. "It was so randy that they decided not to put it on display." She glanced at their pile of clothing on the floor. "So, about those jeans."

"I'm having them framed. Thirsty? There's still some wine."

"Water first?"

"Be right back." In a moment he returned with the pizza box and two mugs of water.

They sat up, propped against pillows with the box between them. She opened the lid, searching for a small piece. "Greg?" You're right. This is the best takeout I've ever had."

He choked on the bite he had just taken and laughed. She snuggled into him.

He grinned and kissed her shoulder. "I thought we had something special. I didn't get why you left."

"My life is in the States and yours is here."

"People move."

"We're not *people*. We're us. You're locked into that project. And I'm taking care of my mother. She's going blind, slowly, but all the same."

"You never told me. Macular degeneration?"

"Yes."

"Wet or dry?"

"Dry. We know there is no cure, but she's doing all the right stuff to slow the progression."

"Both eyes?" He cringed.

She shrugged. "Not yet. Just one and they caught it early."

He pulled back to look at her and frowned. "Can she manage alone?"

"For most things. But I hired an attendant since I figured I could be here for a month. When I did your translation and then went to Biarritz, my aunt was visiting her."

"And when you are home and need to go into New York for a day for some meeting? What then?"

"She can see well enough to manage most things and has a button she can push if she has an emergency. And we have nice neighbors."

He took a deep breath. "Okay. What else didn't we talk about?"

She hesitated. "I don't know if your family..."

He laughed. "The Patel thing scaring you off? Think my parents are old school from India? Mom in a sari?"

"I don't know what to think since you never talked about them. How would I have a clue if they would like or...accept me?"

"Accept you?"

"I'm not Indian."

"Really? I didn't notice." He squinted and adopted a comic barroom swagger. "Anyway, what'd ya have against Indians?"

"Nothing. Obviously. But I..."

He laughed. "You look at this bronzed body and think...*hmmm is he dark because he is Indian or because he keeps his beautiful surfer tan all year?*"

"Now you're making fun of me."

"We don't need any secrets between us. You know where my tan lines are."

She blushed again. "Greg..."

"No. Let me finish. My dad's dad was from India. Part of the brain-drain that fueled the start of Silicon Valley decades ago. He got his citizenship and sent home for my grandmother. My dad was born in San Diego and mom is from Nicaragua. Came to the States as a kid. Naturalized. And she hates curry. See? No worries."

"Maybe I was just setting up barriers because I was afraid."

He smirked at her. "Of what? That they wouldn't love your copper hair and freckles or how you light up a room?"

"It was moving so fast. Or maybe I was caring too much." She glanced past him for a moment then looked directly at him. "Maybe I was afraid of losing you."

"To what? Oh, shit." He smacked his hand against his forehead. "When we first met, working on the paper, and I asked about your family...you told me that your dad had drowned in a fishing accident. When I was late, did you think? Shit! That's when you went off on me. You weren't pissed, you were scared."

"He didn't die fishing. I found his tackle box in the garage while the police were telling mom that they found him."

"He drowned, right?"

"He killed himself. Just swam out to sea. I was six and could read quite well by then. I found a letter from a hospital in the trash and looked up the word 'leukemia' by myself. I pretty much had it figured out before my mother told me what had really happened when I was about fifteen or sixteen."

"Oh, man! You just lived with that as a kid? No wonder you were scared when I was late. I'm so sorry."

"Maybe I hadn't figured out why I went off on you then. But I've thought a lot about how I overreacted—and how much you mean to me."

He smiled. "Seriously?"

"But you made it pretty clear that your research is a ten-year study. And I don't want to live here that long. I can't. I have a life and family and a business in America..."

"The *study's* for ten. I'm not a prisoner here. You translate. You could do that anywhere. My family is in San Diego. Your mom's on Long Island. We could move to Kansas and visit both frequently."

She shivered. He moved the empty pizza box to the nightstand and pulled the tangle of covers up to her shoulders. "I know. Jack would probably say that it's colder than a well digger's ass in here."

She laughed. "He just might."

"Want a shower to warm up?"

She slid under the covers. "Go ahead. I want to float for a little longer."

He slipped out of bed and started the shower. Once he had lathered, she knocked on the wall beside the flimsy shower curtain. "Room for another?"

He chuckled and rinsed off quickly. "Barely room for me." He pulled her in and they embraced.

She turned around and laughed. "You're right. This was a dumb idea."

He wedged into the corner, soaped her back, and slid out of the shower. "Good idea. Bad shower. See you when you're finished."

He dried off, pulled on his jeans, and took the pizza box to the bar in the kitchen. When the box nudged her cell phone, a notification flashed. Missed Call – Jack's Cell. He rushed to the bathroom holding a towel in one hand and her phone in the other "It's Jack."

She turned off the water and listened to the message. "Oh, shit."

"What?"

"Listen." She tapped the message again and handed the phone to Greg. While he listened to Jack sobbing that he was lost and didn't know where they were staying, she toweled off. She took back the phone and hit redial. "Somebody's gotta be nearby that can…" When Jack answered, she shouted into the phone. "Hey Jack! It's Eileen. Just got your message. Can you tell me where you are?"

She rolled her eyes and told Greg, "McDonalds!" Hitting the speaker, she dropped the phone on the bed and started dressing. "Okay. There are lots of 'em. Jack? Is there somebody there near you? Somebody that works there you can hand the phone to so I can ask them?"

The speaker clanked and crackled as Jack dropped his phone on the table and called for someone.

Greg pulled on a sweater. "Finish getting dressed. I'll find out where." He quickly determined that Jack was at the McDonald's near the Louvre and offered a reward to some employee named Olivia if she stayed with Jack until they arrived. She disconnected before Eileen could ask to speak to Jack again.

Greg was searching for his shoes.

She looked at him. "You don't have to. He's my problem."

"How're you going to get there? It's not even seven. It's rush hour and the Metro's gonna be packed."

"Uber."

"Same problem." He pointed to his gray New Balance shoes, which were half under the bed. "Toss me my trainers, will you?"

"'Trainers'? You going British now?"

"Let's go."

She jammed her feet into her tied Nikes. "Got a helicopter I don't know about?"

"Vespa."

Her shoulders sank. "You know they scare me. Is there another choice?"

He zipped up his jacket. "Not really. If you don't want to go with me, I'll go and wait with him until you..."

"Come on." She grabbed her coat and hurried after him as he sped down the stairs and went into the courtyard. A collection of mopeds, bicycles, and scooters were locked to a rail against the wall. His Vespa was silver and had two helmets in the small box on the rear. He unlocked the wheel and started it with a quick stomp on the foot lever. By the time she had buckled her helmet, the engine had smoothed to a calm buzz. She got on, tucked her coat under her, and held tight, alternating between glancing over his shoulder and burying her head in the center of his back as he wove between cars and darted around busses.

He stopped on the edge of the bike lane just past the small McDonald's sign, turned, and shouted above the traffic. "Give me a wave when you see him then I'll find some parking!" She hopped off the back of the Vespa and handed him the helmet. "Olivia is the lady I talked to. The manager," he called after her as she ran inside. She saw Jack huddled in a corner booth, waved to Greg, and rushed toward Jack.

A slim woman intercepted her and asked if she was his daughter. After Eileen explained that she was a friend from his work and his family was not here, the young woman relaxed. "I talked to a man, so I expected him. My apologies."

"You're Olivia?"

"Yes."

"Thank you so much for watching after him."

Olivia patted Jack on the shoulder and then she returned to the counter. Once Jack looked up from his empty paper cup and noticed Eileen, he grinned. "Isabel! I'm so glad to see you."

"You too, Jack. What're you doing here?"

"Got hungry, and you weren't back so..."

"I left a sandwich for you in the fridge and wine. You remember me telling you that?"

"I don't know, Isabel."

Ignoring his mistake, she asked, "Did you eat anything here?"

"No. I ordered, but then I couldn't pay. I musta left my wallet back at the hotel. They still gave me a hot chocolate. That girl you talked to, I think she might have paid for it."

"Do you want to get something here?"

"Okay. Cheeseburger and fries?"

"Sure. Want another hot chocolate?"

"Naw. Water's fine."

Eileen went to the counter, scanned the almost-familiar menu board, and ordered, "*S'il vous plaît, deux 'Le Royal Cheese', trois frites, et un McWrap 'Poulet et Crudités' et, trois Evians*." She paid the cashier and took the ticket. She waited at the edge of the counter for the young woman who had helped Jack. Eileen asked if she could pay for his hot chocolate. The woman declined the offer or reward. Eileen thanked her again. The young woman shrugged and said her grandfather was the same and that she was glad he had friends.

Eileen had just returned to Jack's booth when Greg arrived holding both helmets. He waved at them as he crossed the room with a grin. "Jack! How ya doing?"

"Better since Isabel got here. Hungry? You staying for dinner?"

"Sure. If that's okay."

She smiled. "I took a chance and ordered you a burger and fries."

"Thanks, *Eileen*. Give me the ticket." He dropped both helmets on the bench of the booth. "What am I looking for?"

"Chicken veggie pita wrap. Two cheeseburgers, three fries. And three waters."

"You bought bottled?"

"I didn't have time to argue them into giving me tap water, okay?"

He put his hands up in surrender. "Okay."

After Greg left, Jack leaned forward and took her hand. "I called you by the wrong name, didn't I? Sorry."

"It doesn't matter."

"This is where I met her, you know. It was a café then, and not a very good one. But I'm so sorry."

"For what?"

"For worrying that nice girl, and you."

She smiled at him. "You'll feel better after you eat. But thank you. I know you wouldn't want to worry anyone."

Greg returned with the tray and served each meal. She stared at his burger and sniffed the air. "I'd forgotten how good they are."

"Having menu regret? Wanna trade?"

"Seriously?"

"Yeah. I actually love their pita wrap."

"Done."

Jack spread his napkin on the table and dumped his fries on it. Then he took a huge bite of his burger and looked at Greg. He glanced at Eileen's hair and frowned, muttering, "Is it raining again?"

Greg looked at her still-dripping hair, pushed an escaping morsel of chicken back to the center of the wrap, and laughed. "No. We went...to my gym."

"Got a pool there?"

"No. Just showers. But we had a good workout. Didn't we?"

She smiled at him and said, "I certainly did."

Halfway through the meal, Eileen found her hand shaking. Tears were welling in her eyes. Greg noticed before Jack did and rubbed her leg under the table. He whispered, "It's okay, you know. Whatever happens is going to be okay."

Jack looked up from picking at his fries and smiled. Greg asked him about his first book and how he started a writing career so late and had an immediate success. That launched Jack into a well-rehearsed story on how all the twenty years of writing and revising short stories while he taught at a college in Montana gave him the building blocks and guts to try a novel.

He continued his story, saying how he'd worked on a ranch the summer before his senior year in high school. He said he had never worked so hard and been so sore in his life, which motivated him to put himself through college and become a teacher. He confessed that his lanky frame and weathered face made people believe he was more of an outdoorsman than he was.

When he abruptly pivoted his monologue to the topic of writing, he explained that his chapters were short and self-contained mini-narratives like short stories and that he based his characters on people he knew—but he described them in a way so that no one would guess their identities. For example, his super-masculine spymaster was based on his mother, for her rigor and clarity of moral purpose, not her physicality; she was a petite homemaker.

As he went on, with minimal prompting from Greg, she watched how he settled into an easy conversation. She also listened to Greg in a new way. Not to his words as much as to his tone and caring. He was genuinely interested in this man and his work. The busy restaurant filled and then emptied of the evening crowd.

Jack interrupted his story with a quick glance out the window at the dark street. "What time is it?"

Greg tapped his phone and said, "Almost eight."

"Time to go. Gotta get my beauty rest for tomorrow." He paused and looked at Eileen. "That's the test day, isn't it?"

She nodded. "Sure is. Ready for me to call you a car?"

Jack asked, "How far is it?"

She said, "Just a few blocks to cross at the Pont Neuf, but then it's a half mile to the penthouse."

"Walk'll do me good, if that's okay."

She slid out of the booth. "Greg? Join us?"

He hugged her quickly. "You go on. I'll meet you at the Institute tomorrow and grease the wheels."

She reached for the tray holding their empty food wrappers and cartons. He took it from her. "I got it. Have a good night." He hooked the straps of the helmets in the crook of his arm and balanced the tray.

On their way out, Jack said he needed to use the restroom. As Eileen waited by the door for him, she saw Greg separate the recyclables from the trash, stack the tray with the others, and straighten them. She smiled as she watched him move with confidence and grace. He went to the counter and talked to Olivia. Jack returned and as they walked past the window, she glanced in to see Greg pull a business card from his wallet and give it to her.

When they arrived at the penthouse, Eileen noticed the bottle of Tito's vodka on the counter with a half-eaten sandwich on a plate and an empty water glass in the sink. She glanced at Jack. He went to the counter, slapped both hands on the cool top, stared at the vodka bottle, and avoided Eileen's glance. "I was getting something out of the fridge and saw the vermouth. Made me remember that Marie liked her martinis really cold so I started making one. Maybe to see if I still could. Maybe to just to think about her, I don't know. Then I thought of where we met and ended up at McDonalds."

She stood beside him in silence, waiting for him to say anything else, wondering what she could say to ease his loss when she had just rediscovered her love. When he dropped his head, she put her hand over his and patted it. "Tomorrow's a big day. Why don't you go and get some rest. I'll clean up in here."

Chapter № 11

October 5, 2017
Thursday

The clatter of cans and roar of the garbage truck woke her at six thirty-three. She stretched and smiled thinking of the prior evening. Then she decided that she had better get up and get coffee ready before Jack tried to make it. Tugging on jeans and not changing from her sweatshirt, she padded barefoot to the kitchen, drank a glass of water, and put the filter in the Chemex. As she looked up to turn to reach the container of coffee grounds in the refrigerator, she noticed that the door to the penthouse was slightly ajar. Running the few steps to his bedroom, she knocked and called his name. Nothing.

She knocked again, hoping he was in the bathroom and hadn't heard her. She opened the door slowly. The bed was rumpled but empty. She stepped into the room and called his name again. She glanced at the open door to the bathroom. Empty.

She raced to the kitchen and stared through the rain-splattered window. Nothing. She tried opening the window, but decades of paint had sealed it shut. When she noticed his phone on the kitchen table, she swore under her breath knowing that unless he was returning to McDonald's, she'd never find him if he got lost again.

She dashed to her room and tugged on her Nikes without bothering with socks. Yanking open her window, she leaned out and saw a man almost to the Pont Neuf who was hurrying past the closed book stalls. Black shirt. Khaki pants. No jacket. Not waiting for the elevator, she ran down the stairs as fast as she could without tumbling on the curved staircase.

Once on the street, she sprinted along the riverside promenade, past Notre-Dame toward the Pont Neuf. A quarter mile into her sprint, she lost sight of the man who had turned onto the bridge. The Seine was running high from the rain and growled as it pushed past the stoned banks. Her breath burned as she approached the bulky railing of the Pont Neuf. She took the turn fast and skidded on the wet stone. Then she saw him on the far side of the bridge almost to the statue of Henri IV.

He was leaning on the gritty stone railing of the span. Hands well apart, balanced but with his body forward, like he was leaning on a lectern in front of students or fans on a book tour. He was watching a couple in the park, beside the statue, embracing. Eileen ran full out, slipping on the wet cobblestones. Two old women walked past him toward the market. The tips of his shoes scuffed against the stones as he leaned further over the barrier.

He turned and looked down at the river. She saw that his face was pinched as he watched the water rush under him. She crashed into the barrier beside him, skinning both palms. She grabbed his shoulder and spun him to face her. He stumbled back toward the street. She forced a smile as she tried to catch her breath. "Jack." It was barely a whisper. She swallowed and tried again. He moved away from the rail and looked at her. She took his elbow. "Jack?"

He relaxed and patted her hand. "I'm no Rilke. Just watching the barges."

She glanced around for a safer place than standing at the edge of the railing.

He frowned as he looked at her. "Out for a jog? At this hour?"

The backs of her legs were shaking and on fire. She tugged his elbow and pointed to the nearby bench. "I need to sit. Sit with me?"

"Sure."

Once seated, she pressed her hands against her knees and tried to calm herself. "You scared me, leaving like that."

"I'm sorry. I wanted to get some air. I heard the rain stop about midnight. When I looked out the river had a skim of fog on it, moved like silk above the leaden flow."

She gasped for breath and forced a smile. "That's beautiful."

"Not quite original."

Her hands were shaking. She pressed them harder against her knees. She was still breathing hard. "Your descriptive narrative...that was always your strength. That and plot."

"Thanks."

"That's why mom loved editing you. She said she got to see your brilliance before anyone else." She let her head drop forward. "I think she would have edited you for free."

"Don't tell Max."

She looked at him. "When are we going to tell Max about you?"

He stood and held his hand for her. "Maybe when there's something to say. You are shivering."

She stood. "Ready for a coffee? I was about to make some when I saw the door was open."

"And you came to get me?"

She stalled before answering honestly. "Yes. I was concerned for you. I didn't want you to get lost again or scared."

He patted her hand. They walked back together, in silence. They passed an old man wearing a frayed black overcoat who was opening his bookstall on the river's edge. Once at the street door, Jack tapped the number pad and opened the door when it buzzed. "Think I didn't remember the code?"

"I don't know what to think, Jack."

"I don't either, anymore. I look in the mirror and see a guy so old he might have gone to high school with Moses. But that's not how I feel."

"How do you feel?" She asked with a smile intended to elicit a positive answer.

"Like a pencil without a point." He pressed the button for the elevator and leaned against the wall beside it, waiting for her to enter first. He was shivering. Once in the penthouse, she turned on the kettle of water. As she made coffee, he watched her in silence. She poured their cups and sat across from him. He asked, "Why'd you stay? You got other jobs to do. Doc told me you are a big-deal translator and he was lucky to get you. Me too. But I don't get it. Why'd you stay?"

"Mom couldn't edit your draft fast enough to meet the deadline." Eileen paused and then decided to tell Jack the whole truth. "She'll be pissed that I told you why she couldn't come, but her vision is impaired. She can't work away from home, away from her special computer. I know how important you are to her, so I volunteered. Well, more like agreed. I have bills to pay like everyone else, and we need to build her savings now for when she can't work."

"No. That's why you came. Why didn't you cut and run when you saw there was nothing to work on—that I'm a mess?"

"You are not authorized to make that diagnosis. Greg said so. Let's wait and see what today brings. Okay?"

"Okay. So? What's the rest of it?"

"Maybe I owed you something. Max hired mom to edit your stuff when I was about six. It let her work from home when no one did that. It let her be there for me after school, on sick days, whenever. It's a luxury most kids don't get. In some ways you are a real part of my growing up. A part of our family. Like an uncle who lived far away."

Silence was comfortable between them for a few minutes. She refilled their cups and sat again. "What did you mean out there when you said you are 'no Rilke'? I bet you have outsold him by twice."

"No comparison. There are a lot more readers now."

"You admire him?"

"Interesting writer. Sort of a pig when it came to women, walked out on his wife and kid, took up with any skirt with enough money to be a patron."

"But *Letters to a Young Poet*..."

He scoffed. "Romantic twaddle. He was writing to a fan. A kid. And he was making up the shit as he went along. Slopping out easy platitudes. Full of youthful hubris."

"I liked it."

"When did you read it?"

"In high school."

He opened his arms as if to signal victory. "See? Read it lately?"

"No. Should I?"

"Probably. To see what BS it is. I reread the classics every few years and find something new every time. Some get better. Some don't. Maybe that's a benefit of my mind going south. I can read the same book over and over. Every day's a new day." He laughed.

"What did you really mean? About Rilke."

He fiddled with his cup. "You know how he died?"

"No."

"Some kind of massive infection like septicemia or toxic shock from a rose thorn. Dumbass never wanted his doc to tell him what he had. *A rose thorn!* Super sick, bloody blisters. Forbid him to say what he had when he knew he was dying. That's some kind of stubborn. Felt a lot like me. But that isn't gonna cut it. I gotta face up to whatever is happening and get my shit together. I got stuff to do."

"Like what?"

He stalled. "Isn't that test today? That one, that CMT thing..."

"Sure, it's at eleven."

He pulled out the hem of his black T-shirt. "This okay?"

"Fine. But the pants..."

Jack looked at his stained pants and shrugged. "Yeah, I see."

She filled his coffee cup. "Hungry? You can eat if you want. No restrictions for the test."

"I'm good. Thanks. Maybe I'll buy you lunch afterward."

"I'd like that. Can you shower before we go?"

"Sure. Okay."

After he left the kitchen, she sighed and sank back into the chair. She was too exhausted to cry and too shaky to want any more coffee. When she heard his shower stop, she went to her suite. Once showered and dressed in her black slacks and garnet cashmere turtleneck, she called the Uber. Jack emerged in jeans, the same black T-shirt, and his tweed jacket a moment later.

When the Uber driver pulled to the curb at the Institute, Greg was pacing on the sidewalk in front of the double doors. "Hey! There's an opening right now. I'll take you in the back way." At his grin, she relaxed. Using his key card, he opened a smaller side door and led them past the reception area into a back hallway that connected to the medical wing. When they passed a small waiting room, Greg pointed at it and kept hurrying.

She chose a row of chairs by the window for the light, put her coat and messenger bag in one and sat beside it. She pulled a handful of papers from her messenger bag and found a pen in the side pocket.

She looked up when an older couple entered and sat silently by the door. During the next half hour, she read and reread Jack's three short stories. As she finished her notes on the first one, the older man asked the woman if she wanted to go to the cafeteria. Without answering, she stood. He rose quickly and took her arm. Eileen watched them fall into the same slow stride and wondered how long they had been together, if they still loved each other, and how long love could last.

When she had finished making all the notes she could on his stories, she shoved the pages back into her messenger bag. *Maybe I've been planted here to do something other than edit,* she thought. Maybe it was a day to relax or distract herself with her own book, since there was no other option than to wait and see what Greg would discover. Maybe it was a time to focus on her draft and not worry about what she could not change.

She drifted into reading her draft in Pages on her iPad and was startled when Greg returned, laughing. "What's funny?"

Greg grinned. "I warned Jack that the MRI was going to sound like he's in a trashcan with someone beating on the outside with a stick. He said since he was deaf in one ear, it would only be half as loud. Humor is a good sign, no matter how bad the joke."

She chuckled. "He's managing all this better than I could."

Greg looked around the empty waiting room before he sat across from her. He leaned forward with his elbows on his knees. "Jack's given me permission to discuss his situation with you, without him being present."

"Situation?"

"Yes. He does have some impairment, as you would expect from the aging process alone. A residue of depression. He took the family breakup hard. Now about some of the conversational bumps. He misses cues. He refused to replace his hearing aid that he lost some time back. Says it buzzes. I don't think the balance issue is an inner-ear problem. But I'm not going to make any more observations until I get the scan and lab results." He paused, and then leaned back. "My instinct is that we have a thyroid or other metabolic problem that's contributing to, if not causing, some imbalance that is screwing up some of the wiring."

"Thyroid?"

"I looked at his driver's license. He weighed almost forty pounds more when he got it just over a year ago. He wasn't aware of losing weight, just that he had to punch another hole in his belt. Thinning hair, dry skin, weight loss. Yes, all that can be a part of aging as our senses of taste and smell diminish so food is not as inviting, particularly if we cook for ourselves. And his sense of smell is compromised—you saw this when we did that experiment at my apartment the other day. My money is on a low thyroid or vitamin deficiency from a limited diet, at the minimum. He lives alone in a remote area. Stimulation is minimal and no one checks on him. He's been drifting."

She nodded. "When do the blood tests come back?"

"I put a rush on it, but they weren't in the morning batch. Hoping for tomorrow first thing, if not this afternoon. Okay?"

"Sure. What do we do in the meantime?"

"I'd recommend that you go have a bland, balanced lunch with him, avoid the second glass of wine with meals, and relax today. He's tight as a violin string right now, understandably. Maybe play tourist. I should hear tomorrow, then we can decide where we are going."

"Greg, I don't know how to thank..."

He winked at her. "Come by tonight? I've got some leftover pizza..." She blushed and smiled at him. He stood. "About another half an hour."

She got to her feet and quickly kissed him.

"I'll call you as soon as I know anything."

Jack's hair was mussed when he walked into the waiting room almost an hour later. She stood and smoothed it. "How are you?"

"It was as loud as he said. Let's get some fresh air."

When they were on the street, she moved to his left side so he could hear when she spoke. "Feeling okay about the tests?"

He nodded. "Doc says I might need a tune-up. I like the guy. Tells it straight. What time is it?"

"It's about one. Are you hungry?"

He shook his head. "Not yet. Greg said I should relax. How the hell does he think..."

"He told me to play tourist with you. How about we take a walk through the sculpture garden at the Rodin Museum?"

He nodded and then asked, "Did you know that Rilke lived there at the turn of the century? It was a falling-down fleabag where artists lived on the cheap."

"Really?"

He continued, talking fast to fill the silence and still his worry. "He was Rodin's secretary for a while. That's how he talked Rodin into opening a studio there, so Rodin had a place to hang with his mistress, an American gold-digger whose husband encouraged the affair. I think they were trying to get the old man to turn over his estate to them. But who knows. The heart is a fickle thing."

"So I've heard."

He chuckled. "Fooled them all. Just before he died, Rodin married his longtime mistress, blew off the American, and gave every one of his works to France for this museum. Sort of stiffed his son in the deal, though. All the stuff for a good movie."

She chuckled. "Or a novella? Ever considered writing historical fiction?"

"Maybe. It gets better. Throw in his stormy relation with his beautiful and talented student, Claudia, no Camille Claudel. Just eighteen when they met. He was almost forty. He had his long-time mistress at home in the countryside at Meudon when he started up with her in town. Camille's sculpting matched his in raw power and talent, but her subjects were more daring. Like the one of the older man deserting his young mistress who grovels at his feet. She scandalized her family so they had her locked up in a nuthouse until she died." He shrugged. "Probably take too much research to get it right." She glanced at him, wondering how much time he had.

The remaining walk to the museum was companionable and quiet. Once there, they walked together in a mutual silence in the sculpture garden. The overnight rain had stripped the last of the roses to woody stalks. The angular, bare-limbed trees had pools of amber leaves at their trunks. Only the evergreens seemed intact after the rain. The smell of cedar spiced the chilled air. The sandy pathway crunched underfoot. He pointed across the garden. "Let's go get a closer look at *Balzac*. I always loved its massive bulk. So modern and fresh after the fussy Romantics."

"I think I like *The Burghers of Calais* better."

He continued as if he had not heard her. "The critics hated his *Balzac* almost as much as they hated *The Thinker*. Some of the reviews made scatological comments in the press on both."

"What?"

He nodded. "Suggested *The Thinker* was on a chamber pot, as it were. And that *Balzac* was…ummm…pleasuring himself."

She laughed. "Are you serious?"

He smirked. "Critics! Seems like the cheap shot is the one heard around the world. A snappy, cutting remark. A sound bite, I guess you'd call it today. Ever have the critics rip you a new one?"

"No. I've been very lucky. Each of my translations has been well received."

"Well, it's no damn fun." He stared at *The Thinker* for a moment. "That's kinda like what you do. Create a new form out of something else."

She laughed, louder than she intended. "That? I could no more sculpt anything than flap my arms and fly. I had to take an art appreciation class in college and ended up with a prof who believed in a hands-on experience for every medium. When we got to sculpture, he brought in these mounds of clay the size of bowling balls and made us try to prod it into something recognizable. I think my efforts were the most pathetic of any in the class. Fortunately, he let us pound the clay back to blobs at the end of the class for other students to use. Maybe that is why I am always so impressed with how true artists can manage to find expression."

He nodded. "Ever been to his home in Meudon? He made a garden so he could paint the water lilies. Want to go today? It's just a quick train ride."

She hated to dim his enthusiasm. "It might not be as beautiful in October as his paintings of it. Besides, I think we need to stay in Paris in case Greg calls."

He shrugged. "Of course."

"Can I ask something?"

"Anything. Fire away."

"Why didn't you go to a doctor back home?"

He paused and scuffed the pathway. "I figured there was no point and that if I did, the newspapers would somehow find out and I'd be just one more level of disappointment to my daughter." He turned and motioned toward the museum's café. "Ready for a break?"

"Sure. I'm getting hungry."

As they stood in line to buy a pastry and coffee, her cell phone vibrated. She pulled it from her pocket. "It's Greg." She hurried outside. Jack followed her to the courtyard. She answered. "Yes?"

"Is Jack with you?"

"Yes. We're at the Rodin, about to get something for lunch."

"Has he eaten today?"

"I don't think so, let me ask."

He shook his head to her question. "Just coffee with you this morning."

"Just coffee, two cups, black, this morning."

"Does he seem well oriented now?"

"Yes."

"Can you put him on?"

She held the phone for him. "He wants to talk to you, Jack."

"Hello?"

"Jack. I wanted to ask if you have had any aspirin or other blood thinner in the past week. I know you said you aren't taking any medications, but some people don't think of aspirin, Advil, Motrin, ibuprofen, and other over-the-counter painkillers as medication."

"Nope. No pills at all for about six or eight months. Stopped 'em when my wrist stopped hurting."

"Any vitamin E?"

"No."

"Can you come back in about an hour?"

He looked at her phone for the time. "At three. Sure. What's up?"

"Another test. Don't eat anything between now and then."

"Okay."

"Can you put Eileen back on?"

"Sure." He handed her the phone.

"Where are we meeting at three?"

"The Institute."

"Then we've got time to eat."

Greg raised his voice. "I told him not to eat anything, no more coffee. One glass of water if he's really thirsty. Absolutely nothing else."

"Okay. Why?"

"Details when you get here. But at least I have some good news for him. Tell him that. Let's get as much pressure off the guy as we can."

"That would be great. See you then."

When they arrived at the Institute for the second time that day, Greg met them in the lobby and took them to his office. He sat on the edge of his desk facing their two chairs. "Jack, I appreciate your coming in so fast. Let me go over some things, then explain about the test I lined up for this afternoon, if you agree to it."

His stomach rumbled. He pushed on it and shrugged. "Okay."

"Let's go back a ways. Eileen, you said that when you first saw him at the airport, you thought he might have been drinking. Why?"

She answered quickly. "His walk was kind of unsteady. He was almost swaying and shuffling."

"Jack? What about it?"

"I think she's right. I feel like I'm walking in tar half the time, can't seem to pull my feet up. And I feel wobbly, so I take shorter steps."

"Have you fallen?"

"Yeah. A couple times. But I never got hurt."

"Depending on how you land, sudden stops can produce a mild concussion even though you don't feel it or crash your head into something. It's just not good to jiggle your brain. Jack, the reason I asked you not to eat anything is to make you more comfortable for a test I want to run. But first, I want to give you some good news. The labs are back and show that your thyroid is extremely low. That can lead to some mental fogginess by itself. At the least, I am going to prescribe a daily pill to get you back into the normal range. A normal annual physical would have found this."

"I guess I screwed up, huh?"

"Let's look forward, okay? I'll get some samples for you today and write you a script that you can fill at any pharmacy here. Second, your MRI didn't show any abnormality that is related to dementia or Alzheimer's. None. No shrinking lobes or any of the classic signs. So we can rule out any overt disease of the brain itself. And your balance is not related to your deafness, which would have been a good bet if there were a tumor there. No noticeable rends or tears in the dura membrane. Frankly, I was almost hoping for an acoustic neuroma, a kind of tumor. Which there isn't."

"No shit?"

"So far so good, but there is more. Your loss of the sense of smell initially bothered me a lot because that's a sign of dementia and also of Parkinson's disease. But I think the answer to that is simple. Like they said in med school, when you hear hoof beats, don't go looking for zebras. You look at the usual suspects first."

"So what happened?"

"I think you may have suffered a mild concussion when you took that hit to your nose just before you lost your sense of smell."

"Concussion? Like those football..."

Greg shook his head. "You didn't even need to lose consciousness. Anyone punch you in the face? Any bar fights?"

"No. Always been good at talking my way out of scrapes."

"Your scan didn't show any damage to your nose: obstructions, tumors, or lesions. But the olfactory nerves are fragile. They run through a bunch of small holes in the ethmoidal cribriform plate, here." He pointed to the bridge of his nose. "If the nerve's axons get severed, they rarely recover. But the damage can be in degrees. A complete loss of smell is called anosmia. A distorted sense of smell, like everything smelling like rubber, is dysosmia."

"So, is it going to fix itself? It was just a bump!"

"Even a minor head or facial trauma, damage that ranks low on the Glasgow Coma Scale, where consciousness was not lost, can shear the *filia olfactoria* nerves."

"So, you're telling me it's not going to get better? That didn't even give me a shiner."

"What most people don't understand is that even a mild head trauma can have profound implications. Did you have nausea, sensitivity to light and sound, confusion? Feeling foggy right after the window hit your face?"

"Maybe. Right after."

"A week later?"

"Foggy? Not really, but...different."

"Now?"

Jack waited and looked at his hands before answering. "Now? I feel better than I have in months. I think. I still can't smell stuff right, but I feel clearer in my thinking, mostly because I'm not as worried. But I'm still not me again. Think those nerves are going to heal?"

Greg spoke slowly and directly. "I don't think so. There is no cure for it other than the body's own recovery, which is rare after about six months. I think losing your sense of smell, a low thyroid, and a low-grade depression is why you stopped eating well and lost so much weight so fast. That nutritional deficiency made everything worse."

"Great." Jack dropped his gaze to the floor.

"We're not through here. I'm going to give you a more sensitive olfactory test to see if you have any restoration so we can fine-tune that testing."

"I think I smelled coffee this morning. Smelled more like burnt wood than coffee, but I did notice something."

Eileen said, "But you couldn't smell burning toast a couple days ago—or your clothes on the flight over."

"I guess. Maybe I was distracted then. But not smelling something isn't my biggest worry. Might even be a blessing, riding the Metro here and in New York."

Greg said, "Don't trivialize a loss of smell. People without it are twice as likely to die within the five years after the loss as those who can smell. They lack the warnings we get from spoiled food, smoke, and gas leaks, so if this loss continues, you need to increase your awareness of food safety and install smoke and gas detectors in your house. We can work on that later."

Jack's stomach grumbled and he grimaced. "So that's the next test? I missed eating a croissant at the museum coffee shop for you to tell me I failed a sniffer test?"

"No. It's more complex than that. The test I want to do might give us some important information. It's called a lumbar puncture, a spinal tap. Ever heard of it?"

"Yeah. Wasn't that a rock band? Or a movie? Just kidding. Sure I heard of it, but why do you want to do that?"

Greg crossed his arms and spoke louder. "Look, you are a very lucky man. I can reduce a lot of your fuzziness by adjusting your thyroid, getting a new hearing aid, and improving your diet. All that is going to help, and maybe some counseling if your depression creeps back. That's a trifecta of good news to improve cognition. But none of these fixes address your gait or memory."

"What do you mean?"

"You walk in a guarded manner, with a wide stance and take small steps. You shuffle. I initially thought it was an inner ear, a balance thing, but that didn't match our clinical testing or other results."

"Something else is wrong? Crap, I'm falling apart."

"A lumbar puncture can tell me a lot. The cerebral spinal fluid—we call it CSF—might show specific chemicals that indicate a bacterial infection or a tumor that might be causing increased cranial pressure. And we can take the pressure of the CSF. The body produces about a pint of it a day in four chambers called ventricles in the center of the brain. This new fluid then goes from the brain into the spinal column. It provides nutrients, removes waste, and acts like a shock absorber to protect both the brain and spine. It's what we call a blood barrier, meaning it's a self-contained system, so if you get a virus in your bloodstream, it won't get into your CSF. But it can be breached and let in bacteria. When that storm window hit your nose, it might have broken that barrier, just for a few minutes to let in bacteria. If so, we can treat it. That's one thing we'll look for."

Jack nodded. "Okay. What else?"

"Ever have a hangover?"

Jack laughed. "Who hasn't?"

"Mostly caused by dehydration and too low of a CSF pressure."

"So where is this going?"

"If the CSF pressure is too high, it can bring on memory loss and confusion, impact gait, and look a lot like dementia. And it's fixable. The tap can measure your pressure."

"How painful is this spinal stick?" He slapped his knee. "Never mind. I don't want to live in a fog, so whatever we can do to fix it, I'm in."

Greg smiled. "I'm going to turn you over to a colleague who can do it better than I can. She'll use a local anesthetic before the puncture. You might feel pressure, but not a needle stick. Then you need to lie on your back an hour for recovery. A headache might follow for a few hours."

"But it might give you more info about ways to reverse this crap?"

"Yes. It might."

"How?"

"There are ways to adjust the pressure. But let's not get ahead of ourselves, okay?"

"Let's do it."

Greg called a number from his iPhone and asked for scheduling. "I've got Mister Forrester here, ready for his tap. Which room..." Greg frowned. "When?" He opened the computer on his desk and tapped keys on the keyboard a few times. "Tomorrow? I see an opening at eleven. Let's book him then. Sure I'll give you a confirm in the morning."

Greg scowled at the computer and tapped in a few notes. Closing the screen, he looked over the desk. "Sorry. Her kid got sick at school and she had to leave work early. She's open at eleven tomorrow. I booked it. Okay? Be here a half hour before for prep."

"Sure." Jack glanced at Eileen. "Tomorrow at eleven?"

She spoke quickly. "We'll be here! I can't believe you can do all this so fast."

"It's not me. I have the good fortune to be in a research facility that offers exceptional treatment if the patient allows their case study to be recorded. This is not at all the long-term testing with sample and control groups. But I wanted a way to treat what could be treated and got that written into my contract here. All this testing would take months in the States, or here, even at a good hospital and clinical setting."

Jack said, "But you've already fixed a lot of the problems."

"Because I knew what I was looking for. Eileen had translated my research and knew symptoms. She presented the problem as one of cognition, and that's my specialty. I work with the brightest researchers in the field. You got lucky." Eileen smiled at him. He continued his focus on Jack. "Most patients are too afraid or unaware to bring their concerns to their doctor. Most doctors won't see clinical indicators in their annual five minutes of medicine. And even when they are told of concerns, most won't catch the reversible causes. That's what we are trying to correct here. Develop research that shows what is reversible and how to diagnose it faster. Historically, medicine has been about the extension of life. I think that cognition is the root of the quality of life, more than the physical attributes. I want to extend the quality of life, of *your* life."

Jack nodded as Greg continued. "We're still learning a lot about dementia. Right now I can quote many different studies with somewhat differing results, but here is an overview. Most think Alzheimer's disease accounts for sixty to eighty percent of dementia, but there are other kinds too. About half of patients with Alzheimer's also have some added factor contributing to their dementia. Lewy Body dementia comes from an abnormal protein impacting the neurons in the brain. Its symptoms are more commonly falling and hallucinations. Pick's disease is a frontal-temporal dementia in which there is obsessive activity, usually eating the same food over and over, a decline in hygiene, and social skills. Creutzfeldt-Jacob disease comes from a deformed protein and is a subset of what you might know as mad cow disease. And tumor, stroke, head injury, vitamin deficiency, thyroid, depression, side effects of medication, alcohol or drug abuse, Lyme disease, and a couple of other things can cause pressure on the brain."

"Jesus! All those can fog you up?"

Greg nodded. "Sure, but that leaves twenty to forty percent of dementia coming from something other than Alzheimer's, and some of these causes are reversible. That's where I want to spend my professional life in research and clinical practice, reversing what I can. I'll leave it to others, smarter than me, to work on prevention and managing Alzheimer's and other forms of dementia. There is good work going on in those areas. Most family doctors wouldn't see the simple constellation of deficits that contributed to your problem because they don't always occur in a quick office visit when the doc comes in and sees his patient sitting down, so there are no gait indicators. Besides, they don't know to look for them. I want to change that. I'm working on a new screening protocol and a set of mini-mental tests for computer users."

"Like the one I did?"

He nodded. "We'll still have the test administered in the doctor's office. But a lot of people can't read well or have vision issues and will need to do the test orally. Even when they make a correct diagnosis, about half of all doctors fail to tell their patients about their concern or diagnosis of dementia. Some seem to think that will depress them and make matters worse for the patient or their family, or that there is nothing to do about it. But that 'ignorance is bliss' mentality is outdated thinking and a disservice to patients and their families. They need facts and time to plan and fix what is fixable."

Jack said, "But you did. You saw it and talked straight with me."

"God, it's so simple. Gait, memory, and urinary incontinence, at least in later stages. That constitutes the triad you are presenting. Or as we joke, we're looking for the three W's; wobbly, weird, and wet. Now you are only showing urgency, not incontinence, but the signs were all there. Parkinson's is similar..."

Jack nodded. "That can scare the hell out of you as well."

"Sure it can. But let's look at what we know now. You had a significant hit to your nose, you separated from your wife, and your daughter shut you out of her life when she was pregnant with your first grandchild. You lost your appetite from some normal depression and your diminished sense of smell, so your nutrition was compromised and you were probably drinking excessively to boot. And then your deafness makes it even harder to navigate the world. Jack, you've had a run of bad luck, but it's over now. Things are going to be better, regardless of how this next test comes out."

"Okay. I'll hold you to that. Will your doctor friend tomorrow speak English or do I need Eileen with me?"

"I've set you up with an English speaker. Doctor Marie Bonnard is superb at the clinical technicalities and will be doing the procedure. Trust me, she has magic hands. Sorry we couldn't do it today as I had hoped. Tomorrow morning is just water, no coffee or breakfast, okay? Eileen can join you in the recovery room after the test if you want."

Dinner that night was light at the kitchen table. Vegetable soup and salad. One glass of wine each, no brandy after dinner although Jack requested one. They both retired to their suites. About midnight she heard him in the kitchen and slipped into her jeans.

"Jack? You okay?"

"Can't sleep."

"Me neither."

"Want a brandy like I said before? It'll help you sleep too."

She shook her head. "You need to be fresh for tomorrow. You can't be dehydrated. How about a cup of herbal tea?"

"What's the point?" He walked back to his room and slammed the door.

Chapter № 12

October 6, 2017
Friday

Eileen dressed before going to the kitchen, where she made a cup of tea for herself and tried to edit her novel. When Jack emerged in his robe, she looked up. "Sorry I can't make coffee this morning."

"Me too."

"Hot water with lemon? Herbal tea? I checked. They'd be okay for you to drink before the test."

"Just some water." He pulled a small prescription bottle from the pocket of his robe and rattled the pills. "Gotta take this or he'll read me the riot act."

He popped the pill and drank some water. He looked out the window at the cathedral for a minute, then sighed. "Guess I better get ready, huh?" Eileen listened for the shower and relaxed when she heard it. When he arrived in the living room, he had dressed in his black suit pants and a clean blue work shirt. She wondered if he had washed the one she had seen earlier or if he had brought two identical shirts.

They spoke little during the ride to the Institute and arrived at ten fifteen. Greg was in the lobby waiting for them. Jack gave Eileen a hug and followed Greg. She went to a crowded waiting room and returned to editing her novel. She had come to a chapter break when a nurse found her and took her to Jack.

The recovery room in the Institute's hospital was cheerier than most. With modern art on the walls, comfortable furnishings, and oak doors, it looked more like a residence hotel than a medical facility. Missing were the echoes from the hallway and smell of strong disinfectant. Jack was flat on his back looking at the ceiling. He was still in a hospital gown. A sheet and blanket were pulled up to his chest. His arms were crossed over the blanket. He looked grumpy. Eileen stood beside the bed. "How'd it go?"

"It was okay. Guess we need to wait for Greg to tell us how it really went." He took a deep breath and stared at the ceiling again.

"Let me know if you need anything. Water's on the stand." Eileen sat next to the window and let him rest in silence.

When Greg arrived half an hour later, he walked to Eileen and put his hand on her shoulder. "How's our guy doing?"

"He's behaving and holding still."

Moving to the edge of the bed, Greg asked, "How are you feeling right now, Jack?"

He grinned. "Better than in a long time. Got a whopper of a headache though."

"Given anything for it yet?"

"Nurse gave me two aspirins, or something like it, soon as they got me in bed."

Greg opened the electronic chart on the high rolling stand and nodded. "Good, drink plenty of fluids today and for the next couple days at home. It'll help."

"Sure will."

"How's your back?"

"Little tender when I wiggle. No big deal. Worst part was the shot to numb me. After that, it was just pressure, like you said."

"She's excellent."

"When can I go home?"

"In a couple hours, if you promise to take it easy for two days. That means no lifting over ten pounds or excessive bending. No rowing-machine workouts or the like."

He laughed. "You got my word on that."

Greg paused. "And lie down if the headache continues. Call me if it gets worse. Let's go over what we know right now."

Eileen stood to leave. Jack motioned for her to stay. Greg wheeled the computer to the bedside and reviewed the report in French on the computer. He paused to be sure of his translation before he spoke. "The fluid was clear, not cloudy or bloody. No visual indicators of infection. No cell deformations suggestive of any cancer."

Jack stopped holding his breath. "That's good."

"Protein levels serve as indicators of inflammation and infection. They were less than forty-five milligrams per deciliter. That's telling me that no inflammatory process is present. Your white cell count and glucose readings didn't suggest infection either. These are great indicators that the cultures that screen for infection will come back fine in a few days just like your blood tests."

"Okay. And the pressure thing?"

"Doctor Bonnard called me right away with your pressures."

He started to prop up on one elbow, grimaced, and fell flat. "And I'm way above it, right?"

Greg motioned for him to stay still. "We want to see a pressure between a hundred and one-eighty when the patient is lying on their side. It should go up to about two hundred to three hundred when the patient sits up. Your numbers were right in there."

"Shit. You said if it was high..."

Greg took a deep breath and put his hand on Jack's shoulder. "Look, this is all preliminary. I want you to have some context on what I'm going to tell you. Can you simmer down and listen to me now?"

"Sure. Okay."

"Do you remember what I told you about cerebral spinal fluid?"

"Sure."

Eileen started to ask Greg something but he motioned for her to wait.

Focusing again on Jack, Greg said, "Tell me about it. All you can remember."

"You said the CSF is made in the brain. It's a shock absorber. It takes nutrients to the brain and takes away waste. I thought of it like a sta-dium's taco truck and one a those blue outhouses...all in one."

Greg laughed. "Interesting way of looking at it."

Jack poked his finger at Greg to continue. "And one more thing that's important. It flows back and forth between the spine and brain to regulate the pressure in the brain, in the vessels." Jack took a deep breath and looked away from Greg.

When he thought Jack had finished, Greg corrected one word. "Ventricles. The fluid-containing cavities."

Jack gripped the sheet. "And that was supposed to be high and squish-ing my brain. Now it's not."

"Actually, normal pressure in this type of lumbar puncture does not rule out a specific type of excess pressure in the cranial area. Maybe your brain is being squished."

Jack shrugged. "You lost me. I thought it was one deal. A closed system."

"It is supposed to be. When the CSF is made in the brain, it should move into the spinal column. If that flow is restricted, there can be a pres-sure buildup in the brain that is not immediately registered by the lumbar tap."

"I'm not following you."

"It's like a kink in a garden hose. Something can restrict the flow. Or it's not being absorbed fast enough. You need the pressure in both your brain and spine to be the same. To equilibrate. Equalize."

"Can you unkink me?"

Greg laughed. "Look, if I'm right, you'd be in a small subset, maybe less than five percent of the people with cognition issues. But I'm betting that's what's going on here."

"How can you say that if my pressure is normal?"

"The tap should tell us if the pressure in the whole system is high. That assumes there is no obstruction or blockage or overproduction of fluid. You got a good reading on the spinal pressure. But that does not mean your *cranial* pressure is normal."

"So what now? Just go home and go nuts?"

Greg shook his head quickly. "First, we are going to let you recover from this puncture and monitor your cognition for a couple days to see if it improves. Either way, I want to recommend a lumbar drain. That's going to take a more accurate look at pressures because it stays in for a while and we can adjust the amount of fluid that is drained. This can reduce your cranial pressure. Following me?"

"Yeah."

"If I'm right and you have NPH, Normal Pressure Hydrocephalic dementia, it's fixable, so I don't want you to think we've done everything yet to get you better. We still have test results to get and then we can develop a comprehensive treatment plan."

Jack squinted away tears. "Hydrocephalic? Like Down syndrome?"

"There are three kinds of hydrocephalus. That's one. Without getting into the details, Down syndrome is genetic and is managed by a shunt, a drain that reduces pressure and improves that patient's health and well-being. Another type is caused by the brain actually shrinking and fluid taking up the lost space. That's *hydrocephalus ex-vacuo*. Means fluid filling the void. Your MRI told us that your brain is not shrinking."

"Guess that's good news right there."

"It is. Now, about the third kind. Normal Pressure Hydrocephalus can come from an injury or some disease process like a tumor or some blockage. For patients with a specific blockage, like a bone or tissue obstruction, we can surgically fix it with an endoscopic third ventriculostomy, or ETV. We use a camera and miniature endoscopic tools to make a tiny hole in the floor of the third ventricle. This allows CSF to bypass the obstruction and naturally reabsorb. But you don't have an obstruction."

"So how do we fix it?"

"First, we get another test. If it shows elevated cranial pressure, you'd be a good candidate for a shunt."

"How's that work?"

"A surgeon will implant a short thin drain tube from your brain to a valve that is a little thicker than a quarter. It's usually placed behind your ear. A very small catheter runs from that valve, just under your skin, to your abdominal cavity. It's so small you won't notice it. What you will notice is a return to your normal cognition within days to weeks."

"What happens if I don't get that surgery and a valve?"

"Let's get some results before we speculate."

Jack raised his voice. "If I don't? Call it straight!" Eileen stood and put her hand on his shoulder.

Greg looked at Jack and took a breath. "You'll continue to deteriorate. You'll have difficulty in focusing your eyes, nausea, increased unsteadiness in your gait, leg weakness, sudden falls, drowsiness, behavioral changes, and seizures."

"Shit."

"The bottom line is that continuous high pressure will cause significant cognitive decline, then permanent brain damage, and death, sooner than later."

"When can you do the next test?"

"There are two tests for it. One is a simple lumbar drain. It's like the tap but we remove some more spinal fluid over a longer time and wait to see if the pressure in the brain drops. The test requires a couple of days in the hospital."

"And the other one?"

"Cisternography. It's a really detailed test that is a lot more complex than the MRI or a CT scan. It can measure absorption and give us a lot of information."

"When can you do it?"

"I can't. It's hard to find a hospital equipped for the procedure, actually."

"Can Doctor Bonnard do the longer tap, the drain?"

"I'll call her and get her schedule. I wanted your okay first. Meanwhile, you stay still."

Greg turned to go. Jack called after him. "Doc? You really think it might work?"

He returned to the foot of the bed. "Jack! We couldn't have had this conversation a week ago. You couldn't have followed it. That's why I asked you to tell me what you remembered about how CSF worked. And you did. Look, I don't know if you are functioning better because some of the worry has been removed or it's a response to a pressure adjustment...or both. But that's why I'm betting that we can reverse this."

Eileen followed Greg into the hallway. "Anything else I need to know?"

"Not yet. Can you keep his activity restricted at home to sitting, or lying flat? No leaning over or straining. Park him with a good book. Over the next hour here, let's get him ready to stand by elevating the head of the bed up slowly to a full upright position. That way, standing won't be a shock. Nurse might come in once or twice to elevate, but if you can do it gradually, that would be better."

"Sure." She started to turn to go back into his room, but Greg touched her elbow and she stopped.

"The next day or two is critical. His behavior and cognition is going to tell us almost as much as the next test. Can you push him? Challenge his memory, introduce conceptual thinking opportunities, and see how he does."

"Like what?"

"Maybe get into some esoteric literature discussion or editing minutia and see how he manages it. Can he handle complex thought and memory?"

"Okay. I'll try. Thanks."

Returning to the hospital room, she sat beside Jack.

"Doc have any added words of wisdom?"

"Yes. We are going to elevate the head of the bed slowly over the next hour to get you ready to stand up."

He fiddled with the bed's controls and the foot started elevating. He let out a little snort, lowered it, and found the button to raise the head of the bed just enough to see her easily. "Did you see a gift shop on the way in?"

"Sure. What can I get you? A chocolate..."

He motioned with his hands. "A notebook. Eight by ten if they have it. And a pen, unless you've got an extra on you."

"You promise to stay still if I go?"

He grinned. "Scout's honor."

About fifteen minutes later, she returned with a wire-bound note-book and a gel pen. She laughed as she put them on the rolling tray and moved it in front of him. "Sorry. All they had was purple ink."

"That's fine." He laughed. "Now I can write purple prose."

She laughed.

"Actually, Eileen, I'm just trying to lock down all this new stuff. I don't want to forget any of it."

She nodded and turned on her iPad to read. She found the place in her novel that she wanted to edit and was sinking into its theme again. She toyed with the idea of telling Jack about her draft, then she dismissed the idea. It was too early in its development to ask for any input, especially from him given his situation. Every few minutes, Jack tapped the bed's control paddle and moved the back higher. Within an hour he was sitting almost upright. Eileen looked at him. "How's the headache?"

"Not bad. About the same, even with sitting up."

She checked the time on her iPad and closed it. "They should be releasing you soon. I'll go see what the checkout procedure is."

After medical clearance and signing several forms, Jack dressed and waited in the recovery room while Eileen went to the lobby where there was better phone reception and called for an Uber. The attendant had just wheeled in a chair to transport Jack to the exit and was helping him into the chair when Greg arrived. "Hey, glad I caught you before you escaped. Where's..."

"Getting us a ride."

Greg nodded to the attendant and took the handles of the wheelchair. "I'll see him out."

The attendant left when Greg pushed the chair to the elevator. Greg pressed the button and put his back to the elevator so he could face Jack. "I called Doctor Bonnard. She can do it Monday."

"So soon?"

"Yeah. Why?"

Jack looked at his hands without answering. Greg frowned. "I thought you'd be pleased. What's worrying you? It's almost as safe as the tap you just—"

"How long can I stay clear? How long can I string this out before I slip back into the fog? I'm thinking that if I can go like this a few days or a couple weeks, I might be able to..."

"I don't know. Everyone is different. We usually do the drain right away if a tap is normal but we suspect NPH."

"But do you know how long?"

"No. Jack, I don't."

"What if I went back to work and then we do the drain thing if... when I start slipping?"

"I'll discuss it with Doctor Bonnard, but she's cleared her calendar as a favor to..." He patted Jack's shoulder. "I'll talk to her. I see what you are trying to do."

"Thanks."

Doctor Bonnard reluctantly cancelled the procedure and rescheduled it for the following Monday afternoon. Jack promised that during the week he would take it easy at the penthouse. Once home, Eileen dropped her coat on the sofa and walked to the refrigerator. "Hungry?"

"Starving!"

"That's got to take a lot out of you."

He chuckled. "Is that supposed to be a joke?"

"Sorry. Wasn't meant to be. Sandwich? Omelet?"

"Cheese omelet and some toast—if I didn't kill the toaster oven."

"It's fine. I cleaned it."

He drew a glass of chilled water from the tap on the refrigerator door, went to the table, and watched her start toast, heat a pan, and whip eggs. Once their plates were on the table, he started eating immediately. She watched him and tore off a bit of toast. "Jack? I've been thinking about what you said about Rilke's *Letters to a Young Poet*."

He swallowed hard and took a drink of water. "What about it?"

"That you thought it trite or something to that effect."

"Not trite. But juvenile. Pretentious. As though he were lecturing himself on how to be a poet. Then he returned to that theme again in *The Notebooks of Malta Laurids Brigge*. Some translations have it as 'sketchbook,' not 'notebook.' And that is a big difference. Now, today he might write it as a fictional diary, but a diary then would have been too introspective, egotistical. So he wrote in the third person as an objective observer of this struggling poet. In some ways the earlier letters seem like a draft of his novel."

"Worth reading?"

"Only if you are a lit student. It was one of the first novels of the twentieth century to abandon all the nineteenth-century structure of plot and character."

"What's left?"

He chuckled. "Not so much. Dialogue. Narration. Endless rambling in what would be a stream-of-consciousness flow if it were first person. Had to teach it one year and I hated every line of it."

"As bad as *Ulysses*?"

"Worse. Ever read Sartre's *Nausea*?"

She nodded, impressed that he was offering rather complex illustrations. "Sure. My thesis advisor required it."

"Ripped off from *The Notebook*. I like a story with a start, a stop, and a middle."

She touched his arm. "You seem so calm. So connected today. I thought you'd be a nervous wreck after that test. I know I am. Waiting is not my strength."

"Or mine. But I like your doc. He thinks I might be one of the lucky ones with a reversible memory loss. But, you were there when he told me that, weren't you?"

"Yes. I was."

"Thought so. So until I know different, I'm placing my money on that option. Gotta, or I'd..."

"What?"

He ran the last bit of his buttered toast around the empty plate to get the last bits of egg. After taking that bite, his shoulders slumped. He pushed the empty plate toward her. "Thanks. Hit the spot. You know, I'm dead tired all of a sudden."

"You okay?"

"Yes. Just tired. Think I'll stretch out. Skim my last book. See if I can get any ideas. Even if I miss this deadline, I'm sure that Max could find some way to salvage something of my shredded career. If anyone can manage the PR mess, it's Max. Hell, he might even find a small publisher willing to take a chance on me after I get fixed."

Eileen offered a supportive smile. "It's worth a shot. But you've got to make your health the priority for the next few weeks. This other stuff has to wait."

Jack pressed the idea. "Maybe I could self-publish if all else fails and have Max find a publicist." Once Eileen agreed with his plan, he walked to his suite and closed the door.

Over the next few days, he settled into a routine of reading quietly in his suite, emerging for meals, and retreating again. Eileen and Greg spent their evenings together. On Wednesday morning, as she made coffee, Jack appeared somewhat scattered in his thinking, but was alert and pleasant. When she asked if he had taken his thyroid pill, he couldn't remember. They counted the pills and decided that he needed to take one. She called Greg and the two lovers decided to spend the remaining evenings together at the penthouse. The pair also decided that she should remain there during the day. When Greg arrived after work, they slipped into an easy routine of a run on the treadmills in the basement gym before making dinner, and dining with Jack.

By Saturday morning at breakfast, it was evident that Jack had returned to his earlier level of confusion. But this was not the passive, distracted confusion that she had seen before. There was fear and frustration added to the mix. It manifested in slammed doors and swearing, which were followed by apologies.

Jack seemed to interrupt her any time that she had found traction in the editing of her manuscript. She was revising her second draft to elevate the tension in the story while half-listening for Jack. Late Saturday afternoon she abandoned her work and made a rich soup for their dinner that night. Jack seemed to enjoy having her in the kitchen so he could talk to her while she cut vegetables and chopped onions. Something in the rhythm of cooking seemed to soothe them both. While the soup simmered, she poured a glass of Chablis for each of them and sat at the kitchen table.

Halfway through her glass of wine, she asked how his drafting was going.

Jack thought before responding. "Candidly, I'm still having a hard time weaving plots together, but I've got an idea for the main theme if we can do a book of short stories."

"I've edited your books. Twice now. And I've read them all more than once, to keep the flow and continuity while I edited. But I still can't figure how you build so much tension. How do you do it?"

He leaned back and looked at her. "You're as smart as they come, kid. Why are you asking about my tricks? Gonna write something for a magazine. Feature story?" He scowled at her, challenging her for a reply.

"No! Really, it's for...me. I'm writing a book, or trying to. Not a thriller or a spy something. Just a simple modern love story, not a sloppy romance but about modern life with kids from a prior marriage that ended in death, not divorce. So the kids are on the fence about the dad's new relationship. One of them runs away. Kind of a YA level."

He relaxed. "Don't dismiss the young adult readership. Kids are smarter than they get credit for. That's a theme you need in your book... how damn smart kids are. How they get it."

"Okay."

"Look, any book needs some tension or it gets 'flabby middle syndrome,' whether it's a romance, sci-fi, or mainstream. I used to teach this stuff, so I bet I can remember most of it. Here's my checklist."

She grabbed a pencil and paper from the counter.

"Maybe not in this order but here goes. First, you gotta have a hero that people care about. Vulnerable, so you can be scared for them. Even Superman has his kryptonite."

She wrote this down and looked at him with her pencil hovering just above the paper.

"Next..." He stopped for a moment and looked past her. Then he became animated, with his arms spread wide. "Maybe it's like a love affair that lasts. Lofty goals, high stakes, unpredictable shit that you get through together." He stopped and took in a hard breath. "Yeah. Use high stakes and time constraints. A ticking clock or timer on a bomb. As soon as it looks easy, mess it all up again. Make the villain as big as the hero, and sometimes the villain is not a person but a thing. But all the while, you are getting closer to the big wazoo."

"What's the 'wazoo'?"

"You tell me. It's like Hitchcock's 'McGuffin.' It's the *thing* that drives the plot, what we have to have or have to avoid. What we'd kill to protect. What we'd die for."

She looked up from her notes. "Wow."

"But the real secret is like that jazz man said. It ain't the notes. The music is between the notes. Everybody talks about my action scenes. But the truth is that the tension exists in the silence, the calm, the waiting. That's what makes our nerves jump and hair stand on end. Waiting's a bitch. No matter if you're a kid waiting for Christmas or me waiting for my test results."

"I get it. Thank you, Jack. I appreciate your insight."

"So you really want into this game? It's not easy. Most writers can't support…"

She laughed. "I've got a good day job. I can pay my bills with editing and translating. Don't worry about me."

On Sunday, Eileen did laundry, tried editing again, gave it up, watched a TED talk about creativity, and made a sturdy beef stew. That night Greg came for dinner bringing with him two baguettes and a bottle of Beaujolais. After dinner, Jack asked Greg to see if the fireplace had a gas log or a real one, as he couldn't tell. Once Greg determined it was a gas log, he asked if Jack wanted him to light it. He nodded. Greg fired it up, lowered the flame, and the three sat on the sofa facing it. The warmth was soothing. They listened to a smooth jazz station that Jack had found during the week. Jack went to bed early, leaving Eileen and Greg listening to music and chatting over a brandy while watching the flames.

Chapter № 13

October 16, 2017
Monday

At four on Monday afternoon, Doctor Bonnard performed the procedure by inserting a slim needle into Jack's numbed lower back, just like the spinal tap. But when she withdrew the needle, a flexible catheter, smaller than a pencil lead, remained to drain a very specific amount of fluid from his spinal column during his hospitalization. Continual monitoring and delicate adjustment allowed a more accurate measure of the slow changes in pressure and an evaluation of the potential effectiveness of using a shunt to relieve intracranial pressure.

For the next two days Jack remained in the hospital under medical observation. Eileen stayed with him. She dressed in jeans, Nikes, a cotton turtleneck, and flannel shirt. By layering, she adjusted to the temperature swings between his room, the cafeteria, and the lobby. When Greg or Doctor Bonnard visited for examinations or cognitive tests, she escaped to the cafeteria for a snack, the nurse's lounge to freshen up, or to speed walk around the floor to get the kinks out and get some air.

She skimmed Jack's last novel on her iPad to understand how he paced tension and refresh herself on his style while he napped or wrote in his spiral-bound notebook. Other than having the Institute's name on the cardboard cover, it looked like the notebooks that students used in his classes. It seemed to her that he was writing faster day by day and that his infrequent interruptions to talk to her were significantly more lucid and confident. She hoped that was not wishful thinking on her part.

The morning of Jack's third day in the Institute's hospital wing, Greg arrived with Doctor Bonnard. Both were smiling as she reported that

Jack was indeed a good candidate for a shunt as his pressures and cognition had both improved during the observation.

"Greg? Can you or Doctor Bonnard put in the shunt?"

Greg shook his head. "It's a surgical procedure. I'm a researcher with a limited clinical practice. For this, I'm going to turn you over to another neurosurgeon on our team who will review options with you. I've imposed far too much on Doctor Bonnard as it is. This is just planning. Nobody is going to do anything until all of your results are back from the lab. And that's still a week or so away."

"Options? What kind of options?"

"What kind of shunt to use. I'll let her explain the details."

"So, it's a real operation?"

Doctor Bonnard nodded. "Yes. Expect a couple days in the hospital for observation to get the settings right and make sure any incision is healing properly. Too high a pressure is where you were, too low is like a hangover with headaches and dizziness, and an extremely low pressure can cause seizures, so we want it adjusted right."

"What are my chances of keeping my mind?"

"Excellent. Our success rate is excellent. About eighty percent of all patients eligible for this procedure have significant improvement within weeks of the shunt being implanted. For some, it takes longer. But how you reacted to just the relief from the spinal tap and drain tells me you are an excellent candidate." She patted his shoulder as she left.

"Is it a one-time fix? Plug and play?"

Greg chuckled at his remark. "No. You'll need to start routine medical contact to be sure its functioning right, monthly then quarterly. And it might need to be replaced in six to eight years. But the new ones should last even longer than that."

"I'm so much better now than I was a week ago; do you think it is really necessary?"

"It's not uncommon for patients like you to feel better, normal in fact, right after the pressure is adjusted. But that's temporary."

"Do a lot of people develop this?"

"NPH? We're still trying to get good numbers on it. But now I estimate that five, maybe as high as ten percent, of Americans with a diagnosis of dementia have NPH and are candidates for reversal and control. But I'm thinking that only about twenty percent of those with NPH get a correct diagnosis, and without that, no treatment is available." Greg noticed that Jack was rubbing his hands together and looking at the ceiling. "Jack! Let me again stress that although this is a treatable condition, it's not a one-time fix. It needs surgery and ongoing management, but it will extend the duration and quality of your life."

Jack frowned. "Why can't they get diagnosed like I did? Those other people?"

"First, you need to go to a doctor with your concerns. That stops a lot of people who could get help. Second, that's my specialty. Some of the symptoms mimic other diseases like Parkinson's or other spinal and neurological disorders. And look, the three most evident symptoms are common to the aging process. Walking problems, incontinence, and memory reduction or confusion."

"Shit. How's a person supposed to figure all that out?"

"I expect there is going to be more support for our research and positive diagnostics as baby boomers age. They are a feisty lot and are going to want a sound diagnosis and ways to retain their mental and physical abilities. The next generation is going to be even more demanding as they figure out how to get information that is accurate."

"And the Internet is..."

"Right now, anyone can post anything on the Internet and pass it off as true. As patients and consumers, we've got to learn how to validate the information we get from the Internet and other media. And we have to get the word out to the general public and medical community through trusted sources. That's hard. And getting harder as people pass off nutty stuff as science and ignore sound science as fake news when it is inconvenient to their political agenda. Sorry."

"I didn't have a clue. People need to know this stuff."

"You're right, Jack."

"So? When can I meet with the surgeon?"

"Doctor Le Blanc is seeing a patient here now. I asked her to drop in, just to meet you. Then you can call her office and set an appointment once you are back at your place. She should be by within an hour. Doctor Bonnard has cleared you for discharge."

"Can you tell Eileen? I think she's in the cafeteria."

"Sure."

An attendant assisted Jack in dressing and had him wait for Doctor Le Blanc in the side chair that Eileen had been nesting in for the previous two days. When she returned from the cafeteria, she laughed. "So? Have I been replaced?"

"They're springing me."

"Are you ready?"

"Almost. Signed some papers while you were out, and got dressed. Greg's got another doc coming to talk to me. Soon as that's done..."

Eileen sat on the bed until she heard a woman in the hallway asking for Jack's room number. Eileen went to the door and smiled. "He's here."

Doctor Sylvia Le Blanc was short, nudging forty, and clearly a woman who took care of herself. Her knee-length white coat was unbuttoned and her pearl gray cashmere turtleneck and black wool skirt were closely fitted. She moved smoothly past Eileen with a nod and greeted Jack with a firm handshake.

"You're Doctor Le Blanc?"

"Yes." Jack opened his notebook and clicked the purple gel pen.

"Doctor Patel has referred you to me to discuss your candidacy for ventriculoperitoneal shunt surgery. For simplicity let me refer to it as a VP shunt. What do you know about it so far?"

"I need a permanent drain because I have too much pressure on my brain."

"How do you feel after the lumbar puncture and drain?"

"My low back is still tender, but my mind is as clear as it has been for months. Almost like normal."

"*C'est fantastique.* The operation is fairly straightforward. Simple, really. In about an hour, we place a short tube inside your head where the fluid pools and connect that tube to a one-way valve at the side or back of your head. From it, we tunnel a longer tube under your skin to your peritoneal...lower abdomen, where the extra fluid is absorbed."

He made a few notes and looked up from his notebook. "Before you go on, let me ask you something."

"*Oui.*"

"If I have the operation here, when can I fly home? Back to America."

She tipped her head and looked at him directly. "Flying is a challenge as it is a pressurized cabin. It is the same as going to an altitude of two thousand five hundred meters over the sea, about..." She paused and did the conversion on her iPhone's calculator. "That's about eight thousand feet. Like going to the mountains. Higher than your Denver, I think."

"And pressure, outside pressure is going to affect my inside pressure."

"*Précisément!* That's an important thing you just said. Some people are very sensitive to pressure and get big headaches when flying or going to a ski holiday. Others, it is not too noticeable. We won't know your sensitivity until we—"

"How soon do I need to have it?"

She raised an eyebrow. "How soon do you want to become better?"

"I need to be back in the States. That's where I belong."

"There are excellent neurosurgeons there. Doctor Patel told me that you live near New York City. Could you have the operation there and go in on a weekly then monthly basis for the next six months?"

"No problem."

"Superb. I know several excellent surgeons there personally from conferences and papers. I can give their names to Doctor Patel, if you wish him to be your medical *liaison.*"

"Yes. I like him."

She stood. "Well, I think we have no need now for another meeting, unless you have new questions. It now should be the decision of your medical support in America to select the proper shunt there to meet your needs."

She stood but he held up his hand for her to stay. "How long before I lose my mind again?"

She sat down. "The pressure reduction from your procedure is temporary. It will build up soon, *mais*, but I don't know what 'soon' is for you."

"Hours? Days? Months?"

"Days, I think several days, a week perhaps, but not many weeks."

"But I feel like myself now."

"Which shows that a shunt is an excellent long-term option for you."

"But if I'm trapped here...waiting for test results and as lovely as France is..."

"I understand your concern."

Jack grinned. "One way or another, I want to start making arrangements for the operation in New York as soon as possible."

"*Certainment*. But I suggest you do not fly for at least a week, so you do not stress the puncture point."

He nodded. "I'd still like the pre-operation information so I don't do anything stupid to delay the operation once I am back home."

"I believe that staying healthy by avoiding crowds is key. The week before the operation you start avoiding blood thinners. Vitamin E, aspirin..."

"The drug store painkillers, right?"

She nodded. "Stop drinking alcohol at least a week before. If you get headaches or withdrawal symptoms, tell your doctor immediately."

"No problem."

"Some things you should think about now when you are clear and write down is how you work. Are you around magnets? On the programmable shunt, a doctor uses a magnetic tool to turn a dial inside the valve. In the past, the valve needed to be reset by a surgical intervention.

But there are risks to this benefit that can be managed for your safety. Magnets can reset the flow settings on some shunts. Some headsets have magnets. If you are a real *stereophile* you should check your headphones. Any future MRI you have, you will need to tell them if you get the programmable shunt because that might change the setting, and you need to have it checked before and after and maybe have it revised...reset. After the operation, I want you to get a medical alert bracelet or *un collier ou un pendentif*... how you say, necklace. So any hospital will know if you have a programmable shunt. This is important also if you ever have abdominal surgery for any reason."

"Okay. I guess I need to see what hospitals in New York can do this."

"We have listings of those we have a fraternal relationship with, for sharing diagnostic or offering second opinions. I can give that to Doctor Patel for you."

"Thank you."

"My pleasure." She stood and shook his hand. When she left, Jack closed his notebook and handed it to Eileen. "Mind carrying this in your bag?" As she was about to answer, the attendant arrived and they left the hospital. Once on the sidewalk, Eileen reached for her phone and started to open her Uber app. Jack put his hand on her arm. "Let's walk. I need some real air."

He moved slowly, as though he had a pebble in his shoe. His shorter stride made it easy for her to walk beside him and remain on his left. Suddenly, he stopped in the middle of the sidewalk. "I'm screwed either way, aren't I?"

"What do..."

"If I stay here I can get the operation and follow-up, but I can't live here forever. Max isn't going to adopt me and those chefs aren't going to let me stay in their place for years. But if I go back, I don't have insurance, and I'm not going to be able to get the shunt."

She took his arm and started toward the café with a red awning in the next block. "How about a coffee and we talk it over."

"Or a glass of red?"

"I thought you were going to work on your book."

"You're right. This is such a wild roller coaster of a ride, finding out that I can be me again, and then trying to manage the real-life shit, I hit a roadblock. Classic 'no mon,' no fun' problem. I don't have the funds to pay for it."

At the door of the café she asked, "Is it easier for you to stand at the bar or do you want a table?"

"A table. Outside."

"It's chilly."

"So what? It's too crowded in there."

They took a table next to the clear plastic sheeting that buffered the breeze off the river. He ordered in crisp French and turned to Eileen with tears in his eyes. "It's back. *I'm me again!* I can't lose that. There's gotta be a way."

She motioned for him to lower his voice. "Slow down."

"I don't have time to slow down! It's like *The Lady and The Tiger.* The Stockton story."

"I'm trying to remember it. Didn't a barbarian king use a test of chance to determine guilt? There were two doors. Behind one there was a beautiful lady that the accused had to marry, behind the other a hungry tiger and certain death. It's a choice. Will he get it right?"

"There is more to it."

"What?"

"The kicker. The wazoo. There is no acceptable choice in the end. You got it as far as you went, but there's more. The suitor of the king's daughter is brought up on charges and set before the two doors. Now the princess gets secret intel on which door has the tiger. But she also finds out that the lady behind the other door is someone she hates. So she will lose her lover to death or to another woman. We are left to ponder if the princess points him to death by the tiger or life with her rival. It is the unsolvable problem story."

"I guess I missed that. How are you feeling? Tired after your hospital stay?"

"Not really. I seem to have hit a burst of energy. Not in drafting my next book, but in journaling, of all things."

"Journaling?"

"Done it forever. It's a habit. Last night I filled up the rest of that notebook you got for me writing about the meaning of mindfulness and memory. Had to make notes on the back cover when that last doc was talking to me. Not exactly a Susan Sarandon, no, I mean a Susan Sontag essay, but it's pretty damn good. It's about what it's like to get a second chance at your art, at your life. About how our past makes our present. Like the sunshine that warms us left the sun almost eight and a half minutes ago. Like our moonlight bounced off the moon a second and a half ago. Our reality is made of the past. So too are our dreams of the future. Without the past, we have no future. Our memories are frozen like a fly in amber. When my mind shattered, I didn't know if I could reassemble the shards of my amber. So I'm writing to figure it out and—"

"You're what? I never saw you writing more than a few lines in the hospital." The waiter delivered two coffees. He took Jack's offered euros with a nod.

"I'd think on stuff then let it rip when you were taking your walks or down in the cafeteria. It's like I can't stop. Like I'm channeling something that's been bottled up in me, and now it's not just oozing out, it's spurting." He took a careful sip of the steaming coffee.

"Jack? How long have you been..."

"Been making notes? All along, just to remember what's going on. Right after Greg told me about the trifecta of fixable stuff, it was like some of the fog lifted. It was like I was almost back to being me."

"I'm not following..."

"I write to understand stuff. In my books, I write to understand international politics and intrigue. I need to write to make the connections work in my plots. I've written every part of this trip since I couldn't trust my memory."

"And are you? Making connections?"

He nodded. "Yeah. Deaf in one ear, so I missed a lot of what was going on and sunk deeper into kicking myself, so I slid into depression. Then I ate shitty, lost weight, and messed up my aging thyroid. Punched myself in the nose with that window and lost a lot of my sniffer. I saw some hope again that I could fix most of the stuff that was pulling me into this...fog. I started a very detailed diary, so if I forgot something he told me I could look it up. I had to write it fast, every day, before I forgot. I had to process it. The best way I think on things is through my writing. That's how I know when I'm being square with myself. I've got a good BS detector."

She glanced at him as she blew across the steaming cup that she cradled it in her hands. "Are your notes helping?"

"They're not notes. I have a full narrative and dialogue starting with our first dinner with Greg, I wrote it that night. I've documented all the doctor meetings...and how kind you have been." He patted her hand and cleared his throat. "I shut the door when you were home so the typing wouldn't disturb you. And wrote longhand in the comp books when I had the door open."

"I never heard you typing after that one time."

"Good. When you were out with Greg, I typed almost nonstop..."

She put her cup down without looking. It tipped and splashed some coffee on the table. "How many words...about?"

"Hmmm. No clue. I haven't even numbered the typed pages yet. Just letting them stack up on the floor so the breeze doesn't mess 'em up. I like it chilly when I write."

She stared at him. "How many pages?"

He shrugged.

"Guess!"

"Thirty. Naw, maybe forty or fifty typed pages. Then there's the comp books to type up. I usually don't edit my journals, but this is different."

She gripped the table and leaned toward him. "Are you kidding me?"

"No."

"Double spaced like the stories you gave me when we first got here?"

He shook his head. "Nope. Single."

"Jack, I think you are writing your next book. Either autobiographical or fictionalized. You just might make that deadline after all."

"It's not a book, just my notes to myself. My thoughts."

"Think what a book like this could do for other people who think they are slipping into that fog! It might get some to a doctor sooner and make doctors more aware of…"

He gave a dismissive flick of his hand as if swatting away an annoying insect. "I'm no expert. That's a medical book that ought to—"

"Listen to me! You have a platform of authority from your own experience. You have come back from the fog. God, with your readership, you could touch the lives of millions of people."

"And I'm going to slide back if I don't get that operation. This is only gonna work for a couple more days, then I'll get foggy again. There's no way I have time to type the next draft."

"Why do you need another draft?"

He laughed. "Because nobody could make hide nor hair of it like it is."

She frowned. "I don't get it."

"It's the way I write. Roll a fresh sheet into my typewriter and let 'er rip. No quotes, no margins, just hit the return at the end of a line, do a dash for new dialog, keeps it rolling that way. Leave paragraphing and quote marks for my second run at it so I can see what I want to keep and what's crap."

"What about the short stories you showed me?"

"All third or fourth drafts. Cleaned up."

"Are you telling me you just have one solid block of type on a page, no split between dialogue and narrative?"

He shrugged. "Yeah. Sorry. I'd be ashamed to even show it to you in its current state."

"How many words do you figure to a page?"

"Never paid much attention, but one of the first pages usually looks like three or four pages once I put in margins and double space it for a second draft."

"What?"

"Yeah, a mess. Margins a quarter inch at most. If I get the paper in a little crooked, some letters might run off the edge."

"I can't see how you could have typed that much."

He chuckled. "I'm a speedy typist, but a slow writer. Hell, that's just a few pages a night. Got a prize in high school for typing and kept it up."

"Don't you use a computer at home?"

"Max bought me one once. Slowed me down."

"But all your manuscripts after the first one came to mom on a disk, then later just as a file to edit electronically."

Jack laughed. "Yeah. I guess Isabel really laid down the law to Max that she had to have my stuff that way so she could edit easier, not retype everything herself. So I guess Max musta hired some poor soul to retype my stuff."

Eileen laughed. "Sounds like mom."

"So? We got ourselves a week, maybe less. That's not enough time."

"When we get back, you need to show me what you've written."

"There's no way we can—"

"Jack! I think there might be a..."

He stared at her. "How fast do *you* type?"

"Oh, I'm just an average forty or fifty word a minute typist."

"Then we're screwed."

She took a quick sip of her coffee. "No, we're not! I can dictate about two hundred words a minute, and clean up your punctuation as I go. I'll dictate your notebooks and typed pages, then we can see how they fit together."

"Who you going to dictate to? We don't have a secretary."

She grinned. "My computer has a voice-to-text program. I've really trained it to my voice and vocabulary so it rarely misses a word. I've also modified it to have several punctuation macros. I've got to be as efficient as possible."

"What's a macro?"

"It's a special command. So at the end of dialogue, instead of typing in a close quote, line return, paragraph, indent, and open quote, I do all of it with one word."

"No shit?"

"Now, it's for transcription only. It's not like I'm dictating your audiobook. I have a friend who does that. Takes about two and sometimes six hours of studio time to get one hour of an audiobook. Longer if there are complicated accents or foreign words. She figures the eleven hours average for most books takes her forty hours when she combines research, getting into character, and actual studio time. And that's for a book of about a hundred thousand words—some of yours have been almost double that. Ever listen to yours?"

"Nope."

She shook her head and grinned at him. "You really are a dinosaur, aren't you?"

"Guess so. That sounds..."

She finished her coffee in one long gulp while looking at him. "Remind me! How old are you?"

He laughed. "Old enough to know better."

"Seriously!"

He smiled. "Sixty-four?"

She frowned. "You're sixty-six. I did your paperwork, Remember? Medicare! Do you have a Medicare card?"

"Had one. Probably still in my shoebox of stuff at the townhouse. I guess I could ask her for it."

"Your ex-wife?"

"Technically, I guess we're just separated. I...we never got around to talking through anything. I just gave her the place, and left."

"Then you are still married?"

"I guess, unless she's filed something I don't know about."

"Does she still work as an attorney?"

"Hell yeah. You know we were married just as the swifts migrated into Paris. Sky was dark with them some days. You know the little black birds that kinda look like swallows? They're only here between May and July, then they go back to Africa."

Eileen tipped her head in confusion. "Jack?"

"Well, she's like a swift, always on the hunt. You know they never land, well just to hatch eggs, then they are in the air again. She's tenacious. The top litigator in her environmental law firm."

"Did you have health insurance before?"

"Sure, she had all the perks. Covered Grace and me."

"Did she take you off her policy?"

"Who knows?"

"We need to know. I can call her if you don't want to."

"Oh boy, that's going to be a tough one to make."

"I'll do it. Do you have her number? I'll call her when we get back to the penthouse."

He looked embarrassed. "I kept it in my passport as my emergency contact. I figured she'd want to know if I dropped dead somewhere, for the insurance at least. Still on my phone too."

She looked at her world clock app. "Middle of the day there. I could call now."

"She'd be at work. I don't want to interrupt her there. How about you leave a message on the home phone?"

He reluctantly handed her his cell phone. She called. As expected, it went to message. Eileen cleared her throat. "My name is Eileen. I am editing Jack's book in Paris and he needs some medical care. He was wondering if you had his Medicare card and if he is still covered on your insurance. If you could call back on his cell phone, it would be appreciated. Thank you." She tapped the red button to end the call and handed back the phone. As she stood, she said, "Let's go look at what you've got."

He was jittery during their walk back to the penthouse. In an effort to calm him, she turned to him and asked, "Jack? When did you meet your wife and where?"

He smiled. "Here! Paris. It was a café near the Louvre, *rive droite*, couple streets up from the Seine. Made the best hot chocolate. I'd been writing all morning, from about three, in fact. I needed to stretch my legs. I stopped for a chocolate. It was one of those bright autumn days so I popped for the extra cost to drink it at a table rather than at the dark stand-up bar, as usual. God, the light that day was crystalline. Cool enough to see your breath after a sip of hot chocolate. The light that day! The river sparkled. You could see where the Impressionists got their light values. She'd been in the museum. Had her sketchpad with her. As she walked by my table, it hit the empty chair beside me. I grabbed it before it tipped over. She smiled. And asked if she could leave her big sketchbook on the empty chair. She asked, in French. I motioned to the chair and offered to buy her a hot drink if she would like to sit for a while. I think she took pity on my accented French. She smiled and sat down. That's how we met. A sketchbook. A chocolate. It was October twenty, a Wednesday that year."

He stopped in the middle of the sidewalk, frowned for a moment then looked delighted. As people darted around him, he announced, "*Le Chat Noir*. The Black Cat. It had an image of a black cat arching its back painted on the front window. Hole-in-the-wall kind of place."

She moved to a wall next to the sidewalk and he followed her. She Googled it on her phone and showed him the screen. "Still there. Five Boulevard de Sébastopol."

He laughed. "That's not it. You know that McDonald's I went to on Rue de Rivoli, at Rue de l'Échelle?"

She nodded.

"That's where it was. A victim of time, like me."

Chapter № 14

October 18, 2017
Wednesday

When they arrived at the penthouse, she hurried toward his suite. She flung the door open. The room looked like it had been burglarized or ransacked by a police search. Clothing he had worn had just been dropped near the suitcase, which looked like a huge turquoise clamshell under the window. The bed was unmade. The down-filled duvet had been shoved onto a mound on one side of the large bed and could have hidden at least three bodies.

She glanced at his small desk. The cover of his compact Smith Corona Skyriter had been removed and was on the floor nearby along with several crumpled wrappers from granola bars. A ream of paper had been ripped open. The top curled back like a sardine can. Less than half of the pack remained in its blue wrapper.

She walked toward the typewriter cautiously. It was as if the edges of the room faded to gray and a single spotlight illuminated the typewriter. A page was still trapped against the roller and moved in the breeze as though it were an exotic bird preening a wing. She bent over the page, pulled it out of the typewriter, and gasped. She had not fully understood his explanation at the café about how sloppy his first draft was.

It was a solid block of smudgy type from an old ribbon and keys that had not been cleaned in some time. The d's and b's were filled at the lower half of the letters. The e's were almost missing the lower half of the letter. The o's had filled with ink. But that did not seem to deter Jack. The type covered the page, edge to edge without top or side margins. It was single spaced, without paragraphs. What seemed to be dialogue was not in quotation marks but started with a dash. After reading five or six lines, she found his flow and adjusted her pace to match where punctuation should have been. There were almost no typing errors. But when there was a misspelling or the wrong tense of a verb, or a stronger word choice had been discovered, the correction followed the error. She smiled as she began to understand his process and knew why her mother demanded a well-typed draft to edit.

He never went back to correct the error, he just moved forward. He kept moving, without interrupting the flow when he was writing, but occasionally left himself choices or alternatives to consider when retyping it. She looked up at him. He was fidgeting then shoved his hands into his pockets, almost holding his breath waiting for her response.

"Jack? Is this how you usually do your first draft?"

"Sorry. I sorta bypass the rules when it's cooking. This way goes faster. Don't need to stop and reload. Saves me lots of paper. I smooth it in the next time I type it, and the next, and the next. Took forever that time I had a cast. Poking away, hunt-and-peck style."

She quickly asked him, "How many drafts did you do on your last book?"

"Eight or nine before I sent it to Max. So you see there's no way…"

She nodded, rushing through his explanation to get back to her question. "And then he had it retyped or scanned and corrected on a computer so we got an electronic file to edit, right? I get it."

"Yeah. That's how I do it."

"How long did it take you to do that page?"

"I don't pay much attention to time when I'm writing."

She stared at the block of black. "There's no white space at all."

"That's what I've been telling you. I just jam it in. Fast as I can."

"That's gotta be a thousand words, at least. Maybe thirteen or fourteen hundred. Where's the rest?"

Jack started to bend over. She stopped him and picked up the stack from the floor. "Careful, I don't do page numbers since I'm the only one messing with it."

She nodded quickly. "Oldest at the bottom?"

He leaned against the desk. "Yup. That way if I get stuck, I just read my last page, and it sorta kicks in."

She added the page she had removed from the Skyriter to the stack, put it to the right of the typewriter, and held her hand on it until Jack closed the window. "How long did it take you to type all that?"

"Been at it every night since I met Greg, so that's almost three weeks. Filled in earlier stuff in those comp books."

"And I never heard you, after that one night?"

"They soundproofed the suites. Remember that Goth girl saying how he was a fussy sleeper? Needed quiet?"

"No. I didn't. Besides, I heard your shower running."

"I left the doors open so the bathroom didn't steam up. It's creepy quiet, that's why I open the window sometimes, so I know there's something alive out there. I guess I forgot to close it when we left for the hospital a couple of days ago. Anyway, I wrote in my comp books so I wouldn't wake you up. Then I thought, *What the hell, if I wake her up she'd let me know.* But you never did."

"Never heard you after that once."

"Good. But I also used my comp books for notes when I had to leave my door open, when it would have been weird to shut it."

"Okay. Where are they?"

He opened the side drawer of the desk and pulled out two composition books. "I dated the entries so I could figure out where to put them if I got to a second draft of the typed stuff."

She looked at the stack again. The typed pages beside the typewriter now were stacked with precision. She started counting them. She was quiet as she finished her count. "Fifty-three! Not counting your notebooks."

"See, it's really jammed together and messy."

"Okay. I get it. Jack?" She held up one page. "I bet this converts to at least four pages if it's pretty solid narrative, or five or six if it's a long run of dialogue."

"Maybe, but I don't know how long I'll have even if you get the format right." He pointed to his head and forced a smile.

She grinned at him. "I can get a rough draft into your hands tomorrow, day after at the most. You *will* have time to edit with me."

He laughed. "There's no way in hell that..." He started to leave the room.

She took his arm. "Like I told you at the café, I have a dictation program on my computer. I can edit for format and grammar as I go. Can your typewriter do that?"

He made a face at her and patted his typewriter. "Can your Apple thing run without a battery or being plugged in?"

"About as good as your cell phone. You'd better plug it in tonight. The battery was almost shot when I called her."

He picked up his phone and started out of the room. "Touché."

"Let me cancel with Greg before he leaves the office and then look over what's here."

She went to her room, shed her coat, left it on the bed, and called Greg. He answered and she blurted, "I gotta cancel tonight!"

"You okay?"

"Yeah. He's written something that... Greg! My God! He's got a huge pile of papers he's been typing all along. I think it might be about a two or three hundred–page manuscript. But it's a mess and I need to start transcribing tonight, and he's got notebooks too." She dug his notebook out of her bag and dropped it on the bed.

"Slow down. I can barely understand you."

She sucked in air but didn't slow a bit. "Greg! I was terrified when he showed me his room. I felt like Shelley Duvall in *The Shining*. You know where she finds that typewriter with a typed page still in it and his manuscript in an open box beside it? And it's all the same line over and over?"

"Yeah. What was it? That 'quick brown fox' typing class thing?"

"No. 'All work and no play makes Jack a dull boy.' How about that for irony? I was afraid he'd gone all Jack Nicholson by typing the same thing over and over. But he didn't."

"What..."

"He's written his journey back from darkness. Now if I can get it into manuscript form, even one that needs a lot more editing, we might be able to save his career."

"Fantastic! Get to it! Bye."

She clicked off and shoved the phone into the pocket of her pants.

Jack stood in the doorway laughing. "Oh, I heard that. The crazy guy used an Adler Universal 39, way too heavy to travel with. But I liked how its carriage return looked like the head of a golf club." He laughed. "Had one once, monster of a machine. West German, when there was such a thing. Had this little do dah on the top that let you put the paper to the edge and pull a lever so it was ready to go in one pull. Not like rolling it in on my little guy. Silly instructions too, called the carriage return the... the..." His voice became suddenly a falsetto. "A 'line space lever,' if you can believe it!" He took a breath and regained his composure. "But the best writing tip I ever got was off the Adler manual's cover."

He waited for her to ask and stared at her silence as she hurried back to his suite.

Finally she said, "Well?"

"It said, 'First read, then write, it pays.' Get it? They wanted you to read their manual, but I took it another way. Still, the sound of that machine in the movie echoing in that big hotel lobby..."

"Still use your Adler?"

"No. Gave it to a student. Promising young woman. See her stuff occasionally in the *New Yorker*. Some days I wonder if she still has it. Then there was another..."

"Jack! I need quiet now so I can look at your draft."

He retreated to his bed and carefully reclined on it, clasping his hands behind his head as he watched her. She turned over the stack and started at the beginning. After she had read several pages of the densely typed text, she nodded. It worked. The macho style that she had edited in his thrillers was missing. There were no twisted subplots that looped and dove around the action of the characters. Gone were the florid descriptions that were overly detailed about breast shape and size or how much cleavage was on display or how Simon's loins felt or what new gun he was using.

What was there was fresh, intimate, and brutally frank. This was a travelogue of fear, of one man's meticulous record of losing his memory and writing all he could of the challenge and loss. A journal of courage. His scream against that loss. How people are their remembrances. No, he was not going to go gently.

Then she read about the tests and sunlight that began to cut through the fog.

She fanned through several more of the unnumbered pages and returned the stack to a neat pile. "Clear enough for me to add punctuation as I dictate. I think I can get almost all of it by morning, if I can pull an all-nighter."

"I don't see how..."

"Let me take a run at it. You get some rest, so that tomorrow you can read what I'm able to transcribe."

Jack held out the speckled books and spiral binder from the Institute's gift shop. "And the comp books too?"

She grinned. "That ought to make the word count for a novella at least."

They both jumped when the lobby door buzzer shattered the moment. As she walked to the intercom, she said, "Did you order delivery when I wasn't looking?" She pressed the intercom button.

"So, what's a guy gotta do to get up there with you two?" a playful male voice asked.

"Greg?"

"Yeah. I was already on my way over..."

She buzzed the lobby door open and returned to Jack's suite. "Let me dictate your typed stuff first, but I don't think I can…"

Greg took off his coat, draped it over the smaller of the two sofas, and walked back to join them. "Can't do what?"

"I was just saying that I needed to dictate his typed stuff first then I'd try to get to the handwritten material. If I can get a good draft out of the typed material, it might just work. But the notebooks…"

Greg reached for them. "Can I see?"

She handed him the dog-eared books.

He flipped through several pages. "You going to be using that desktop computer?"

"No. Dictation software's on my laptop."

He nodded toward the office. "Then, fire it up, and I'll start on these."

"You'd type it for Jack?"

He grinned. "I came by because I wanted to be sure he was still okay. No, I wouldn't do this for Jack, but I would for you."

She blinked away tears as she walked to the office. She started the desktop computer, typed in the password, and stepped aside. Greg slid into the chair. "You using Word?"

She shook her head. "Pages, Apple's word-processing software. It goes faster with my program."

"Okay. Check my format."

"No need. Just use the default. I'll format it in Pages later."

"Cool."

She kissed the top of his head and whispered, "Thank you."

Jack looked bewildered at their computer chatter and stared at Greg. "You really gonna type it all?"

"Gonna try. Go relax. I'll ask if I can't read something. Or I'll mark it and we can fix it in the morning."

"Sure."

Jack turned toward his suite and almost lost his balance. He grabbed the door jam for a moment to get his bearings then walked to his room.

Greg motioned to her. "Hey. Take a look."

He handed her the opened book. "God, that's gorgeous. He must have just scribbled that note I saw earlier. Look at some other pages."

Greg boasted, "I got the easy job. I haven't seen handwriting like this for years. I guess he went to school when kids actually had to learn to write."

"How much is there?"

"So, sixty pages, wide rule, a margin. Three books. Bet I beat you."

She chuckled. "Bet's on. Stakes?"

"Pizza at my place. Loser brings the wine."

She grinned. "Bet's on."

"Is my banging on the keyboard going to screw up your dictation?"

She shifted her laptop to her other hand. "No. I've got a noise-cancelling mic on the headset. But I'll work in the kitchen. There's a power plug there and good lighting."

She set up her portable Mac and let the programs load while she got the stacked pages from Jack's room. He was at the typewriter rolling in a fresh page. "Eileen? I don't know how this ends."

She patted his shoulder. "We'll just tell Max to hold a place for an 'Afterword' in the draft. How's that? Get some rest."

She took the stack to the kitchen, put it in front of her, and pushed the laptop back slightly, so that where a keyboard normally would have been, the stack now sat. She glanced around the kitchen then returned to the office. Greg looked up from typing. "Don't interrupt me. I've got a pizza riding on this."

"Seriously? I need a ruler to keep my place, it's such a blur."

They searched the desk drawers and found one. He stood and kissed her.

She slid the kitchen chair closer to the table, balanced the ruler on the top page, put on a Bluetooth headset, and opened a new document she called "Jack." She cleared her throat and began reading his pages.

He had documented everything said to or about him by Eileen or

Greg as his guides in this investigation of why he was changing. He characterized Greg and the other doctors as his medical detectives and searchers of truth. Heroic in their quest. Moral and empathetic in their dealings with him. Hopeful when he had lost hope.

After a few pages, she moved the stack aside and had only one page on the table in front of her at a time. That way the ruler moved easier, and she was able to hold her place in the text. She numbered each page with a pencil as she finished it.

It was all there: the process, the dialogue in detail, albeit without any hint of punctuation. On the right margin at the bottom, several words lost letters when the paper had been inserted into the platen at an angle. She stalled trying to decide what the word was, then made a guess, put an asterisk beside it to ask about it later, and moved on.

His typed version began with that first dinner with Greg. His report of their meeting had captured most of those events with the innocent perspective that he had that night. He assumed that Greg was Eileen's friend with enough pull to get their table. The style was simple, less complex than his plainspoken daily speech. Short sentences. Some repetition. Basic.

After an hour, her voice started to get scratchy. Greg noticed, left his work in the office, and made her a cup of tea with honey. Without breaking her pace, she nodded appreciation, and took a sip.

From that first night his typed pages recounted their time in Paris from his view. She started crying once she realized that the entries before the tap were flat, juvenile, lacking perspective, and only recounting the most basic of facts.

At nine, she took a break and went to the living room to do some stretches. Greg left the office and leaned against the wall beside the fireplace. "You owe me. What wine…"

"Finished?"

"About an hour ago. Big lines. Easy reading."

"Why didn't…"

"Didn't want to break your flow. Can I make something for you to eat?"

"Not pizza! How about an egg, scrambled? I gotta get a shower and wake up."

"I'll check in with Jack and see if he's hungry, okay?"

"Actually, why don't you guys go out for a bite and bring me back a sandwich or something? I really don't want to stop."

"Sure."

By the time she showered and changed into jeans and her *Hamilton* sweatshirt, they had gone. She drank a glass of water and took a spoonful of honey before resuming. As she dictated, she found Jack's style changing after his evaluation by Greg. She heard it in her own voice. A new level of writing had emerged. His style became more complex. The sentences were compound. His attitude was reflective and insightful. The asides were moving and philosophical. Another shift in his style toward more complexity occurred the day after the spinal tap. He wrote of the procedure with clinical accuracy while adding an emotive and nuanced reflection on the meaning of the test and of memory. He became both philosophical and hopeful.

When they returned just after ten, Greg carried a container of soup and a square box. She glanced at them as she finished dictating a few more words. Before greeting them, she tapped a few keys on her computer and took off her headset. She stood and ran her fingers through her hair. "Have a good dinner?"

Jack smiled at her. "How's it going?"

"Good. Just finished leaving the hospital after the spinal tap."

He pointed to his room. "I'll be in there if anyone needs me."

Greg lifted the containers. "A whole quiche Lorraine and onion soup, both of which are still hot."

"Great."

"Onion soup or quiche?"

"Both. Can you put the soup in a mug?"

By the time she had returned from the bathroom, a steaming mug of soup and a wedge of quiche were at a place set on the high counter, well away from her computer.

She took a sip and sighed. "Perfect!"

"I had them leave off the cheesy crouton."

"Good call." She cut a bite of quiche and balanced it on a fork as she asked, "How was yours?"

"Easier than I thought. He dated every entry so it should be pretty easy to merge the two. Yours dated?"

She nodded and took a long draw on the soup. "Same here. Like a journal, but really insightful, you can see his recovery in the way he is writing, it's like a display of a writer's early work in a lifetime collection. I can see he is maturing intellectually. That style change is something I have never ever seen in a book."

"Jack told me how afraid he is of slipping back."

She nodded as she took another bite of the quiche. "Did he tell you I called his wife about insurance?"

"No. What..."

"Haven't heard back yet, but I left a message on her home phone. He wouldn't let me interrupt her at work."

"Really?"

"I'm guessing that there is some complicated stuff there." She picked up the edge crust of the quiche and nibbled it.

"Can I dictate for a while? Give you a break?"

"Thanks, but it'd take longer to initialize your profile than we'd save, besides I'm doing the punctuation as well."

He faked indignation and puffed up his chest. "And I wouldn't know punctuation?"

"Wouldn't know my macros that speed it up." She winked at him. "I'm sure you're a fine punctuator." She drained the mug and used her fork to capture the few strands of onion that stuck to the side of the mug.

"How far..."

"I'm almost halfway through his stack." She glanced at her iPhone. "Started about six, almost midnight now." She nodded. "I figured about eleven hours."

"How'd you get that?"

"The average audio book is eleven hours of listening time for a hundred thousand–word book. So I figured, I dictate faster than they narrate, and his total was less than the usual... so by sunrise..."

"What can I do?"

"Give me the stuff you typed. Call the file 'Jack 2.'"

"Okay!"

"If you can't find a thumb drive in the office, e-mail it so I can add that material when I finish this." She stood, stretched, and motioned to the quiche. "May as well leave it out so I can nibble when I take breaks."

"Okay. I'll put the soup in the fridge."

As she started for the bathroom she called back, "Containers are under the stove."

When she returned, he kissed her. "Don't push yourself too hard."

"How about just hard enough?"

"What if this took two days to do, and you called it a night?"

"Jack might not have two days left to read it and comment. Didn't you ever cram for an exam in college?"

"Actually..."

"Of course not. Well, I did and I know I can jam through this. I'll set my phone and take a break every hour for food and potty, is that okay, Mister Worry-Wart?"

He grinned and pointed to the sofa. "Sure. I'll be there when you finish."

She motioned toward her suite. "Bed's more comfortable."

He winked at her. "I know, but I'll be here."

She took a couple bites off of the quiche that was in the box and chugged a glass of water. As promised, she set her phone's alarm to vibrate in an hour and slipped it into her rear pocket before settling back into her dictation. In what seemed like minutes, the phone vibrated. She slapped it with annoyance and pulled it out of her pocket. She left her headset on, grabbed a few more bites of quiche, did a couple of stretches, and resumed dictating.

She glanced into the living room and saw that Greg was asleep on the longer sofa. She relaxed her shoulders and smiled. Then she felt that the room had a chill that she hadn't noticed while she was working. She paused her dictation program, pulled the afghan from the back of the smaller sofa, and covered him.

She finished dictating the typed pages, did her usual final save of the file to her computer, then saved it in the iCloud and to her Dropbox account as well. She stood, stretched, and then noticed that the sunrise had turned the kitchen a honeyed hue. She filled the electric kettle, went to her bathroom and splashed water on her face and neck, used the toilet, and made it back to the kitchen before the water boiled. She poured the hot water over a teabag in her cup and started to sit at her computer again. She stopped herself, went to the office, and opened the first composition book intending to check the dates. When Greg woke, they would figure out where to enter his typed material. But there was no need to wake him or Jack yet. This was her time.

She sat in the office and opened the first composition book. His penmanship was clear but slightly shaky. It began with an account of Max demanding the unwritten manuscript, Jack's impulsive counter-demand to go to Paris to fill in the blanks and add color to the book. Pages later, he recounted meeting her at the airport, and detailed his disappointment at not meeting Isabel, but a trip to Paris was still a trip to Paris. She chuckled at his candor.

The next entries were dated at the top of a page. She followed his perspective on meeting Greg at the touristy restaurant and how he seemed like a nice man. A considerate and interesting one. She smiled and noted that it almost duplicated his typed version, so she would need to edit for redundancy before just sliding Greg's file in by dates. The next page was after the disclosure that Greg was a doctor. It showed his anger at being scrutinized over dinner and his embarrassment at being clumsy, of missing parts of the conversation, of being duped by sparkling water that he took for Champagne. The ink and words radiated anger and fear.

The notebook had fragments of days that were either incomplete or missing from the typed pages. All were dated so she saw the progression from hopeless to hopeful. From simple language to complex. She knew most of the next observations as she was with him for his medical appointments. The last entry in this book was of making the appointment for the spinal tap. It disclosed his fear that the spinal tap would paralyze him, leaving him in a wheelchair, impotent and unloved. Stunned, she closed the book and decided to get her tea before opening the second book.

In the kitchen, she added honey to the Earl Grey that had become too strong in the cup. She left the teabag on a saucer and took the tall mug to the office. After a sip and a stretch, she tucked one leg under her and opened the second notebook. It started in a style that was objective, an essay on modern science extending life when the quality of life may not merit an extension. Thoughtful. Reflective.

The next pages continued with the same journalistic account. The last entry in that notebook was not dated, but just had a title of "bridge." She shivered as she realized it was his thoughts on the morning that she saw him walk in the dawn light along the river, turn to cross the Pont Neuf, stop just before the park, and stare at the two young people kissing by the statue. That's when she ran downstairs to catch him, to see if he was wandering lost to McDonald's again.

Eileen sighed and remembered how she had been irritated at him, cranky at having to race down the stairs into the cold morning without her coat. Embarrassed to be out with her hair uncombed. Shivering in her jeans, without socks or a jacket. Panicked that he might wander away since his cell phone was still on the kitchen table and she wouldn't be able to contact him. But this was not her account. He knew nothing of her concerns. He was a man losing what made him his own person. Losing his memory of love and loving.

She paused to reflect what it must have felt like inside his mind, slipping and seeing brief moments of clarity before it went gauzy again. Not trusting his recall or his judgment. She opened the book and started reading again where her finger had held the line. He wrote that the lovers at the statue were only moments away from when he and Marie were those lovers, and how his life had unraveled. How he had lost love and now was losing his reasoning. Death was as simple as living, and possibly easier.

He wrote that life and death were not so very far apart as he stood on the bridge deciding whether or not to just lean forward a bit, tip over the rail, and drop into the fast-moving current below. With a shudder, she thought of her father and how the sea had given him the release he sought. She shook her head and struggled to focus on the fact that this was Jack's musing on which of his insurance policies would be the better to use. A death policy would mean an early retirement for his wife and never having to worry about money again. But then, his long-term care policy would cover him in a facility where he might not know if he had been fed or not or if she had visited him. He wondered if she would really believe he just fell into the river. He glanced at the lovers, knowing he could never again be that man in Paris with the intensity of the love he had discovered and still had for her. He took a breath and let the stone of the railing grind into his palms as he shifted his weight forward, lifted himself, balanced on his palms. His boots slowly left the walkway. His toes were scuffing against the side of the wall when suddenly she was beside him and he felt her hand. He shifted his weight back to the walkway.

His observation suggested that she hadn't noticed the small change, his decision to live. He wondered if she had believed his lie when he said that he was just looking at a passing barge. But in that small moment, she had saved his life just as she and Greg were working to save the life of his mind.

She closed the book, rose quickly, shut the office door, sat at the desk, and sobbed. Greg opened the door and held her. "You read it?"

"I had no idea. I thought he was just wandering off. Leaning over the rail. He could have..."

"But he didn't. You were there. No one knew. No clue in any of his tests or interviews."

She was barely understandable, muttering into his shoulder. "But. But. It was so close."

He held her tighter and stoked her hair. "It's better now."

Eileen jumped when Jack's cell phone rang. The caller ID said "HOME." She pointed to the phone as she pulled a tissue from her pocket. "Can you get it? It's his wife. I called...insurance."

Greg answered it. "This is Doctor Patel."

Eileen reached for the phone.

"No. He's not in a hospital. Let me put you on speaker and have Eileen, his editor who called you, explain why she phoned, then we can talk."

Over the next few minutes they let her know that he needed a corrective surgery and had to decide whether to get it in France or return to the United States. The surgery was essential but costly. She reported that she found his Medicare card where he had left it and that he was also still covered under her health insurance policy. She asked to speak to Jack. Eileen said he was asleep, but that she would relay her request.

After the call ended, Greg looked at Eileen. "Well, that was some good news about the insurance."

"She sounded concerned and supportive; maybe there's still a chance for them."

"Maybe. Sounded like she just got the message. She cared enough to call here in the middle of the night there. Grab a shower. I'll make some coffee, then we can merge the files."

She nodded. "There's some overlap. It's not just a clean insert."

"Want me to print mine so we can compare them?"

She nodded and left. After showering, she returned to the kitchen, which now smelled of fresh coffee. Jack was at the tall counter with his hands wrapped around a steaming mug. He was leaning forward listening to Greg, who was across from him. Jack's cell phone was on the counter between them.

Greg pointed to Eileen's computer and then to Jack's stack of typed pages. "Eileen said it's over seventy thousand words, and that's before she loads in the notebook stuff I typed into the other computer."

Eileen came to the counter and put her hands on Greg's shoulders. She smiled at Jack. "You're officially a novella, if you were in the fiction aisle. My draft is just over two hundred pages now. Shorter then your usual work, but nonfiction is more forgiving on length. Your fans might expect you to push out several hundred pages of daring-do and complex plots, but this is different. And it's important."

Jack shook his head and gave her a goofy grin. "You edited it all in one night?"

"I wish. It's only a rough first draft at this point, but close enough to submit just to meet your contract requirement."

"I can't believe..."

"It'll take another close read to edit and smoothing over, and you'll need to clarify a few words I couldn't make out, but at least we can hit the deadline. It still needs an ending, and I need to merge in your notebook stuff. But we're gonna make it." She looked at the cell phone on the counter as Greg poured a cup of coffee for her.

Jack smiled and looked at Greg. "He told me. I called her."

Eileen smiled back at him. "And?"

Jack grimaced and said, "It's complicated." Then he turned to Greg. "Can you tap me again? Do another lumbar drain? I need some more days of clarity to finish my book and then fly home for the surgery in New York."

Greg sat and ran his hand over the dark stubble on his chin. "We used the lumbar drain as a test. It's not risk free."

"Couldn't your Institute give me another one?"

"I don't see that as a medical necessity. I won't recommend it."

"Who would?"

"I'm not going to doctor shop for you. The surgery in New York can be set up soon, and I don't want you subjected to any risk of infection or other complication that might delay your return or put a successful outcome there at risk. What you need to do now is limit alcohol, get exercise, and eat well to get ready for the surgery."

"But..."

"I can't. Call your wife again. Get a doc there and a schedule the appointment now."

Jack clenched his fists. "I'm not her problem!"

"I can make some calls for you."

He glared at Greg. "You'd do that but you won't give me a few more days of..."

"That's the best I can do."

"As my doc?"

"As your friend." He finished the last of his coffee and went to the office to review the printed version of the material from the notebooks.

Eileen joined him and closed the door. "He really wanted..."

"I don't care what he wanted if it would compromise his already delicate situation."

"Delicate?"

"He's had both a tap and a drain. Any puncture is a site for infection or leakage. I don't know how fast the pressure is going to return or if it is going to be enough to increase his risk of stroke or other issues, but I do know we can finish this up and try to help get him scheduled in New York." He handed her his pages with a few pencil lines striking out phrases. "I crossed out the meandering and duplicative material from the notebooks. Now you need to see what repeats the stuff you've already entered."

"Okay." She kissed him and rubbed the stubble on his chin. "Cute. I like it. Reminds me of the better parts of our vacation when you didn't shave for days."

He grinned. "Get to work, woman! I gotta clean up and get to the Institute. See you tonight."

She shrugged and made a face. "This is going to need a lot more work. I'm sorry."

"No. You misunderstood. I'll bring over dinner and hang just long enough to see if I can help. You can eat while you're editing. I'll take care of Jack. He knows he's slipping again and is getting frustrated."

She hugged him. "Lifesaver!" She walked him to the door. They kissed.

When she turned, Jack was grinning at her. "He's a good man."

"Yes, he is." She nodded toward the kitchen table. "You want to work there or in the office?"

He marched into the office. Once they were seated across from each other, Jack said, "Shoot. What do you need?"

"I need some decisions on style so I know how to smooth your draft. Your language was pretty simplistic and angry when you were fading, then your word choice and sentences got more complex and sophisticated after the tap. How do you want me to present that? Want to keep the different tones or smooth it to a uniform narrative?"

"Can't you do both? Keep my choppy stuff inside quotes and be all grown-up and consistent in the narration?"

"Good idea." She hesitated. "About your family? I think the book might benefit from a little more on how the separation impacted you. How it contributed to your isolation."

"Nope. Marie's got enough on her plate without getting her into the spotlight."

Eileen persisted. "But if your readers knew..."

He folded his arms over his chest. "Sorry. She's out of bounds. No."

She shrugged. "Okay then." She picked up the first of the composition books. "Greg typed all the handwritten material."

"Want me to read it on the computer?"

"No. Let me print you a copy. Just read the stuff that is lightly shaded that I think is repetitive. I'll show you."

"Okay. Let's do it."

"If there is anything there that is critical, just tell me, and I'll be sure it is included."

The next week was committed to editing, to getting the book's pace and tone right while keeping Jack's style, to finding the words in the narration that he would have used if he had been able to discover them in his fog. She smoothed his account of the steps into oblivion and back while retaining his limited and often contradictory voice within his quotations. She sequestered herself in the windowless office and emerged only for necessities and to hand Jack printed pages to review and edit while he was still able.

It was early Friday afternoon, October 27, when she finished smoothing the last of the transitions between his typed pages and the notebooks and entered the last of his edits. She let out a whoop to match her fist pump.

Jack hurried into the office. "Is it?"

"It is! All I need to do now is break it up into four files so I'll be sure it sends as an attachment and not be too big. So I need to concentrate and do it right the first time."

"Want me to be quiet or leave?"

"Leave! Go get a bottle of Champagne. A good one. I'm going to pop it when you tell Max to open his e-mail."

She laughed as she hit the send arrow on the last of the four messages with a file attachment. She was still laughing as she danced into the kitchen and hugged Jack. "We made it!" She looked at her phone's world clock. "It's about eight there. Friday morning."

"Yeah, he'll be in the office. Probably pacing, swigging Pepto, and wondering if we..."

Jack had put the glasses on the counter. She glanced around. "Where's the bubbles?"

"In the freezer for a little more chill."

She tapped Max's number and handed the phone to Jack. She pulled the bottle out of the freezer, ripped off the foil, twisted the wire, and found that her hands were shaking. She released the wire cage, held her palm over the cork until Jack told Max to look in his in-box, and then held the phone next to the cork as she let it pop. After pouring their glasses, she waited for Jack to finish talking to Max and hand her the phone.

Max was breathless. "Did it. My God! You really did it. Number twenty one!"

She asked, "You okay? You sound..."

"Yeah, just can't really believe it. I don't know why Jack wants to give me ulcers."

"I think you are going to find it really terrific. Not just the place-holder I thought it might be. It's heart and soul true. Not perfect, just ready for more editing. And the ending, since there isn't really one yet, Jack wants to hold as an 'Afterword' or maybe 'Epilogue' might be better. You'll see that as a placeholder."

"What'd you mean there's not an ending? Not a peep from you, then this? How can he have a thriller spy novel without an ending?"

"You'll see. It's not his usual work. Trust me! It's a great read."

"I'm printing it now. Talk soon."

They collapsed into chairs at the kitchen table. She poured two glasses of champagne. They tapped their glasses together. Jack put down his glass and pushed it away. He looked at her. "We need a real celebration. On Max!"

She smiled. "A dinner out at..." The buzzer from the outer door broke her thought. She tapped the screen to activate the security camera, saw Greg making a face at her, and buzzed him into the lobby.

Jack was serious. "No. I changed my mind. A small party here, on me, for everyone who has helped me through this madness. I mean everyone! Receptionists to my neurosurgeon, Doctor Le Blanc, Greg, obviously. The kid who walked me through the MRI process. The bloodsucker. The doc who tapped me. All of 'em and their dates."

"What are you thinking? Wine and finger-food?"

"Hell no! A full-blown Halloween party on the thirty-first. We're not leaving until the next day. Remember how Max found the cheap flight back?"

Greg joined them. Jack handed him his untouched glass of Champagne. "Celebrating? You finished?"

Eileen hugged him and smiled. "Sure did! I thought you had to go to work."

He took a sip. "I did. Then I decided to call in and burn some vacation hours. What was he yelling about?"

"Max is reading it now. Jack wants to throw a Halloween party for the people here."

Greg laughed. "*Un allo-een' party?* That's just as popular here as Thanksgiving. It is *no in zee French culture.*"

She shook her head at his mangled accent. "They've adopted it now. Everyone here loves a dress-up costume party with masks."

Greg smiled. "Corn candy! I haven't had it for, what? Three years?"

She shook her head. "Candy corn?"

"Yeah, that's it."

"Okay. I'm in. Let's make a list and see what's here and what I have time to order from Amazon or have mom send."

Greg held up his hand. "Actually Tuesday the thirty-first is not going to work. There's a huge training session Monday and Tuesday in Geneva for about half the people he met."

Jack shrugged. "So we have it over the weekend. How about Sunday? That should let us get an invite out to those who helped me here. Can you phone them, Greg?"

"Sure, tell me who you want, and I'll text them. I've got all their contacts. What time?"

"Sunday here, six to whenever, wine and pizza on me. Tell them they can bring a date, guest, whatever.

Chapter № 15

October 28, 2017
Saturday

Eileen slept until noon on Saturday. Once up, caffeinated, fed, and showered, she dressed and pulled on her coat and slung her messenger bag over her shoulder. Just as she was about to leave, she turned and rapped lightly on Jack's door.

"Come on in."

Eileen opened the door slowly and saw that he was dressed, lying on top of the duvet, and propped up on several pillows. His last book was on his lap. She smiled. "Just checking to see if you need anything before I leave."

"Nope. I'm fine. Made myself a sandwich and plan on reading today. Trying to get that new plot in mind."

She smiled knowing that he was eating better and had put on enough weight that he no longer had gauntness to him. "Anything I can get you while I'm out?"

"Where you going?"

"Caterer for meat-and-cheese platters for the party and Monoprix for some costume stuff if I get lucky. Then Galleries Lafayette."

"Nope. I'm good. Think I'll just take it easy today. Party tomorrow ought to be something."

She lingered and tried to evaluate his mood and awareness. He laughed. "Stop it! I know what you're doing." He paused, then continued. "I'm really okay. Go do your thing. And, no. I don't need you here overnight if you and Greg..."

"Got your phone handy?"

He pulled it off the bedside table and waved it over his head. "Charged and everything."

"Okay. Enjoy the book. I hear it was a great one."

As she turned, he called, "May as well leave the door open."

After checking the refrigerator to insure that there still were easy meals for Jack, she left. Walking several blocks to Monoprix, Eileen was grateful for the lining in her trench coat and warmth of her good wool slacks as the temperature had dropped. In spite of the bright sun, the air was brisk. The store was crowded and her progress through the aisles was slow. Once at the housewares area, she found a replacement for the French press coffee maker that she had broken only a few weeks earlier. She wandered the aisles of the store clutching the box of her new glass press until inspiration struck. Laundry bags and hampers in a variety of colors captured her attention. The tall round one in a bright yellow was perfect: two feet around, waist high and made of light cotton on a plastic frame. She grabbed one that was collapsed in a sturdy plastic wrap and went to the school supplies area where she located a green fabric marking pen and some black and orange construction paper. In the aisle with travel-sized cosmetics, she found a small sewing kit.

While waiting in line to pay, she checked her phone for the time. Almost four. She then stopped at the McDonald's where Jack had gone. At the counter she asked to speak with the manager. Stepping aside, she waited a moment before a young man approached her. Their exchange was rapid in French.

"Yes? How can I help you?"

"I need to speak to the other manager. She's a slim young woman. Olivia, I believe is her name. Could you tell me when she arrives?"

"She is here now, but not on duty yet. Can I say who you are?"

"She won't know my name. Just say she called me when that man was...lost here."

"Good. Yes, she told me of it. If you wish to be seated I will advise her of your request."

In a few moments, Olivia arrived, and sat across from Eileen. "You wished to speak to me?"

"Yes. First, I wanted to thank you for your kindness to my friend. Second, I wanted you to know that he is much better now and is having a party tomorrow. A silly American costume party for what we call Halloween. It's the night before your *la Toussaint*; what we call All Saints' Day, but it will be this Sunday evening at six. If you care to come and bring your boyfriend or husband or partner..."

"Costume? What type of costume?"

"Jack has this idea of having it be like your occupation, but anything is fine." Eileen pulled out a small spiral notebook from her purse and wrote as she spoke. "Here is the address and my mobile number if you need to call. Any time after six in the evening for pizza, snacks, and wine. He would be delighted if you could come so he could see you and thank you again before he goes home."

"Thank you. I will see if it is possible."

Eileen gathered her messenger bag and parcels from Monoprix and was almost to the door when her iPhone buzzed. She answered it just outside the doorway when she saw it was Greg.

"Meet me for dinner."

"I'd love to...but I've got a couple more errands to run today."

"What? Maybe I can help."

She stepped away from the busy McDonald's door. "I need to get a scarf for mom. A good one from Galleries Lafayette."

He raised his voice. "There? It's..."

"I know, it's not Monoprix. But this is a special gift."

"What time do you want to meet?"

"How about six?"

"Can you make it four-thirty?"

"Sure. Where?"

"How about we meet at the tasting bar. First floor. Blue tiles—"

"Tasting?"

"Petrossian caviar or salmon if you prefer with your Champagne."

She laughed. "Great way to start shopping."

"So we get the scarf then, and if the weather stays good, we can get a bite at La Terrasse."

"On the rooftop?"

"Right. Watching dusk fall over the city is crazy beautiful. The late sun makes Sacré-Cœur and the Eiffel Tower just glow."

"At four-thirty then. Bye."

She arrived a few minutes early and barely managed to stow her purchases in her large messenger bag before she went into the main building. As usual she was overwhelmed by the opulence. It always seemed to her that the stained glass dome and arched galleries over-looking the massive atrium resembled the opera. It was as much a treat for her nose as her eyes. On her way toward the caviar bar, she passed the cosmetics section. Booth after booth offered custom blends and practiced artists to demonstrate high-end cosmetics. Scents from the different perfumes and cosmetics on display mingled and competed as she hurried past the perfumes and wondered if Jack would miss these explosions of aroma.

Passing through the foods area, she saw gems of chocolates and delicate pastries all promising to be the perfect end to a dinner party. She slowed as she walked past a case with numerous types of bread, an-other with a dozen varieties of smoked salmon, and a charming display of American imports, which included jars of French's Mustard, Heinz catsup, and relish from Wickles Pickles seeming to tumble out of a large picnic basket. She chuckled to herself at the idea of things so familiar being considered exotic.

She spotted the caviar bar and walked toward it, slowly evaluating each of the remarkable foods offered. He spotted her, not for being an American, as she moved as easily as a local through the crowd, but her hair. No one had her auburn curls with those natural copper highlights. She turned. He smiled. No one had her freckles, her intelligence, or her passion. The black trench coat and black knee-high boots looked very stylish, possibly French, but she was clearly her own person, an American. He grinned when she turned and smiled at him, with the smile she had in bed.

She waited for him just outside the seating area at the caviar bar. He took the messenger bag from her. She gently grasped the lapels of his long black leather coat and kissed him quickly on the lips. "Glad you called."

"Me too."

"Let's get the shopping over with then go to the rooftop."

"Sounds good."

On their way to the escalator, Eileen glanced at the extraordinary selection of timepieces as they passed the displays of Rolex, Tag Heuer, Cartier, Patek Philippe, Piaget, and others. He hurried to keep up with her and dodged two women who were chatting as they meandered in the center of the aisle. Once on the floor that featured women's fashions, she wove her way quickly past the incredible displays of designer clothing and made for the accessory counter. A tall rack of floral and patterned scarves stood seven feet high and displayed more than a hundred scarves that ranged from short ones that barely would hide under a lapel to long ones that would wrap three or four times around a neck and still provide a generous cascade of flowing fabric. These were not for warmth or protection against the cold of the coming winter. These were pure adornment and finery in both material and execution.

She stopped and glanced over the fountain of fabric. He whispered, "Holy shit. I never imagined there could be so many..."

She looked at the display case. On the glass a meticulous arrangement of nearly fifty scarves formed a perfect rainbow of colors, from the purest white through the spectrum to a shimmering black scarf. Some had small discrete patterns while others were pure radiant colors of fine silk. All were folded to precisely the same square and lined up against their neighbors to make an uninterrupted flow of color.

Before the tall sales associate could approach, Eileen had found the perfect scarf. It was a rich rust with dots of amber. Not wanting to disturb the intricate display, she pointed to a folded square of silk and asked to see it. Nodding, the woman turned and extracted one from a drawer behind her. She presented it in a manner suggesting that it was the only one like it in the universe. She held it on her outstretched palms then let it unfold and tumble open. The slightest draft of a passing customer made it ripple and shimmer.

Greg grinned. "Wow. That's so delicate."

Eileen unconsciously wiped her hands on the sides of her coat before taking the scarf. "The colors are perfect for her." She turned to the sales associate and asked the price. Eileen inhaled quickly, smiled, and nodded, then requested a box for the gift, but declined to have it wrapped, thinking about going through customs in a few days. While she paid for it, Greg wandered back to the towering display and found a long scarf that precisely echoed the copper highlights in Eileen's hair, glanced at the price, shrugged, and carried it to Eileen. "What do you think of this one?"

"Beautiful, but *très chère.*"

The sales associate nodded to him. "The perfect color for her."

He grinned as he handed the woman his credit card. "I thought so too."

He draped the scarf over her shoulder and looked into her eyes. "*Belle.*"

Eileen picked up the end and looked at the fabric. "It is."

"Not it, you." He gently put it around her neck, held the ends, and slowly pulled her toward him. They kissed. "Thank you, Greg. I love it." She smiled as he took Isabel's boxed scarf and carefully slid it into the messenger bag. After Greg was presented with his receipt, he took Eileen's arm and they went to the rooftop terrace restaurant.

After having a glass of Sancerre and sharing a leek quiche in the heated domed restaurant of the terrace, they walked around the rooftop watching the tourists point out all the familiar landmarks. Although it was getting brisk, they lingered until six to watch the special illumination on the Eiffel Tower. Greg put his arm around her when the golden lights on the tower were overwhelmed by an added 20,000 lights that started their pulsing dance. "On the hour until one. Corny, but I like it."

"Me too, but it is just a bit busy."

He kissed her neck when the light show ended five minutes later. "Think Jack can manage without you tonight?"

She smiled at him and nodded. "Yes. But I'd better call to be sure."

He pushed aside her scarf and nibbled the back of her neck as she called Jack's cell phone. She pressed her back against him and smiled when Jack answered promptly. After Jack assured her that he was okay and able to make a sandwich for himself, she said she would see him tomorrow.

"He's fine."

"Good. Hey, you never told me what your mother said when you told her about finishing Jack's book."

Eileen looked stricken. "I didn't. I told her I was going to be buried in work. I ought to…"

He laughed. "Call her now."

She turned and made a very short call. Afterward, she gave him a hug. "She's thrilled!"

He looked at her half smile. "And? There's something else. What?"

"She's hired an assistant! A temp."

Eileen was silent as they left the terrace and used the elevator. Once out on the sidewalk in front of the huge store, Greg waited for her to say something about her mother's assistant. When she didn't, he pointed down Boulevard Haussmann. "You know Proust lived at one-oh-two during the First World War?"

"I think I might have read that somewhere."

"Want to walk by it?"

She gave him a shy smile. "No. I have a better destination in mind."

He had his arm around her waist during the walk to his apartment. Once there, they kissed slowly and deeply before taking their time in undressing each other. He was stiff immediately and laughed out loud as he opened the drawer of the bedside table and thought of baseball scores.

"What's funny?"

"Nothing. Just happy." He kissed her and took his time in pleasuring her. They mapped the geography of their desires and delighted in their discoveries.

Close to midnight, he kissed her awake before he grabbed a robe and disappeared. She heard the clatter of a glass against the tile of the kitchen countertop and the sound of the refrigerator door slamming. Greg shouted, "Close your eyes!"

He arrived with a glass of milk in one hand and a huge Toblerone chocolate in the other. "Okay. Open 'em."

She saw the triangular cardboard container and laughed. "Now that's my Proustian dream...you and chocolate."

"Not a madeleine?"

"Never!"

"I remembered that you liked this even more than some of the other chocolates they had in Biarritz." He opened the end of the package slid out a quarter of the chocolate, and peeled the foil away. He snapped off a triangle of the morsel and fed it to her.

When she moaned, he chuckled and said, "Stay."

She nodded. "Umm. I am. Jack's okay tonight without..."

"No. Don't go back to the States."

"I have to get Jack..."

"After that. We could get a better apartment here. A real one!"

"I can't."

He leaned on an elbow and looked at her. "Why not? You travel back and forth to work here. Planes are gonna fly both ways in the future. You can visit your mom..."

She reached for her turtleneck on the floor beside the bed. "After all she's done for me, I couldn't just—"

"You're grown up, you can do..."

She pulled on her top.

"You forgot your bra."

"I didn't forget anything. It's cold."

"So? Come here."

She sat up and crossed her arms. "Why? So you can lobby—"

"Eileen, what she's done for you is raise a fiercely independent and loyal daughter...a woman who needs her own place in the world."

"I have my—"

"You're trading places with her and you don't need to." She turned away from him and sat on the edge of the bed. He continued. "You're not her mother. You are not responsible for her. We can help her, but that's a decision, not a duty. Not any more."

"But..." She slipped into her bikini panties and stood to pull on her slacks.

"Caring for her at the expense of your life is not what she raised you to do. I hear that when you talk to her. You keep waiting for something to go wrong, but it is fine. God! She just hired an assistant on her own."

"But if—"

"Life is full of iffy stuff. Just look at Jack. If something goes wrong, we'll fix it. Okay? You can care about her and for her without being in the same house. You can partner on your work and still be independent."

"But after Dad..."

He stood and leaned against the wall, his robe bunching at his shoulders. "You were a kid—"

"She never had time to find another man—"

He spoke louder. "What I was trying to say, was that you were a kid and still look at his death from a kid's perspective. He didn't just abandon you and your mom. It's never just one thing. Never. Trust me on that."

"And if I do?"

"I'm not going to abandon you."

She turned and hunted for her boots. He silently sat beside her. When she found them she held them, sat back on the bed, and looked at him. Her cheeks were wet. He reached for her hand. "What if, in your father, your mom had found the right guy, her one and only, the love of her life, and she felt that she didn't need anyone else? Or *want* anyone else? Maybe that was enough love for a lifetime. Had you even considered the possibility that the life she had as a single mother raising you was the life she wanted?" Eileen dropped her boots. He pulled her up, pressed her against his chest, and wrapped his arms around her.

After several deep breaths, she whispered, "No. Not really. I always felt like there was something missing. Something I had to try to fill."

He smoothed her hair. "It's not your job anymore. Never was. It sounds like she is independent and wouldn't want anything less for you. Would she?"

"Probably not."

"What scared you off—from us?"

"Being together. It was too perfect. But that wasn't real life. It was a vacation. You invited me on a whim to go on a surfing trip knowing I don't surf."

"It wasn't a whim. You said you were working on a book, one that you were writing, and wanted some quiet time to write. We'd worked together so well, like we had known each other for years. I saw a sexy, brainy, caring woman. I thought you could write while I surfed for a while, then we could have the afternoons and nights together. It was fast but it seemed so right. It scared me."

She chuckled. "You, scared?"

"I wanted to see who we were away from our work project. See you as your own person. Maybe the writer you want to be, not just the brilliant translator and editor you already are."

She snuggled deeper against him and took a long breath. He smelled of sleep and chocolate. "Why didn't you tell me?"

He whispered, "Stay here."

She pulled back to see his face. "Why? Why would you want to take a chance that I'll get scared and run away?"

"Because I love you and we can get over the little stuff."

She smiled. "What about the big stuff?"

"Like what? Growing old together?"

She laughed. He grinned. "See. We're already making progress."

"What if we change?"

"We all change. We'll become more of who we already are. I'll risk it. Besides I don't think you'd ever hurt anyone intentionally. You are the kindest... Look how you helped Jack."

"I couldn't walk out on him."

He raised his voice. "My point exactly."

She shrugged. "I needed the money."

He chuckled and gave her a quick squeeze. "I call BS on that. Jack told me that Max had other jobs lined up for you that you could have started immediately. You took this job as a favor to Max and for your mom."

She tried to find a defense. "In part..."

"But you stayed to help Jack, didn't you?"

"Maybe."

He teased her. "And?" He adopted a fake Freud accent and stroked his chin. "I 'sink dis vas some subconscious desire to zee me again.' Isn't that right?" He watched for her reaction and burst out laughing. "You look like a kid with her hand in the cookie jar."

"Of course I wanted to see you again!" She shook her head. "But I don't want to be dependent on someone who is going to leave me like—"

He pulled his head back to watch her face. "Your dad? Did you ever consider that he didn't run away from you? He quit life in a powerful way...maybe in a way that he thought was a gift of freedom to you and your mom. I don't think we can ever know why someone decides to commit suicide. You saw your mom's pain. You were scared. That's what you remember. But what you don't see is how brave your mom was in raising you alone. I see that fierceness in you, but you don't admit it." She sighed and looked away from him. He leaned in front of her. "You're smiling. What is it?"

"I just remembered something. I was maybe five. My parents took me for picnic at the shore. We were Jersey people then. They bought our place on Long Island a few months later." She snuggled against his chest. "A picnic just meant taking some sandwiches or a pizza to eat out of doors. Late summer. The weather turned after we got set up and it started sprinkling. The few people on the beach scattered so we had it all to ourselves. Then it really started raining. Mom grabbed the pizza box and put it in the back of the station wagon. I climbed into the back seat. Dad tossed in the blankets and started the car. But then she turned and held out her arms and pulled me into the front seat. She asked my dad to turn off the car and fold the backseat flat. So we ate our picnic in the rain in the car, on sandy blankets, and laughed, and had the beach just for us when it cleared. That's how they were. We had our picnic in the rain. Anyway, she saved the day."

He grinned. "Just like you are saving Jack, his career, and him. But you don't have to save her anymore. Not alone. We can deal with it together. Okay?"

She kissed him and shook her head. "You are something! In a million years…"

"What?"

"If someone would have told me I'd be in Paris with you after how we left things in Biarritz because of a bestselling author who was slipping into dementia—"

"But you caught him."

"No. You did. It was just a lucky coincidence that I translated your paper and…"

He grinned at her. "And what?"

She shrugged. "That's not true. I really don't believe in coincidences. I wanted to see you again. But I almost didn't call."

He pulled back to watch her face. "Why?"

"I'm not sure. Embarrassment and I guess I didn't want to seem like an opportunist."

"For getting Jack help?"

She shrugged. "I know it sounds silly now, but how would we have ever met again?"

"There'd have been a way. I have a conference in January in Baltimore."

"And you were—"

"Going to call you, even after your e-mail telling me to drop dead."

"That I didn't send!"

He shrugged. "Okay. I'll never mention it again if you won't."

"That's a deal."

"You think Max is going to talk the publishing company into accepting his draft?"

"If anyone can, it's Max."

"Eileen, this book could change lives. And it's not just about Jack having normal pressure hydrocephalus. Heck, that's such a small percent of the causes of dementia. But if more docs put NPH and other reversible causes of dementia into their screening protocol, we'd change more lives for the better. Letting people know that they need to get a professional opinion, not just do a Google search and self-diagnose, would do wonders." He laughed.

"What?"

"I was just remembering a post my mom sent me. One of those silly things on Facebook. It shows a librarian at a desk and the caption is 'Google will give you a hundred thousand answers, but a librarian will give you the right one.' You were the right time, right place for Jack."

"I had second thoughts about intruding. About calling you. I really did."

"*Il faut cultiver notre jardin.*"

She chuckled, then frowned. "*Candide* by Voltaire. Tend your garden."

"Right, but how big is your garden? You let him in and changed his life, maybe saved it. His book is going to change lives. That's *his* new garden."

"Where's this going?"

He looked down at her and stroked her hair again. "Eileen, it's your garden, not your mom's. I love that you are torn between caring for her and being your own person. But you don't need to be one or the other. It's a false equivalency. You need to care as much for yourself as you do others."

She huffed and frowned at him.

He shook his head and continued. "Why'd you ride across this city during rush hour on the back of my scooter when you hate scooters?"

"Because he needed me."

"I need you."

"I love you, Greg."

"Thank God! I thought you'd never say it! But at least you didn't tell me in an e-mail. How lame was that?"

She kissed him and felt him respond. "That was *the* most romantic thing ever. The bravest."

He shook his head. "No. You get the bravery award for that ride in traffic on the Vespa."

"Maybe I can learn to ride it, in the country."

He shook his head dramatically. "I'm selling it."

"Since when?"

"When I figured you wouldn't move here, and I won't need it when I'm back in the States. To be honest, I've been making calls."

"What?"

"What if I took a position at Johns Hopkins?"

"John Hopkins? In Baltimore?"

"*Johns* Hopkins! Poor guy was given his grandmother's last name as his first name. They've offered me an interview. If you won't stay in Paris, how do you feel about Baltimore?"

She kissed him and grinned as she began to untie the belt of his robe. "I love crab cakes, but why not a New York hospital or research—"

"Considered it, but Hopkins combines the best in research and clinical practice that I want. And. If." He was having difficulty concentrating as he opened the bedside drawer.

"That's the reason you'd go back? Give up your research here?"

He was on one elbow beside her. "No. You are. It's a two-hour train ride to visit you, if you still need to live with your mom for a little while longer. After we move in together, it's just two hours by train for you to visit her, or she could move closer to..." He kissed her forehead and then pulled back. "Eileen? I don't have all the answers, but if you want this as much as I do, we can make it up as we go along."

She kissed his neck, pulled him closer, and whispered. "*Au pif.*"

"What?"

She chuckled. "I thought you'd know that French slang. To improvise, at random. Here they say, 'of the nose'; we'd say 'play it by ear.'"

"Well? Wanna *au pif* with me?"

She grinned as she felt him against her and kissed him again.

Chapter № 16

October 29, 2017
Sunday

That morning, Greg woke early and made coffee, which he brought to her in bed. She laughed as he set her cup on the nightstand. He frowned. "What's funny? I thought this was a romantic gesture."

She tossed back the covers and grabbed his robe off the floor. "It is, but they never have to pee in the movies."

He shouted after her. "I know a fun breakfast place! You up for an adventure?" He scowled when he heard the shower start, knowing there would not be enough hot water for him. A few minutes later she crawled back in bed, wrapped in his robe, and picked up the cup. "I need to make some decorations. Just a couple pumpkins cut out of construction paper."

"I'm good at crafts. Then can we go for breakfast at my place?"

"Casual, I hope?"

"Very. Soul food."

"Mama Jackson's in the twelfth? I've been there. It's good."

"No. A new place in the twentieth."

"You're crazy, we don't have time for that."

"I'm only crazy about you." He grinned. "I'll shave later, let's get ready. Call Jack while I shower."

She took a gulp of his coffee, grimaced, and dressed quickly. After making ten pumpkin cutouts, they left the apartment. He pointed to a Metro sign and said, "This will be the fastest way." Soon they arrived at the glaringly white interior of the Philippe Auguste station. Once above ground, he took her arm and they walked to the small restaurant. When he opened the door, the scents of strong coffee, sweet syrup, and frying sausage swirled around her. The small room was done up as a bayou juke joint, complete with burlap on the walls, and B.B. King pounding out the blues, his Gibson wailing as he stretched its strings into a human voice.

Greg handed her a paper menu that he had grabbed off the counter. They sat at a scarred wood table. The menu was classic Alabama low country: grits, greens, and fried most anything. Brunch featured shrimp on grits, three-egg scrambles with sides of country sausage, molasses ham, or a pork chop. She decided to go for the sausage gravy and biscuits with one scrambled egg. He frowned at her. "I don't know if they can make something that small here, but I'll ask." She laughed as he got up to place their order at the counter. He turned back and called, "Orange juice or coffee. It has chicory in it."

"OJ's fine."

She smiled at the collision of French and English in the restaurant's few early morning patrons. Then she traced the carved lettering on the tabletop. Most were old-fashioned hearts with an arrow through them. Initials with a plus sign between them. A couple of peace signs flanked a "Kilroy was here" graffiti from World War II, complete with the goofy face with a big nose staring directly at the viewer with hands on either side of the face, as if looking over a wall. When he came back a couple of minutes later, she asked, "Think these are real?"

"Mean old? Doubt it. The owner asked me once to scratch something. Does it with her regulars."

"Did you?"

"No. But I could now if you want."

"What would you carve?"

"Our initials. Like a ten-year-old schoolboy with a penknife and a crush."

"Is this just a crush?"

"No. I'm past that. Even before you came back, I knew..." He paused when a lean man in denim overalls and a red-and-white checked shirt delivered their food with a broad smile. "Enjoy, now. Hear me?"

"Thanks, Jessie."

She looked at him in awe. "How often do you come here?"

"Just enough to qualify as a regular, I guess." He pushed the grits and fried eggs aside to get a better angle on cutting his pork chop.

They ate quickly. Halfway through her meal, she closed her eyes. He watched her then asked, "You okay?"

"Just trying to figure out this gravy. It's maybe the best I've ever had."

"Good sausage, but I think it's the pepper. Fine grind and lots of it."

After they ate and she was finishing her juice, he stood. "Be back in a second."

He left the table and went outside for a moment. When he returned, he handed her a folded paper. "Here's your map."

She read the heading. *Cimetière du Père-Lachaise.* "You're taking me to a cemetery?"

"*The* cemetery! Don't tell me you never visited Proust's grave here. Or Jim Morrison's. Come on!"

"Actually. No. That's creepy."

"No it's not. Come on. At least you can make your Proust pilgrimage. Besides, there are some cool monuments and sculptures in there."

"This is not a side of you I like."

"It's almost Halloween! Finish your OJ and let's boogie."

She stood. "Who says that anymore?"

"My dad. You'll love him. He's got all these old-time sayings he loves to trot out."

"How does your mother put up with you two?"

"She's a saint. We both agree."

He took her arm and they walked toward the cemetery entrance. She stalled at the gate. "Are you sure about this?"

"Absolutely. I need to thank him in person."

"He's dead, you know."

"Guess that's a good thing. Being here and all."

"Not funny."

The cemetery pathways were freshly swept. The fine gravel crackled under their feet in the still morning. He consulted his map several times before finding the correct path in the huge cemetery. After a long silence, she asked, "So, why are you thanking him?"

"He brought you to me. That simple."

She took his arm and leaned her head on his shoulder for a few steps. He stopped and looked at her. "I did get it right. Didn't you do your thesis on him?"

"It was brilliant in its time." She laughed. "The book, not my thesis. Which translation of *À la Recherche du Temps Perdu* did you read...or did you read it in French?"

"Want a confession? I've never read it."

She laughed. "What! You knew where he lived on Haussmann..."

"Wikipedia. *Britannica* online. I'm trying to impress you."

She stopped and stared at him. After a few steps he noticed and turned. She grinned at him and shook her head. He walked back and put his arm around her.

He had difficulty finding Proust's memorial. He looked at his cemetery map again and again. Finally she pointed. "Here! It's here."

"No wonder I didn't see it. It's so much lower than the surrounding tombs." She approached the modest marker, a simple, rectangle of black marble, looking like a king-size bed with a cross that was raised slightly on the flat monument. On it was a black vase with white lilies that had wilted to a coffee color. *Marcel Proust 1871–1922* in gold letters was deeply carved on the foot of the slab. Greg gave a little salute to the black marble slab. "Well, Mister Valentin Louis Georges Eugène Marcel Proust, I thank you. If you hadn't written *Swann's Way* and the rest of it, she never would have had to translate it for her thesis and if she didn't get her big-deal degree, she never would have gotten a super-agent like Max, and if Max hadn't steered her to my translation because he was known for having a super-translator in his stable of talent..." He turned and kissed her. "Since we're here, want to see Jim Morrison's or Oscar Wilde's monuments?"

"Nope. I still need to make my costume and get the place set up for the party."

"I ordered the pizzas already."

"The meat-and-cheese trays are being delivered, so that's done. So? What are you coming as?" He just grinned and put his arm around her as they walked toward the Metro station.

By three o'clock Sunday afternoon, Jack had showered, shaved, and slipped into his turtleneck and stained khakis, both of which had been washed. When he heard the front door open, followed by a clatter, he went to the living room to investigate.

Adele, who had picked them up at the airport a month earlier, dragged in her battered camera case and backpack, looking the worse for wear. Her black eyeliner had smeared and she seemed tired. Her vintage Rolling Stones T-shirt was knotted at her left hip. Her black jeans were strategically ripped at the knees. Jack couldn't decide if it was a fashion statement or if she had been in an accident, so instead of asking, he just took her camera case. "Here, let me help you, even if you can bench press—"

"Eileen told me that you had a big health scare. I'm really glad you're gonna be okay."

"She tell you I got my book in on time?"

"No. I think she was more concerned about you."

Jack looked away for a moment. "Pretty scary there for a while. Once I'm back in New York, I'm going to get an operation that's going to keep me well."

"That's great. Well, I better clean up and get into my costume."

Jack smiled. "Oh, who are you going to be?"

"Me? Just another homeless gal living off the goodwill of a patron."

"Hmmm. That's intriguing. A hint?"

"H.G."

He shrugged. "Party isn't for another couple hours, so you've got time for a glass of wine after you get ready."

"Cool. What're you going as?"

"I hadn't really thought about it."

"I know where there's a chef's coat and toque, that big hat, if you want to be a chef."

He chuckled. "Thanks, but I think I'll go as me. That's hard enough these days."

"Okay. I need to shower and change, so see you in a few."

He had intended to open a bottle of Sancerre, but paused at the wine refrigerator in the kitchen, turned to the refrigerator, and pulled out a carton of orange juice. He poured a glass and left it on the counter. He sat at the kitchen table and looked at the cathedral. Then he got up and stood at the window, watching people scurry along the promenade. He wondered if they knew how fast their life could change.

He felt that his life was going to be very different in the coming months. A new book. A new writing style. Finding himself again. But without her. He caught his breath. When Marie loved him, the world was right and he was brave enough to manage anything. She was the perfect mother to their child and his soulmate, if such a thing existed. He stopped himself when he heard the door to the guest room open.

Adele waved at Jack as she entered the living room. He frowned for a moment. Who was this gorgeous waif in a floor-length black sheath with a slit that stretched all the way up to the middle of her thigh? Black opera gloves past her elbows, and a cigarette holder a foot long. Then he beamed at her. "Adele?"

"Do I know you?" She teased him with a sidelong glance.

"H.G. It's Holly. Lovely gown you have, Miss Golightly."

"Thank you, Jack."

He laughed. "Holy shit! You look just like Audrey Hepburn in that Capote one... *Breakfast at Tiffany's.*"

He marveled at her transformation. The spiked hair was now combed forward into perfect bangs and her shaggy ponytail had been wrapped into a stylish up-twist. Pearl earrings replaced the safety pins in her ears. Her nose ring was missing. She moved like a model on a runway. She made her voice go wispy. "Thank you so much for inviting me to your party, Mister Varjak."

"Oh. He was the George Peppard character. The impoverished writer kept by—"

"Patricia Neal..."

"He reminds Holly of her brother Fred, who is in the army."

She laughed. "I love that movie. Why don't you go as Paul Varjak? All you need is a suit and a skinny tie. Maybe carry a trench coat over your shoulder like in the scene when they visit Tiffany's."

"Do you think anyone else will get it?"

"So what if they don't? We'll be absolutely adorbs."

"Adorbs?"

"Yeah. Adorable."

He shrugged. "I don't have a trench coat."

"I do, and since it's just a prop, it won't have to fit you at all. Got a dark suit and narrow tie?" He nodded. "Then go get dressed. I'll set up the bar. Just wine, right?"

"Just wine. In that outfit?"

"Why not? It's easy. You ought to see the weird stuff I have to do on the set as a 'go-fer.' Go for this. Fix that." She adopted a shrill voice. "'I need a Perrier. No, not this one, I want the one with lime in it.' Then I get to climb a ladder and adjust a reflector or maybe I get to buff up a shoe when some model stepped in dog shit on the sidewalk. Gawd!"

"Sounds challenging."

"But fun too. Want me to put out a cheeseboard or something?"

"No thanks. They got it covered. Greg is bringing pizza. Eileen ordered some meat-and-cheese plates."

By the time Jack had changed into his white shirt and black suit, she had put a half dozen bottles of red wine and a galvanized tub for ice on the counter. The first six bottles of Sancerre, Chablis, and Champagne were chilling in the pullout drawer of the refrigerator. She had placed two dozen party wine glasses on the kitchen granite counter and left the crystal Lalique and Riedel stemware safely in the cabinet.

She looked at his wrinkled suit and shook her head. "Good thing this is a costume party—we can pass those wrinkles off as part of the character. Where's your tie?"

He pulled a rolled-up dark tie from his pocket. She made a face. "Way too wide. But I've got tape."

She retreated to her room with the tie and returned with it taped into a straight line an inch wide. She pulled up his collar, slipped the tie around his neck, and quickly made a perfect knot.

He held the end of the tie and asked? "God, were ties really this thin in the sixties?"

She nodded, stepped back, and looked over his outfit. She stared at his scuffed brown hiking boots and shook her head. "That's it? You're wearing those?"

"I forgot to pack good shoes."

"Yeah. Okay. It'll have to do. I looked up the movie poster online to get my hair right." She grinned. "Want me to give you a trim and style it to match the poster?"

"You cut hair?"

"I do everything when I'm shooting fashion. That tape on your tie, we use it to adjust the dresses on models or instead of a bra if there's too much nipple exposure." She chuckled at his discomfort when she said this. She squinted at his shaggy hair. "Yeah. Easy to trim the edges, a little comb to the side. A low fade to a part and side comb."

He laughed. "A what?"

"Tight sides and back, long on top. It'll look sharp. Sort of a sexy *Mad Men* look on top and almost Army whitewalls on the sides. Trust me."

"What the hell. I'll probably get my head shaved for the operation anyway. Why not?"

She tossed him a kitchen towel and pointed to the stool at the massive kitchen island. "Grab a seat. Be right back."

Jack sat down and draped the towel over his shoulders. She returned, gloveless, with a hair trimmer, scissors, a comb, and a small can of hair spray. She adjusted the setting with a dial and pressed the button on the front of the small trimmer. Standing behind him, she gave him a totally clean neckline and an easy fade from bare to a half inch near the crown of his head.

"How's it going?" he asked over the low buzz.

"Good. You have a nice shape to your head. This is going to look so rad." She circled around him and matched the sides to the fade an inch above his ears while leaving the top long. Then she grabbed a comb and scissors and trimmed just enough to make the comb over not be shaggy, gave him a part on the right, and ratted the front for a bit more height. As she smoothed the top with her fingers, she said, "Yup. That's the look I was going for. Cover your eyes."

"Why?"

"So I don't blind you with hair spray."

Once plastered in place, the haircut was flattering. He folded the towel, retreated to the guest bathroom to look in the mirror, and grinned. He rubbed the back of his neck and twisted to see the sides. He shouted to Adele. "Not bad! I think this is going to be an interesting night."

She put away her equipment and returned. She leaned over to mop up the hair with a wet paper towel. He took it from her and smiled. "Let me."

The electric hiss of the front door lock releasing caused Adele and Jack to look at each other and grin. She quickly tugged on her gloves and grabbed her cigarette holder from the counter. He extended the crook of his arm. She took it as though they were really going to the party in the film. Eileen walked into the living room lugging her heavy messenger bag and froze. "Who?" Once she recognized Jack and Adele, they all laughed.

Eileen motioned for them to turn around. They spun in a showy way. "My God, you both look fabulous!"

Adele hurried to help with the bags. "Got your costume in there?"

"Kinda. I found some things at Monoprix that I need to pull together..."

"Need some help? We're all set here. Just waiting for the pizzas and the deli delivery. Bar's set up. I'll open the reds about five thirty."

Jack smiled. "And I'll get the door if someone rings."

Adele followed Eileen into her suite and placed the bags on the bed. Eileen pulled the coffee press from the bag and handed it to Adele. "Can you put that in the kitchen?"

"Why? They've got three more in the pantry."

"I broke theirs."

Adele snickered. "As if they'd notice. Just blame a caterer, so—"

"I broke it. It's on me."

"Got it." Shaking her head, Adele stowed it in the kitchen cabinet and returned in time to see a variety of merchandise strewn across the bed.

Eileen liberated the bright yellow laundry hamper from its wrapper. It expanded into a tall fabric cylinder held open by hoops of plastic at the top and bottom and three side ribs. Fabric markers in red and black were in their plastic packages.

Adele put her hands on her hips. "What's the plan here? What're you going for?"

"A pencil. Going to make a stubby pencil, with a red eraser bottom, the green lettering of the Dixon Ticonderoga pencil up the side and a beige turtleneck. Then I'm going to make a black pointed hat as the pencil's lead. That's what the construction paper's for."

"She's got a hat. A Vietnamese conical hat in black lacquer that would be a perfect point."

"Think she'd mind?"

"It's just a hat they used as a prop in one of their videos, not one of her antiques."

While Adele went to fetch the hat, Eileen dug through her purse for a stub of a pencil and started lettering the side of the round laundry bag to match it. When Adele returned, she helped cut a hole in the bottom of the hamper to slip over Eileen's head and then cut armholes on each side. After trying it on and adding the hat, Adele nodded approval. "You still need that eraser part and a couple green bands at the bottom."

"Thought I'd draw them on next."

"She's got some pink tea towels we could tape on for the eraser. Won't hurt them. Want me to do that?"

"That'd be great. Thanks."

Within a few minutes, they emerged as a Dixon B1 pencil and Holly Golightly, again with gloves and a foot-long cigarette holder. Jack howled with laughter when he saw Eileen's pencil costume. They all taped the construction paper pumpkins on random walls and the mantel. The entry buzzer interrupted Jack's continuing laughter. He answered the door while Adele put small bags of M&M's from the pantry into several bowls and placed them around the living room.

Greg arrived in a baggy maroon tracksuit that somehow looked good on him. He extended his foot to show off his high-top Converse Chuck Taylor All Stars. The shoes' black canvas had significantly grayed with age. The white circle over the ankle and logo on the heel were the last archeological clues as to the shoes' former glory.

Jack frowned. "So what are you? I don't get the relation to your job. Adele's an artistic homeless waif."

Greg smiled at her and put out his hand. "Hi. I'm Greg. Great costume."

Jack continued, "Eileen is a pencil and I'm a writer but..."

He turned and pointed to the lettering on the back of his jacket. "I'm a basketball player, but..." Written across the shoulders of the tracksuit in silver glitter was "FREE AGENT."

Adele stared at him. "I don't get it."

"I'm a free agent. A ball player about to change teams. I'm moving back to the States."

Jack looked at the still-open door. "Eileen said you were bringing pizza."

"I paid to have it delivered."

Eileen motioned to the kitchen. "We thought that with four ovens here, we can keep them all warm and serve them as needed."

Adele turned the ovens to the low setting and pulled pans from a cupboard. "May as well pre-heat them now."

Jack stared at him. "You're really moving back?"

"Yes."

Eileen put her arm over his shoulder. "Isn't that great?"

The pizza delivery arrived at six. Several pies were placed on pizza pans in the warmed ovens. As the delivery woman left the elevator, the outer door buzzed. She passed a vampire in the lobby.

When the penthouse door opened, Jack laughed and stood aside. A tall man, suited in black with a lace collar, was splattered with blood. Upon entry, he pulled his cape in front of his face so it formed a solid shield in front of him. The hideous laugh that he emitted caused Adele and Eileen to stop and turn toward the door. The woman in the skimpy maid's outfit behind him laughed and followed him into the penthouse. Greg called to him. "Julien! Over here!" Julien, the phlebotomist, removed his false vampire teeth to greet Greg. An unpleasantly realistic stain extended from his crimson lips down his chin onto the neck of his white lace collar. Greg pointed at the bar. "Red or white?"

"Red. Only if it's a vintage RH positive." Adele and Jack played bartender while she sipped Champagne and he nursed a ginger ale.

Arnaud, the MRI technician, arrived wearing a tuxedo and carrying a set of cymbals. "You see," he explained as he slammed them together, "the noise of the machine is my costume."

Pierre, the intern who had shepherded Jack through the MRI process, came as a female nurse, complete with a blonde wig and an impressive set of falsies. His girlfriend wore pale green scrubs, had her hair tucked into a surgical cap, and sported Pierre's name badge on a lanyard around her neck.

The receptionist from the Institute arrived as a bumblebee. To insure that the correct initial impression was made, she buzzed as she entered the room. Wires extended from a large pair of sunglasses suggesting antennas and bug eyes. A black turtleneck gave her black bug arms. Black tights completed the skinny bee legs. She had sewn alternating strips of yellow and black feather boas on a summer beach shift that came to her knees. No wings were required to make the point.

Doctor Marie Bonnard was dressed elegantly for an evening out, but arrived at the Halloween party with an icepick in her hand. She took a glass of Champagne, sipped half of it, and left soon afterward apologizing that she and a friend had tickets for the theater. She abandoned the icepick on the counter.

About eight, Ahmed, the slim radiologist who took the MRI, arrived wearing a paint-smudged smock over a puffy down jacket. His face was hidden behind a white beard, suspended from clear eyeglasses by sagging elastic bands. A dusty brown fedora hid his short dark hair. He held a painter's palette and paint-crusted brushes.

Jack frowned at the man for a moment, wondering who he was and what his costume represented. Then he saw the slim woman behind him who wore skintight jeans and a sweatshirt with the reproduction of Monet's water lilies on it. Jack laughed and said, "Oh you're a painter."

Ahmed assumed a gruff voice and answered, "*Non! Je suis Claude Monet.* The painter of light." He took off his dusty fedora and waved it over his head in mock anger. "That is what I do, I make images with different kinds of light." His girlfriend grinned as she pointed to the picture on her chest and then to her boyfriend.

Greg came over and stared at Ahmed before nodding his approval. "Radiologist. Pictures. I get it. Cool costume. *Allez-y entrez.*"

As more guests arrived, clustered around the cheese board, and spoke French, Jack tried to explain Halloween pranks. "On Halloween we say, 'trick or treat.'" He paused. "It is an odd thing and actually a threat, if you think about it for a moment. We knock on a door ask the homeowner if they want a trick, like TPing their trees or give us a treat. Like these little bags of M&M's."

Ahmed flourished a paintbrush as he asked, "What is this TPing?"

"Never mind. Have some more wine. Okay?"

A clutch of young men who worked in the hospital lab arrived, obviously having had several drinks on the way to the party. After fiddling with some controls on the music system, Jack found another channel that had danceable American pop music from the eighties. Some of the guests danced, but most just talked louder.

About nine, Greg found another music channel, this one featuring the songs of Tom Petty. Jack sidled up to Greg. "Always liked his music."

"Me too. How you doing, Jack?"

"Pretty good, considering I'm just drinking ginger ale. He was a real favorite of mine, back in the day. Shame to lose him. Hey, can you be sure to play *American Girl* and then cut the music for a minute? I want to give a special toast to Eileen." A few minutes later it came up on the playlist and Jack yelled for everyone to listen to it. As the song concluded, he shouted, "Hey! I have something to say!" The room became silent. Jack cleared his throat. "I want to thank you all, not just for what you did for me, but what you do every day to make people better. And I want you all to know how grateful I am to Eileen, who had the courage to bring me out of darkness into a new light. So thank you all, and here is to my American girl! Eileen, who saved my life!" He applauded and the others joined him.

As the applause ended and people resumed chatting, Olivia arrived wearing her McDonald's uniform. An elderly man was at her side. Jack recognized her and hurried to greet her. "Olivia! Come in."

She hesitated at the doorway. "He is my father. But we have no costumes for your party. I just got off work and his...attendant, for the night had an emergency."

"Well, I'm glad you both came."

Again, she hesitated. "Is Doctor Patel here? I wanted him to see my father so we could thank him personally for the referral he made to help my father."

"I'll get him. Please come in and have a seat on the sofa." Jack looked at the elderly man and sighed. There was an abstract quality to his presence that was frighteningly familiar. Jack kneeled beside them. "Wouldn't you like a slice of pizza and some wine, or juice?"

The older man raised an eyebrow. "Pizza?"

"Lots of kinds. All cheese. *Tout fromage ou fromage avec canard* and figs." He struggled for the translation.

Eileen arrived behind him and finished his thought for him, "*Figues.*" She turned to Jack. "It's almost the same." She extended her hand to Olivia and nodded. "*Je suis très heureuse de vous voir ce soir et de rencontrer votre père.*" Jack looked at her.

"I told her that I am so very happy to see her tonight, and to meet her father."

The man announced, "*Canard pour moi.*"

Jack watched Olivia for approval. On her nod, he hurried to the warming oven and extracted a slice of duck and fig pizza. He grabbed a napkin and delivered it. "I'll get a fork if you want. *Une fourchette?*"

"*Non, merci.*" Olivia smiled at Jack. "Thank you, but a small glass of water..." Eileen got it and then went to find Greg. By ten, Jack was struggling to follow a fast exchange between two young men who seemed to be arguing over a soccer game. The fatigue and emotion of salvaging his mind and his contract had wilted him. He said a fast good night to his guests and retreated to his suite. Just after eleven, Adele coaxed the last of the partiers to depart by bribing the lab boys with the last of the pizza and a good bottle of Barolo.

Greg turned down the music and found a mellow jazz playlist. While Eileen changed into jeans and a turtleneck, Greg and Adele started gathering the glasses, lining them up on the long counter like soldiers sorted by rank and battalion. Adele threw all the crusty spatulas and silverware into a sink of warm water to soak while she collected the plates in stacks. After rinsing the utensils and loading the plates, she started the dishwasher.

When Eileen returned, she started washing the glassware. Adele dried. Greg took the towel from her and pointed to the couch. "You've done enough! Go relax."

She ripped open a bag of M&M's and propped her legs on the arm of the sofa, letting her high heels dangle in the air. "Thanks." She searched her handful of candy and carefully selected two yellows. "Not a bad last-minute Halloween party here." Adele laughed as she kicked off her high heels, one almost making it to the door of her room beside the office.

Greg said, "Your costume was the clear winner."

Jack sauntered in, pulling his skinny tie loose. "Hers? I thought mine was pretty good."

Adele laughed and got up. "I thought you'd crashed."

"Just needed some quiet." He held up an empty glass. "And some water."

She posed next to him. "Just like the movie poster!"

Greg nodded. "You nailed it."

She scooped up her shoes. "Time to change into something comfortable, then I'll take down the decorations."

Jack came to the counter and sat on a high stool watching Eileen and Greg wash the glasses. "You two look like you've been together for a while."

Greg looked at her. "That's the plan."

"I hated the parties we had to throw for her law firm. Business bullshit. But after! That was the best part. The quiet. Washing dishes. Getting the house back in order so we could be us again. Going to bed tired. Together."

Adele returned wearing her torn jeans and a denim work shirt. Her hair was still in the sophisticated updo. She peered at Jack and studied his face. "You look different tonight. You're not the guy I picked up at the airport just a month ago lugging that chunk of iron you call a typewriter and saying you were going to finish your book, I figured you for some cray cray."

"A what?"

She stopped removing the paper pumpkins that were taped to the walls and gave a half smile of apology. "A crazy guy. An *inpressive*."

Eileen cocked her head and looked up from washing a glass. "Impressive?"

"No. *In*-pressive. Insane and impressive. You have a spark. Kinda like that guy who wanted to jump over the Grand Canyon on a motorcycle."

Jack threw his hands up in the air in a mock panic. "First time I've been compared to Evel Knivel! How come everyone saw what was happening except me?"

Greg traded out a wet dishtowel for a dry one. "Go easy on yourself, Jack. That's the way dementia is. It's a sneaky son of a bitch at first."

"Well, it's been a hell of a ride. I came here as a fraud. Never figured I'd go home. I'd lost what made me...*me*. My family. My memories. How to write. How to think. It all was sliding away."

Adele gave him a thorough looking over. "I gotta say, you're a realsharpie now, and I'm not just giving you some haircut swag. You really are some kind of brainiac pulling off a whole book in a *month*. And you look better too. It's like you're going someplace."

He chuckled. "You can say that again!" He pointed at Eileen. "But she'd just edit out what I just said as a cliché."

"When are you flying home?"

"On Wednesday. The first."

"Cool. I'll be done with my shoot. I'll drive you."

"I'd like that. Be a good bookend to the trip." He started for the refrigerator and stepped behind Eileen.

Adele looked at Greg, who was putting away glasses in the cupboard. "So, Mister Free Agent, when are you going back?"

"It's going to take about a month to transition the work here to others. My new job in Baltimore starts in January."

"So what's up for December?"

He grinned at Eileen. "Going to take a little break. Hang around Long Island. Meet the mom. Catch a Knicks game."

Eileen froze. "Basketball? You like basketball?"

He sensed danger and answered slowly. "Sure and other sports. I'm not obsessed."

"Baseball. What's your team?"

Jack was behind her about to refill his water glass at the refrigerator. He looked at Greg and mouthed "Cubs." Greg tipped his head. Jack made a "C" with his free hand.

Greg smiled. "I've always liked the Cubs."

"I knew there was something special about you. Right from the start."

Chapter № 17

November 12, 2017
Sunday

I t was drizzling in Long Island when Eileen left for Manhattan just after six thirty in the morning. In spite of the three fender-benders on the expressway, she arrived at Jack's hospital and found parking just as visiting hours started. He was eating breakfast when she stopped at his door and glanced inside the room. Jack smiled at her. "Come on in, I'm decent."

"You're looking pretty chipper today. Better than yesterday. And a lot better than Friday."

"I was pretty out of it on Friday."

"Yes, you were!"

"Thanks for being here."

"Sure."

She draped her wet coat over the back of the one chair beside his bed and sat down, holding her messenger bag on her lap.

Jack motioned to his tray. "Want some toast? Got more than enough." She dug a bagel wrapped in a napkin from her coat pocket. "Thanks, but I bought this from the cart in the lobby. You better get released before I start gaining weight." She nibbled on the bagel. "I called Greg last night. He had already talked to the surgeon, again, so I didn't have any news for him, except to say that you looked good."

Jack laughed. "I can't imagine I looked like anything but a shaved drowned rat."

"Trust me. You are looking swell."

"How's his deal with Hopkins coming along?"

"All set. Starts mid-January. He's having Thanksgiving with us on Long Island. Then we're looking for a place in Baltimore."

Jack squinted at her. "We?"

"Greg and I. Mom's new assistant is working out well. I'll be just a couple hours away."

He chuckled then winced. "Meeting Isabel over turkey! You'd never let me get away with that in my books."

"Yeah. It's a cliché, but that's the way the scheduling worked out." She chatted with Jack until a nurse entered the room. He obviously did some serious weightlifting in his off hours and could have had a side hustle as a bouncer at a high-end club. Eileen stood immediately. "I'll leave you gentlemen to do your thing."

The nurse smiled at her. "Just going to take his vitals and change the dressing. Give us fifteen."

"Sure." She grabbed her messenger bag and walked around the hospital floor twice then went to the cafeteria, where she bought a can of Diet Coke. When she returned to Jack's room, his eyes were closed. He appeared to be asleep. The Redskins-Vikings game was playing on the small television set mounted above the whiteboard, which had the day, date, name of the physician and the nursing staff on duty that Sunday. She quietly walked to the bedside chair and sat down. She took the Diet Coke from her bag and cleared her throat, not knowing if Jack was dozing or not. She whispered, "Think they'll hold on to the lead?"

Jack said, "Who?"

"You messin' with me?"

"Yeah. I've been following it just fine. Just resting my eyes."

She glanced at the fresh gauze square behind his ear. "Sure you were. Headache still there?"

"Getting better by the minute. Good game if you like the Redskins." Jack grunted as he shifted his pillow and raised the back of the hospital bed. "When are they gonna change that dumbass name, anyway? It's so…"

Eileen leaned toward the television and squinted at the running text under the action. "Keenum's pass is good. There goes the game."

He moaned. She looked at him. "You okay?"

"Just tired of being here already. But I guess they need to 'observe' me another day or two, like I'm some lab rat."

"Grumpy?"

"I feel like me again, and don't want to be here any longer."

"I guess that's good, but you need to stay put. Like Greg said in Paris, your big issues are avoiding infection and getting the valve adjusted correctly. But I guess your doc here has already drilled that into your skull, pardon the pun. Just a couple weeks to a month in New York after you get released, checking in with them, then you should be ready to go back to your cabin."

"I've been thinking about that. That tall lady you saw here yesterday."

"With the clipboard?"

"Yes. She's a social worker. Asked me about my post-release plans. Really pissed her off when I said I didn't have any."

"Max said you were staying with him!"

"He invited. I declined."

"Stay with us while they get your new gizmo dialed-in. You can have my room. I can drive you into the city for..."

"Greg's going to be there."

"We've got enough room, so consider it, okay?"

He smiled. "Wasn't too smart, me living alone in the woods. If I'd even met with a bunch of old codgers for coffee in town once a week, they might have tipped me off to how I was changing and needed to see a doc."

"As obstinate as you are, you still need other people. We'd be..."

"Make that independent."

"You're editing *me*?"

"Thanks, but I've put you and Isabel through enough."

"One way or another, you've got to meet her soon. She's pissed that you won't let her visit."

"Okay. Soon." They watched the rest of the game and some news to-gether, commenting occasionally as if they were on a sofa in some den in a comfortable home and not a hospital room. Eileen opened her laptop when Jack started napping after lunch.

Midafternoon, Max hurried into the hospital room with a briefcase and skidded to a stop at the foot of Jack's bed. He tugged down the vest on his pinstriped suit and stared at Jack. "Whoa. That's some haircut you got! What happened to the long-haired mountain man?"

"Thinking about being a city boy again."

"Sorry I couldn't make it yesterday."

"No sweat. Eileen's been keeping me company."

"They loved your draft. The e-mail I got this morning..."

"On a Sunday?"

"Time means nothing to them. Anyhow, they had a few tweaks here and there. Nothing major. But here's the big news. At their editorial meeting Friday, they decided to delay the pub date since it's not exactly Christmas reading. More like an Easter book. Add more legs to the suc-cess story of the last chapter." He looked at Eileen, who stood to give Max the one chair. "So, with that delay, you still could have Eileen do the final edit and work in their tweaks, if that's okay with you."

Jack grinned at Eileen. "Yup. She's amazing. We worked well under *pressure*. No pun intended."

Max put his briefcase on the floor next to Eileen's chair and faked a groan. "Not with the bad puns again."

"It's who I am. Sorry I sorta went to shit for a while."

"Who can anticipate these things?"

Eileen stood and moved toward the door. "I'm gonna run. Let you guys catch up. Be back tomorrow, okay?" Jack gave her a casual salute.

Max grinned at her. "Good work, kid."

After she left, Max opened his briefcase on his lap. "So, the art de-partment sent me a PDF of the mock-up of the cover." He handed it to Jack who looked at it, the ceiling, then at the cover again.

"Well? I know that face. What's the problem? It'll look better on a slick proof—I just ran it off on my color printer at home, but it'll look better... You don't like the title, the font, the artwork... What?"

"Naw. That's all fine."

"Then what?"

"Eileen needs title credit. I want her name on it."

"What? 'As told to'?"

"Nope. Equal billing. And I want a French translation, by her."

"Are you shitting me?"

"Just do it, okay? And let's get a real picture of me for the back jacket maybe after my hair grows back a little."

Max nodded as he tossed the mock-up into his briefcase and slammed it shut. "Okay. If you're sure." He picked up his briefcase and walked to the foot of the bed.

Jack squinted at him. "Max? What is it? Are you pissed I want her to get credit?"

He shook his head quickly. "That's a good thing."

"Then what's up?"

"She called me last night. From Chicago."

Jack barely whispered. "Who?"

"Her! The mother of your child, that's who. She's got some big trial there. She wanted to know when you were going to have your operation! You never told her?"

"What'd she want?"

"To know what's up with you. Why you haven't called her!"

Jack propped himself up on one elbow. "What did you tell her?"

"The truth."

Jack winced. "What part of it?"

"All of it, you dumb schmuck. I never could figure why you'd leave her."

Jack whispered, "She left me."

"You're the one who moved..."

"Come on. You know what I mean."

Max ignored Jack. "If you'd just kept your hands to yourself and your zipper zipped."

Jack sat taller, clenched his jaw, and stared at Max. Forcefully, he said, "I did."

"What? Thank God. At least I don't need to worry about one of those 'He grabbed me by the whatever ten years ago' headlines."

"Nope."

"You can't tell me you never... On all of your book tours? With any of those sweet adoring coeds at your lectures?"

"Nope. Tempted? Sure. But no—not once. Max?"

"Yeah, buddy?"

"I'm glad you told her. I need to see her. I've been thinking about her. About us. And bigger stuff too, now that I can think again. Like how my country's going through something like I did."

"What do you mean?"

"I'm known as the optimistic American. I've got a good sense of what's right, and I say so in my spy-thrillers."

"That's your trademark. Straight talk, good values, with a screaming hot plot line."

"Something has changed. Maybe I just needed a fresh look. Or to pay better attention, but we suddenly appear to have no sense of shame about our history or respect for the truth."

Max walked to the side of the bed and leaned toward him. In a lowered voice, he said, "Jack..."

"No. Let me finish. Without that sense of tragedy, of perspective, how can we celebrate our victories? America has done some fantastic things. But we seem to be stalling out. Celebrating the wrong stuff. Going from melting pot to crackpot. I wanna know how we can find our moral compass again."

"When did you get so smart?"

"I'm not. I just had time to stop and look around. Maybe it was just being out of the country or losing my mind. Most of us can't stop for that look. We work like we're hamsters just moving our shitty pile of wood shavings from one corner of our cage to the other. We're afraid to look up and see that someone left the cage door open and we can escape."

"You lost me."

"What I've been thinking is that maybe America has its own self-induced dementia. Maybe we just want to forget shit. Ignore income inequality, discrimination, the homeless, jobs. I could go on and on. But this current pettiness in politics is far outweighed by our strength and resiliency as a people, and that's the part that's getting lost. Look how the folks in Huston forgot color and income during Hurricane Harvey. It was just people helping people."

Max smirked. "And lost it when it came to Puerto Rico."

"Maybe some of those guys in D.C. did, but not everyone. I just read today about a big-deal chef, José Andrés, who went down there and served over a million and a half meals, and he's still working there, not at one of his high-end places. Restaurants in San Francisco were driving meals over to Santa Rosa and Napa when those damn fires swept through wine country in California before the feds even heard about it on the news. That's the strength of this country. We help each other."

"So? We've always had good guys when we need them."

"We used to be better as a government, doing what individuals can't. We've got to stop defending whatever foxhole we've dug for ourselves and listen to the other guy. Without dismissing another perspective as 'fake news' or a 'distraction.' Hell, that's a game for pickpockets and magicians, not our national discussion. So I'm thinking...maybe it's time for me to put my money where my mouth is. Contribute what I can in what's left of my writing career."

"You gonna write all *this* down?"

"When I figure it out. We need people to stand up and fix the thousands of little things that the big things lean on. And the big things too. You know in France everyone has basic health care, and more of their babies grow up than ours. Our infant mortality is where Sweden's was forty years ago. We're supposed to be the best and brightest, so why do we let babies die while we moralize about abortion rights and dither about the age a kid can buy a gun while Congress is cutting funds for health and mental health? We believe Internet crazies over science, fear vaccines, and wonder why third world diseases are now coming here. What the hell are we thinking?"

"We're not. I think you have something to say, Jack, and why not now? Hell, I can send my last kid to a state school."

"Max?"

"Kidding. But you're right—it's time to stop ignoring the dead elephant in the American living room. If you want to try another non-fiction, I can shop it. I don't know how your imprint is going to take another surprise. But I'll give it my best."

"I trust you, Max. If there's a way, you'll find it. When I can, I want to get rid of some stuff at the cabin and then travel. I want to rediscover the America I thought I knew before the 2016 election. We've gone nuts. I want to figure out why, and maybe, just maybe, help us get our mind back. I want to take a long drive and talk to people. Farmers and academics, craft brewers, IT kids, and homeless people. Sort of a de Tocqueville meets *Travels with Charlie*."

From the doorway, a slim woman in designer jeans and a loose red sweater asked, "Need a driver?"

Jack turned toward the door and smiled. "Marie?"

She walked toward Max. "Good to see you again, Max."

He pivoted quickly. "You too, Marie."

She gave Max a hug. "I was hoping to find Eileen here and thank her for calling..."

"She just left."

She nodded quickly. "I saw her in the hall. Recognized her from the selfie you shared with me. I introduced myself. We had a nice chat. She's a lovely young woman."

Max moved toward the door. "Well, I better get back to the office and send some e-mails about the cover changes and your new demands so they can scream at me Monday morning. Good seeing you again, Marie."

"You too, Max. Thanks."

They watched Max fumble with his briefcase as he hurried from the room. Both started to talk at the same time, stopped, and laughed. Jack reached for Marie's hand and pulled her to the edge of the bed.

Before she sat, she paused. "This okay?"

"Sure. How long have you been standing there?"

"About the time you started your rant about trying to find America's heart again."

"Oh."

"Are you serious about a road trip—doing a Don Quixote?"

He nodded. "Time I grew up and did more than entertain the masses."

"Eileen said you needed to stay in the city for a while."

"That's what they tell me. I'll start looking for a place as soon as they'll let me get a newspaper. Stay in a hotel until..."

She laughed. "A paper? All the ads are online now."

He chuckled. "It's true. I am a dinosaur."

She took his hand. "You don't need another place."

He frowned. "What?"

"Come home."

He ground his teeth and glared out the window. When he looked at her again, he struggled to control his voice. "No way in hell! Don't you think it might be a little bit crowded with all three of us there?"

She looked at their hands and held his tighter. She spoke softly. "It's over. Never really started."

"How'd you know I was here?"

"When I hadn't heard from you, I called Max. He let me read the draft."

"You read it?"

"It's brilliant. But, you didn't need to protect me and make it sound like you just moved out. I know I screwed up our marriage. I told Grace."

"Why'd you do a damn fool thing like that? You two are like the *Gilmore Girls*. I couldn't put a wedge between you."

"She needed to know. Your opening to the book..." Tears slid down her cheeks.

He squeezed her hand. "Are you okay?"

"I don't know anymore. I miss you so much. I don't know how to say it, but I hope you will come home."

After a long silence, he asked, "You really read it?"

She pulled a tissue from her pocket and dabbed her eyes before she recited. "Most of Paris was still asleep when the rough stone railing of the Pont Neuf dug into my palms. To my right, I watched a couple near the statue of Henri IV. They stood on the exact spot where I had once kissed the most beautiful woman in the world, my bride of three months. But this morning, I was alone, balancing on my palms, toes barely touching the bridge, and leaning too far over the dark water. I wondered if I should just lose my balance or if my life was worth living without her or my mind."

"Hmmm. Did I really write that?"

She smiled at him. "Remember that Post-it you had stuck to your computer screen for the longest time?"

"*Respice finem?*"

She nodded. "Consider the end. You told me it means think about your future, your legacy, take the long view, not just the end of one of your books. Jack, I don't want *us* to end. I want us to begin a new chapter."

She leaned down and kissed him.

In the doorway, a younger version of Marie held a car seat baby carrier with a small blanket over it. "Want us to come back?"

Jack smiled. "Grace!"

"I wanted you to meet your grandson. Can we come in?"

"Hell yes! Bring him over."

Acknowledgments

There is a myth that authors work in isolation writing what they know. If that were the case, most books would be short and dull. While we may write alone, our work tangles with thoughts and experiences of others. This community enriches our lives and work, through the research and scholarship of others, a friend's sage observations over a cup of coffee on a rainy morning, or the generosity of someone answering an inane question that opened a pathway to a greater understanding. It has been my good fortune to have personally thanked many who contributed their time, experience, expertise, and encouragement along the way. But several contributors to this project merit added attention.

Two women planted the seed. Ann, to whom this book is dedicated, did reverse her NPH dementia and set a standard of grace and courage for all who knew her. My appreciation as well to Eugenia L. Welch, the President and CEO of Alzheimer's San Diego whose work has expanded my understanding of the complexity of dementia as well as the need for public education and funding for research in this critical health care area. But there is a great gap between inspiration and the book before you.

First and always in her support of my writing, from exploration of an idea to the last draft, is my sister, Maureen Shanahan. Her encouragement and critical eye are invaluable. She has the superpower to be able to read the tenth draft with as clear an eye as the first, apply her formidable range of knowledge, and offer improvements which are consistently thoughtful, well placed, and often humorous. My brother-in-law, Dennis F. Shanahan M.D., M.P.H., generously shared observations and guidance based on his many academic and professional achievements. He is my go-to science and medicine guy on an astounding range of matters.

For all things French, my appreciation goes to Sarah Foulon for her sharp eye and gentle wit.

On the technical side, I am proud to call Laurie Gibson my editor. She contributed her deep knowledge of both the art and science of writing. Her clear vision of this project and technical prowess are unequaled.

Because the medical research referenced in this work continues to evolve and everyone is unique, individualized medical evaluation and assistance is essential for anyone with cognitive concerns. Any errors of fact or fictional excess in pursuit of the story are mine alone.

A Disscussion Guide

1. Why was author Jack Forrester cleaning his rifle before deer season opened?

2. What were your first indications that Jack had cognition issues?

3. What did Jack intend to accomplish by going to Paris?

4. Why did Eileen Ross, Irene's daughter, go to Paris to work on Jack's book?

5. What is agent Max's relationship with author Jack?

6. Why does Jack buy college student Sam Greene a coffee at the airport?

7. How does Jack relate to Adele, the chef's personal assistant and independent photographer?

8. Why did Jack adopt a Hemingway style in his new writing in Paris?

9. Do Jack and Eileen use literary references to enhance or avoid issues?

10. Why did Jack react as he did to the taxi driver over the Highway 91 shooting in Las Vegas?

11. Why did Greg and Eileen break up? How did they reconcile?

12. Why did Jack go to the bridge the morning of his examination?

13. What did Jack and Max think about submitting a memoir in the place of the fiction Jack usually wrote?

14. Why did Jack throw a Halloween party in Paris?

15. Will Jack and his wife, Marie, reconcile?

16. What is next for Greg and Eileen?

17. Are the themes in this book relevant to your life?

18. What did you discover about dementia that was new to you?

www.ingramcontent.com/pod-product-compliance
Lightning Source LLC
Chambersburg PA
CBHW052026020726
47501CB00004B/1260